VANDERJACK WAS IN NO MOOD TO BE HECKLED BY GHOSTS.

"You won't get any more steel just by sitting here!"
said the Balladeer.
"This isn't doing you any good,"
said the Apothecary.
"You're not a warrior; you're a drunk,"
said the Cavalier.
"Drinking is no substitute for true thought,"
advised the Philosopher.
"True thought? He hasn't had a true thought in months,"
said the Aristocrat.
"No prey in sight, so no motivation,"
said the Hunter.
"The sword's magic is wasted on him,"
said the Conjuror.

Vanderjack called the ghosts the Sword Chorus.
So long as he gripped Lifecleaver's hilt, the souls of those
who had not yet been ready to die haunted him.
Seven souls had been snared by the sword's curse,
and they had come with the sword when he acquired it.
The legend had it that with two more souls,
Lifecleaver would break. So far, at least in his opinion,
everybody he had killed with the blade had deserved it.

Vanderjack made every effort not to test the
legend's veracity.

TRACY HICKMAN

Presents

THE ANVIL OF TIME

The Sellsword
Cam Banks

The Survivors
Dan Willis
(November 2008)

Renegade Wizards
Lucien Soulban
(March 2009)

TRACY HICKMAN
Presents
THE ANVIL OF TIME • VOLUME ONE

The Sellsword

CAM BANKS

Tracy Hickman Presents The Anvil of Time

THE SELLSWORD
©2008 Wizards of the Coast, Inc.

Published by Wizards of the Coast, Inc. DRAGONLANCE, WIZARDS OF THE COAST, and their respective logos are trademarks of Wizards of the Coast, Inc., in the U.S.A. and other countries.

Printed in the U.S.A.

Cover art by Daniel Dos Santos
First Printing: February 2008

9 8 7 6 5 4 3 2 1

ISBN: 978-0-7869-4722-5
620-21535740-001-EN

U.S., CANADA,
ASIA, PACIFIC, & LATIN AMERICA
Wizards of the Coast, Inc.
P.O. Box 707
Renton, WA 98057-0707
+1-800-324-6496

EUROPEAN HEADQUARTERS
Hasbro UK Ltd
Caswell Way
Newport, Gwent NP9 0YH
GREAT BRITAIN
Save this address for your records.

Visit our web site at www.wizards.com

This book is dedicated to my wife, Jessica, whose love and support has kept me alive through all of my mercenary endeavors.

PROLOGUE

Palanthas, 422 AC

The Journeyman was surrounded by ghosts. He sat at a small desk in one of the rarely-used archival basements of the Great Library of Palanthas. The shelves were crammed tight with volumes and reached all the way up to a ceiling shrouded with cobwebs. Bearing the soot from a thousand years of oil lamps and the dust from a thousand years of being barely browsed, the archival basement was creepy enough. The ghosts made it downright macabre.

The Journeyman's lamp, perched on the edge of the desk between a pile of historical treatises and a large omnibus of Nordmaaran horse poetry, sputtered as yet another spectral figure sailed by. They were the ghosts of Aesthetics who chose not to pass on through the Gate of Souls to the hereafter, but instead preferred to continue their work in the library, just as they had when they were living.

The ghosts were visible only by the light of a naked flame, which revealed the translucent outlines of dead librarians drifting back and forth. Upstairs, where the living Aesthetics worked, the ghosts were never glimpsed; the magical lamps set into the fine polished desks of the East Wing couldn't reveal their presence. Down in the basement where all the old and unused books came to die, a candlelit parade of souls was omnipresent.

The Journeyman never spoke with the ghosts. He wasn't sure they'd respond or even hear him, for one thing, and he couldn't escape the crawling feeling that went up and down his spine whenever he was close to one. Others had, or so he assumed, because the Senior Council of Aesthetics that presently ran the day-to-day affairs of the library included at least one spectral representative at its table.

The Journeyman rubbed his temples with aching, calloused fingers and tried to put the ghosts out of his mind. Some months earlier, he was assigned by the late Bertrem, former head of the library, to the remote City of Lost Names. There he was instructed to use the mysterious Anvil of Time's time-traveling properties to investigate the past and uncover the truth behind many of history's legends. Bertrem had chosen him, he said, because he was unremarkable in appearance yet knew a little about a lot of things. The Journeyman was taken aback by the unexpected honor, but one does not turn down the head of the library.

After one or two excursions, the Journeyman determined that he didn't have a large enough reference collection on site at the Anvil, so he made his way back to Palanthas. With the help of a fisherman who had turned to smuggling under the rule of the Dark Knights, the Journeyman stole into the city and to the Great Library.

At the Anvil, he had nobody around to keep him from his research, neither alive nor dead. In the library, on the other hand . . .

He heard the hurried *slap-slap-slap* of an Aesthetic's sandals coming down the basement stairs. The ghosts swiftly vanished into the darkness as the new arrival emerged into the lamplight.

"There you are!" she said. Stella Cordaric, exotic with her raven hair and caramel-colored skin, was one of the living Aesthetics. One slender hand grasped the bunched-up hem of her robes; the other waved in her usual loosely frantic way.

"Yes?" the Journeyman said, noting her excitement. "Trouble?"

"In the streets," she said, words running together excitedly like a gnome who'd been given a three-function wrench for Yule. "The Dark Knights. All of Lord Kinsaid's occupation forces. Somebody heard they were getting ready to leave. They're cleaning house."

The Journeyman squinted. "Leave? But they've had the city under martial law for over thirty years. Why now all of a sudden? Is something happening? Should we get out? We should get out."

Stella grinned, showing gleaming evidence of Ergothian pirates somewhere in her family tree. "No, this is good news!" she said. "The Dark Knights leaving? No more curfews! Come on upstairs, we're all of us watching through the windows."

The Journeyman started gathering together his papers, tossing books and scrolls into a worn knapsack. "No, no. I have to get back north. I can't stay here. Not in another city being invaded." He shuddered at the memory of a previous excursion through time.

"Another city? Invaded?" she asked, watching him pack.

"Never mind. Are you sure there's nobody chasing them out? Is it the Knights of Solamnia?"

Stella looked back in the direction of the stairs. "I'd know more if I were still up there watching out the windows." When she turned her head to look at him again, she was grinning even wider.

"No. I think I really need to leave. Is it safe on the streets?"

"Maybe. Look, do you need some help? Some of the spirit Aesthetics are down here, right? They're very helpful. They're always helping me."

The Journeyman, standing, cocked his head to one side. "What? The ghosts? No. How could they?" He gave the darkness a searching glance—no sign of them anymore—and stuffed the final sheaf of papers into his knapsack.

Stella shrugged. "Just a suggestion. I've always liked ghosts. The way they move things around. You know. Like this." She wriggled her fingers at him.

"No, I don't know what you mean. Look, Stella. Is there a way to the waterfront? I need a boat. The Dark Knights must have the whole of the Old City locked down."

"Hmm. Let me think. Oh! You know, if they're leaving, and it's the Solamnic Knights coming in—though I think I heard it was some lady wizard—not Jenna, the other one—anyway, if it's the Solamnic Knights, then my brother Etharion's probably leaving too. The Legionnaire? You met him. He smuggled you into the city last week."

The Journeyman shouldered his knapsack and lifted the oil lamp from the table. Shadows skittered across the shelves, and he was sure he saw a row of ghostly faces watching him. "He was your brother? The trout fisherman with the bad teeth?"

Stella shook her head. "Those teeth are fake. Yes, that's him! He's with the Legion of Steel. I'm sure he can smuggle you out again; he's a master of disguises. His Legion cell was only in Palanthas to watch the Dark Knights, anyway. If the Solamnics are coming in, he'll be following Lord Kinsaid and his men out."

"That will have to do," the Journeyman said, following Stella to the stairs. "I appreciate it. I'm sorry. I can't afford to be caught . . . all my notes. You understand."

Stella turned and punched the Journeyman in the upper arm, making him almost drop the knapsack. "Silly. Of course I understand. Now come on! You'll have time to watch the liberation of the city from the windows while I send word to Etharion. One of the Aesthetics is baking cookies. He can show you the recipe, and then you could help him. You're multitalented."

Rubbing the shoulder, the Journeyman let out a long, tortured breath. "I'm a terrible cook, Stella. The library in Solanthus was nothing like this. And Bertrem must be rolling in his grave."

Stella giggled. The Journeyman followed the *slap-slap-slap* of her sandals up the stairs, leaving the ghosts to their silent routine in the absence of his lamplight.

CHAPTER ONE
Nordmaar, 351 AC

The sellsword was surrounded by ghosts.

Vanderjack sat with his boots up in a roadside bar in the middle of a rainstorm. A leg was missing from his table, so it had been propped up on a barrel of cheap wine. His clothes were soaked by the water leaking through the roof. He had used the last of his steel coins to pay for the mug of watery beer awaiting his pleasure; one hand rested on the hilt of his sword, Lifecleaver, which lay beside the beer. He was in no mood to be heckled by ghosts.

"You won't get any more steel just by sitting here!" said the Balladeer.

"This isn't doing you any good," said the Apothecary.

"You're not a warrior; you're a drunk," said the Cavalier.

They were his own personal ghosts. When they appeared, they looked like ordinary people, albeit transparent. Their voices sounded like echoes, and when they moved or expressed any activity, it was all flickering shadow. They didn't glow, as one might expect, although firelight seemed to catch in their incorporeal forms and illuminate them the way it does in a glass figurine or a precious gemstone.

Actually, the ghosts haunted the sword, so Vanderjack called them the Sword Chorus. He had bought the sword from his mother, an infamous Saifhumi pirate, on her deathbed. Or at least that was what he told everybody, but in truth he hadn't really paid for it at all, which he supposed was only fair, given the sword's curse. So long as he gripped Lifecleaver's hilt, the souls of those who had not yet been ready to die on the end of the blade haunted him.

So far seven souls had been snared by the sword's curse, and they had come with the sword when he acquired it. Legend had it that with two more souls, Lifecleaver would break. Vanderjack made every effort not to test the legend's veracity, and so far, at least in his opinion, everybody he had killed with the blade had deserved it.

"Drinking is no substitute for true thought," advised the Philosopher.

"True thought? He hasn't had a true thought in months," said the Aristocrat.

"No prey in sight, so no motivation," said the Hunter.

An enchanted sword such as Lifecleaver was a vital asset in this day and age. Although he had little of it anymore, Vanderjack made his steel by killing people. The so-called War of the Lance had been won, the Queen of Darkness had been defeated, her Temple of Darkness destroyed. None of that meant the fighting was over, however. The dragonarmies had retreated to the five corners of Ansalon, tenaciously holding onto lands they had conquered during the war. There weren't enough knights in shining armor to hold back the tide, so the free nations of the world had taken to paying people such as he for protection.

"The sword's magic is wasted on him," said the Conjuror.

Vanderjack exhaled and muttered, "All I'm trying to do is have a blasted drink." He lifted his hand from the sword, and the shimmering phantoms around him vanished.

When standing, the sellsword was over six feet tall, with muscles that had been much harder when he was twenty years younger. He was still relying on his dark Ergothian complexion and shaved head to make him stand out among the other mercenaries. Vanderjack had many imitators, several of whom were being rounded up to answer for the numerous jobs he'd done and enemies he'd made. He'd heard many rumors about his own demise. If it weren't for the ghosts in the sword, he'd be wondering if he were a ghost himself.

Vanderjack reached for his beer. As his fingers closed about it, the mug shattered.

"Ackal's Teeth!" he cursed, snatching up his sword from the puddle of beer and leaping to his feet. The Sword Chorus swirled back into his vision again. A crossbow bolt was still quivering in a wooden post a yard away from him, the source of the exploding mug. "That was my last beer!"

"What did we miss?" asked the Balladeer.

"We're under attack!" said the Cavalier.

"Be quiet for one blasted minute," barked Vanderjack. There were no other patrons in the common room; it wasn't a busy time of day, and it wasn't a good enough bar. The bar's owner was still dozing under an awning over in one corner, oblivious. All he could see outside through the open window was rain, but the bolt couldn't have come from anywhere else, so he ran to the door and ducked outside. The ghosts sailed after him in his wake.

Outside, the rains of Nordmaar were warm and heavy, as they always were in early summer. The road between Pentar and Jotan wasn't paved; rumor had it that old King Huemac had decreed it, but the dragon-army invasion put an end to any public works. King Huemac's captive son, Prince Shredler, had more than enough to worry about, so the surface of the road was an inch of mud. Thirty feet from the bar, wheels deep in the slick sludge, Vanderjack saw, was an expensive-looking carriage was under attack.

Vanderjack took in the immediate situation with a seasoned veteran's eye. He hadn't been the target after all. The carriage had a single driver, the owner of the crossbow that had robbed him of his beer. A passenger inside the carriage was fending off one of the six assailants with a narrow sword. Despite the rain, Vanderjack could still make out wings on the carriage's attackers; they were draconians.

Draconians were the scaly reptilian soldiers of the dragonarmies. They were created from the eggs of the dragons of Light, eggs that had been stolen from the Dragon Isles and subjected to dark rituals. Takhisis, the Queen of Darkness, had told the good dragons not to interfere with her holy war against the free people of Krynn, or she would destroy their eggs. When the good dragons learned that the eggs had been used to spawn the abominable draconians, they had entered the conflict, and that had been the beginning of the end.

Some years after the end of the war and the triumph of the forces of the Whitestone Armies and their good dragon allies, those few draconians who survived had been reduced to grunt troops for the surviving dragon-armies or, more often than not, mercenaries just like he was. The draconians threatening the carriage, with their red tabards over chainmail hauberks, belonged to the Red Wing of the dragonarmies holding Nordmaar. The carriage's occupant was in serious trouble.

"We have to help that man!" said the Aristocrat.

"Well, he looks rich," muttered the mercenary, wiping water from his eyes. "He might appreciate the assistance."

The Cavalier shook his spectral head. "Mercenaries. Have you no honor?"

Vanderjack smirked, setting off across the road in long, easy strides, sword held out to the side. "Do I look Solamnic to you?"

The closest of the draconians didn't see him coming. Vanderjack ran right by the first one, bringing the sword up in a lazy arc that took the draconian's horned head clean off at the neck. The mercenary was at the carriage before the draconian had toppled forward, turning to stone and landing heavily in the muck.

Vanderjack hated draconians. He'd fought alongside them once, when he was on contract with the Blue Dragonarmy, and learned all of their worst traits up close and personal. Consequently, when he later switched sides and fought with the Armies of Whitestone against the Dark Queen's forces, he knew just where to hit them and just what to do when they died. They were baaz draconians, which meant a quick kill was the only way to avoid having your sword trapped as their death throes turned them to stone.

"Two closing in beside you!" warned the Hunter. Vanderjack spun in place, his sword slicing a lethal trace through the rain and through the upper bodies of the draconians the ghost had warned him of. Their stony faces were frozen in shock.

To the casual observer, the mercenary appeared to have eyes in the back of his head, for he was the only one who could see or hear the Sword Chorus. Most of the time the ghosts settled for incessantly heckling the sellsword. In battle, however, Vanderjack had learned to listen to the Sword Chorus's warnings, responding so quickly to his opponents' actions that onlookers could scarcely believe his skill.

The carriage driver had loaded another bolt into his crossbow. Vanderjack ducked around the side of the carriage as the other draconians caught on to his presence. In so doing, the mercenary smacked the side of the carriage driver's seat with his sword and shouted, "Aim for the head!" The driver swung about, following one of the draconians with his crossbow, and released. The bolt struck its scaly target just beneath where an ear would be on an ordinary soldier. It was enough. The baaz fell dead against the carriage with a thump.

Vanderjack stood ready by the window of the carriage. The carriage's occupant, a sharp-nosed man in soaking-wet velvet clothes, looked as if he were trained in the fancy style of dueling that nobles in Palanthas favored. He was completely out of his depth. "Stay inside!" called Vanderjack. "I can handle these lizards."

"You will die with the baron!" hissed one of the two remaining draconians. It was typical baaz bravado. They weren't the brightest of their kind, and they were often drunk; those fighting him did seem a long way from being sober.

"I don't think so," said Vanderjack. He stepped to the side, feinting with Lifecleaver, and the first baaz fell for the misdirection. Vanderjack took the draconian's arm off with the follow-through, and kicked outward. The draconian fell backward into his companion, who yelled with surprise and fumbled with his own broadsword.

Vanderjack pressed the attack, catching one draconian after the other in the abdomen, where the armor was a poorer-quality chainmail. The links parted under Lifecleaver's magically keen edge, and the draconians were stone-dead a second later.

The driver leaned over the side of the carriage. "Milord! That's all of them!"

The baron was wiping at his face with his voluminous sleeve. "So it is," he said. "And we have this one to thank for it."

Vanderjack watched as the petrified bodies of the slain draconians crumbled into powder and became mixed in with all of the rest of the mud. He let the rain wash the greenish black draconian blood from his blade, and nodded once at the baron. "Well, I'm used to draconians."

"How can I repay you?" asked the baron.

"The noble thing would be to help him out of the mud and see him on his way," said the Balladeer.

"You don't need to be paid for the rescue," said the Apothecary.

"It wasn't much of an effort," agreed the Conjurer.

Vanderjack ignored the ghosts. "Steel is the universal thank-you." He grinned, sliding the sword back into its scabbard.

The baron didn't seem shocked. "Of course," he said. "And in fact, I may have something even more lucrative for a stalwart fellow like yourself. Let's talk about it somewhere dry."

Vanderjack gestured behind him with his thumb. "The bar leaks."

The baron opened the door of his carriage. "Ah, but my manor does not."

Vanderjack shrugged and climbed up beside the baron. The driver stowed his crossbow and snapped the reins. The horses lurched forward, pulling the carriage out of the mud and along the road. With his sword safely sheathed, Vanderjack enjoyed the trip without the running commentary of the ghosts.

As they departed, a black-robed figure stepped out of the shadows of the bar, watching as the baron's carriage grew distant. Oblivious to the rain, the figure walked out into the center of the muddy road, looked down at the remains of the draconians—mainly armor—and poked at them with one boot until it found what it was looking for—a corroded medal bearing the symbol of the dragonarmies. Pocketing the medal, the robed figure headed for the bar; the rain washed away all that was left.

* * * * * *

A gnome walked brazenly along the boardwalks of Pentar with his poleaxe over his shoulder, heedless of the stiff breeze coming off the ocean. He was easily half the size of the other marketplace patrons, who jostled and shoved their way through the weathered stalls and booths, shouting out their offers to the vendors.

Pentar's seaside market was unique in that it extended out over the water with wooden walkways connecting converted flat-bottomed boats and buoys. The gnome skipped over the gaps in the boardwalk, ducked under the arms of two humans engaged in the early throes of a brawl, and leaped up onto dry land.

The gnome, whose name was Theodenes, was a thousand miles from Mount Nevermind. The gnome homeland, built within and on the slopes of a dormant volcano, held no attraction for him; he was a mad gnome, his kinsgnomes had decided, and better off elsewhere. Theodenes, not one to argue too long with anybody, agreed, and he had taken his life's work of journals and logbooks, piled them onto the back of a mule, and struck out for adventure.

That was several years and countless annoying tall people earlier. Odd jobs repairing and tinkering with buckets, skillets, plows, and yokes had kept him solvent along the road to wherever he was destined. There were no classes in entrepreneurship at the Mount Nevermind Collective Scholastic Learning Academy for Gifted Gnomes, despite Theo's insistence that somebody would one day like to make a living off the pervasive gnome culture of invention. No, Theo had to come up with a working hypothesis for earning steel all by himself. It was unorthodox, but he was mad, after all.

Theodenes didn't look mad. He looked like every other gnome. He was short and slender, with a large head and a big nose. He had a wispy white beard and a receding hairline, and his eyes were bright blue. His skin showed the signs of years of travel in the world outside of Mount Nevermind; he was even more tanned than his kinsgnomes.

Seedy wharfside buildings loomed over him. He continued along, slipping into an alleyway flanked by oxcarts, over a midden pile of seashells and used fishing nets, and finally into a crowded square within earshot but out of sight of the floating marketplace. A sign bolted above a door read Monkey's Ear Tavern, just like the name on the note in Theo's pocket.

Inside the Monkey's Ear, which was quite spacious for a gnome but cramped for the taller folk, a small gathering of ne'er-do-wells, scoundrels, and rogues was clustered about a long table. At the table, a broad-shouldered old salt with a missing eye was taking names and writing them in a ledger, occasionally arguing with one of the miscreants and thumbing over his shoulder.

Behind the seated man, three of Pentar's Seaguard stood with arms folded, cutlasses hanging from their belts, giving troublemakers a watchful glower. The Seaguard, once a dependable organization of maritime peacekeepers, were nowadays paid off by criminals and mobsters and had become little more than enforcers. The three in the bar could have been brothers and probably were. Pentar was a town filled with siblings who shared work, especially dangerous work.

Theo casually walked up to the table and looked about for a place to stand in line. As he turned his head from left to right, he swung the enormous poleaxe about, as if he'd forgotten he had it with him. Cries of outrage and yelps of pain ensued, and a space quickly cleared around him. The recruiter at the table glared in his direction with his one good eye.

"We don't hire on kender," he barked, looking Theodenes up and down.

Theo was short, yes, and had the same build as a kender, possibly. But nobody could mistake a gnome for a kender. Would a kender have his shock of white hair? Or his proud and sizable nose? Was any kender known for such brilliant blue cobalt eyes, or a most excellent mustache and goatee?

"I am a gnome," announced Theo indignantly. "I am nothing like a kender. Indeed, I am offended by such an association! Why, even in my beardless youth, I could not have been mistaken for a kender. Kender are all burglars and thieves and scallywags. I, if you please, am Theodenes, a gnome and a master of locks, portals, gates, fasteners, sundry latches—"

"We don't hire on gnomes," interrupted the recruiter.

"Well now, I don't believe that was the purpose of my visit."

The recruiter snapped his fingers and pointed at Theo. Immediately, the Seaguard thugs behind him leaped forward with their cutlasses flashing.

Theo took a step to the right and swung the poleaxe up and over his head. The first Seaguard thug sailed over the recruiter's desk and into the path of the swinging blade, falling to the beer-stained floor of the tavern with a cry. His severed right hand, cutlass still firmly in its grasp, kept on going, tumbling over and over and into the shocked crowd.

The second Seaguard brute narrowly avoided the poleaxe, grunting with surprise. Theo looked up at him, one bushy white eyebrow arched, and brought the poleaxe around again. As he did so, he twisted and tugged with a one-two-three on the haft of the poleaxe. A series of rapid clicks sounded; the axe head collapsed in on itself and formed a wicked spear point. It lanced right through the upper thigh of the Seaguard.

The gnome leaped over the pole of his trapped weapon to escape the third Seaguard thug's cutlass. He grabbed the polearm, tugged it free, and looked directly into the eyes of that cutlass's owner. Another twist of the haft, and the spear head became a wickedly curved hook. The bushy eyebrows narrowed.

"What are you waiting for!" shouted the recruiter, who was standing, sweating. "He's half your size!"

The last Seaguard formed a scowl and feinted forward with his blade, hoping to at least goad the gnome into reckless action. Theo responded by sweeping the hooked polearm in a wide arc, scraping the floor, and catching his opponent around the ankles. The Seaguard toppled like a fallen vallenwood.

The recruiter blinked in astonishment. The gnome's weapon—a poleaxe once again—was at his trembling throat.

"As I was saying. I, if you please, am Theodenes, a gnome and a master of locks, portals, gates, fasteners, sundry latches . . . "

He inclined his head to one side, in the direction of the three maimed thugs lying with a great deal of cleared space around them, the other scoundrels and rogues backing away and keeping their distance.

". . . and other obstacles."

CHAPTER TWO

Vanderjack stood in a dry, comfortable room looking up at an empty spot on the wall above a fireplace.

The baron, who had introduced himself on the three-hour carriage ride to his manor house as Lord Gilbert Glayward, had left the sellsword in the cozy room to dry off. Vanderjack quickly determined that there was more expensive artwork in that one room than he had ever seen in his life. There were portraits of long-dead aristocrats, quaint scenes of rural Solamnia, and random pieces of sculpture depicting kingfishers and crowns and roses. A handful of odd-looking Nordmaaran tribal statues, such as cats and apes, provided contrast.

Some of the art was missing, however. Vanderjack wondered if Lord Glayward had been selling it off. There were few nobles in this day and age whose family coffers were still full. Glayward's manor house was nice, but judging by the occasional dusty mantel or picture frame in there, he'd have a hard time impressing any of the muckety-mucks in far Palanthas.

The sellsword wasn't sure what he thought of the

18

Knights of Solamnia, or Solamnia in general. During his time with them, as one of their auxiliary, he'd had to endure their Oath and their Measure and their rigid fraternal behavior. It was said that in the past three hundred years, their reputation had grown from bad to worse; accused by the common folk for bringing about or failing to prevent the Cataclysm, the Knights had been chased out of their ancestral estates and forced into the role of expatriate nobility on the island of Sancrist. There, alongside the gnomes of Mount Nevermind, the Knights had spent three centuries obsessing over what had happened and wallowing in their own guilt while the rest of the world dragged itself out of famine and despair.

All of that made them extremely difficult to get along with. Even worse, when their glory was restored by one knight's sacrifice at the High Clerist's Tower, most of Solamnia expected that knight's brothers to be as brave, noble, and courageous as he was. Far from it. Vanderjack had run into a handful of valorous men in plate armor while he was in the pay of the High Council of Knights, but most of them kept away from the front and let mercenaries such as he make the charge.

"Magnificent," said the Cavalier.

The Sword Chorus floated about Vanderjack, voicing their own impressions of the baron's wealth.

"Clearly a man of refined tastes," said the Balladeer.

"Keep your hands to yourself!" warned the Aristocrat.

"Contemplate this life of austere devotion to Solamnia," added the Philosopher.

The others all joined in. Vanderjack half listened, ignoring most of the commentary, which was evidently about how he could be living a more productive life in any number of professions that would offer more useful employment. When Lord Glayward returned, the sell-sword removed his hand from Lifecleaver's hilt, and the ghosts vanished once more.

"I see you're admiring the art," the baron said.

"I'm not really a good judge of it." Vanderjack smiled. "But I can tell you've got roots in Solamnia. How did you end up here in Nordmaar?"

Lord Glayward dismissed a servant, who had delivered a plate of meats, cheeses, and other things arrayed around a tureen of soup. He helped himself, and indicated for Vanderjack to do the same. Vanderjack shook his head.

"My family is all Solamnic nobility." The baron shrugged. "But of course, after the Cataclysm, when the commoners blamed them for bringing about the anger of the gods, or not doing enough to stop it, they were among the many that left it all behind them."

"I see. And your family made it all the way here."

The baron nodded. "Nordmaar was very welcoming to displaced nobles like my great-grandfather. The natives aspired to be more like the Solamnics. Or so the legends say. Before the Cataclysm, none of this land was above the water, you know! So it was all here for the taking."

"I'm sure that's what the Red Dragonarmy said ten years ago too." Vanderjack grinned.

The baron flinched but managed a conciliatory smile.

Vanderjack quickly changed the subject. "So, Lord Glayward. You said you had a job offer?"

"Oh yes! I'll have my aide bring the paperwork. Do excuse me for a moment." The baron crossed back to the big oak doors, and called through them. Moments later, a woman stepped into the room with a stack of papers.

The new arrival was the ugliest woman Vanderjack had ever seen. Her reddish-brown hair was chopped off at the jawline and had no shape to it; it was as though she'd gone at it with a dull knife. Her eyes seemed spaced too far apart, her nose was enormous, and her mismatched ears stuck out. Her limbs were slightly crooked, and even when she stood up as straight as possible, she had no womanly figure to speak of.

The baron noticed Vanderjack staring and coughed. "May I introduce my aide, Gredchen?"

The woman bowed curtly. "An honor."

Vanderjack said, "If you say so."

"Gredchen, Vanderjack here saved my life on the road to Pentar this afternoon. It was quite a stroke of luck, as I am in the market for somebody with his talents."

Gredchen studied Vanderjack the way she would a crack in the woodwork or a dent in the good silver. "Indeed, my lord."

Conscious of her disapproval, Vanderjack decided to continue his discussion with the baron instead. "I can't give you any references. I'm not with anybody at the moment, and I don't have any of this new Shinarite protocol, but I'm familiar with most forms of contract."

The baron relieved Gredchen of her paperwork and began sorting it at a table by the fireplace. The woman arranged writing implements and ink but continued to study Vanderjack. Vanderjack decided not to worry about that since people stared at him on a daily basis.

"I have in mind a short-term arrangement," the baron said. "Short term because I can't afford to wait. You see, there's something I want you to retrieve for me."

The sellsword frowned. "That's not usually what I do."

Vanderjack had carried out a search-and-retrieval job once before, for the elves in Southern Ergoth. Complete disaster. He didn't like to think about it, and there was only one other person who knew about the details and he was safely tucked away in Mount Nevermind. If you'd call that safe.

"But it's a matter of great import. And I believe I can offer you substantial compensation."

Vanderjack crossed his arms. "Such as?"

The baron said a figure. Vanderjack coughed. He hadn't been paid that much in twenty years. Gredchen looked equally astonished.

"My lord, how . . . " she began.

"Never mind the amount! Gredchen, the red wolves are at my door. You know as well as I do what the stakes are."

Vanderjack leaned forward and lifted an eyebrow. "You may know the stakes, but I don't. Are you going to get around to telling me what this is about?"

"I need to you to go into occupied territory," the baron said, lifting a sheet of paper covered in cursive writing. "Just inside the Sahket Jungle, near North Keep. Castle Glayward in fact."

Vanderjack's eyebrows arched even further. "Your castle?"

"Before the invasion, yes."

"You want me to go to your castle in Red Wing–occupied Nordmaar. Did you leave something valuable there?"

"In a manner of speaking," the baron said. "I want you to rescue my daughter."

Vanderjack looked up at the ceiling. "Ackal's Teeth," he said.

The baron and his ugly aide stood there for a while,

watching the sellsword expectantly. Vanderjack rubbed his face and groaned. Women were usually nothing but bother.

"All right. Where do you want me to sign?"

******

It was raining heavily in Wulfgar, Nordmaar's City of the Plains. Water ran in curtains from rooftops and turned the famous horse arena into a lake. The distant Khalkist Mountains blocked out the setting sun, but the heat of the earlier day gave strength to the humid air.

This is what passes for summer here, thought the Red Dragon highmaster. She stood on one of the balconies of the Palace of the Khan, looking down upon the city from an impressive height, taking in the steamy view while sipping from a tall glass of chilled wine. Highmaster Rivven Cairn was blonde and half-elf, the latter evident in her upswept ears and arched eyebrows. That alone would have been enough to make her stand out in Wulfgar. The highmaster wasn't content with that, however; she was never seen without her garish red and black armor and the curving elven sword worn on her back.

The Red Wing of the dragonarmies under Highlord Phair Caron had occupied Nordmaar almost ten years earlier, one of the causes of the War of the Lance. Caron was gone, killed in Silvanesti and replaced by Verminaard. Verminaard was gone, killed in Abanasinia, and replaced by Emperor Ariakas himself. Ariakas was gone, replaced by a succession of would-be highlords. The current claimant, Karelas, was skulking in the ogre lands of Kern, while Rivven Cairn, highmaster to all of them, held Nordmaar alone.

Rivven watched as a messenger ran up the streets of the city, through the main gates that led to the sloping approach to the palace, and on through the various open courtyards. She set her glass on a side table and took her horned great helm from its stand by the bed. When the young boy finally burst in through the royal bedroom doors, flanked by a pair of baaz draconian guards, she was ready.

"Hand it over," she said, her voice resonating though the mask. The terrified messenger handed her a scroll sealed in red wax. Rivven waved him off, and as the draconians roughly escorted the boy outside, she broke the seal—that of her black robe mage in Pentar—and scanned the scroll's contents.

"Aubec!" she shouted, getting to the last line of the message. Her chief aide, a stocky, bald Nordmaaran who had thrown his lot in with the dragonarmies years earlier, appeared in the doorway moments after.

"My lady?" he said, watching the highmaster pace back and forth. "Troubling news?"

Rivven crumpled the scroll in her mailed fist and shook it in Aubec's direction. "Idiots!" she shouted. "The wizard Cazuvel writes that somebody in my army took it upon themselves to make an attempt on Lord Glayward's life."

Aubec nodded. "Overzealous," he said.

Rivven Cairn removed her helmet and threw it onto a nearby armchair. "I will not abide this kind of behavior from my officers. I don't care how bored they are or how much the baron mocks them over the lines of occupation. We have a system here, and it works."

Aubec shrugged. "He lives yet?"

"They failed, yes. Some Ergothian swordsman intervened, and I lost six draconians." Rivven kept pacing back and forth. "I'm not going to be able to get any more of those from Neraka either! Incompetents."

Aubec produced a sheet of parchment and crossed to a writing desk. "I shall draw up the necessary orders of reprisal to Captain Annaud, my lady."

"Cazuvel has been watching Annaud for the past three months," Rivven said. "Annaud's going to wonder how I got hold of this information. He'll start to ask questions, and that'll annoy Cazuvel. I need Cazuvel. And he's more useful to me when the captain thinks he's working for him."

The red Dragon highmaster was, like others in the upper echelons of the Dragon Queen's forces, quite conversant with arcane magic. She was not in the late Ariakas's league, nor even that of the white Dragon Highlord Feal-Thas. The moons of magic were just a means of tracking the passing of days to her.

But Rivven had acquired a number of minor magical skills in her time, enough to bolster her considerable martial talents and enough to get a good read on blackrobed mages such as Cazuvel. The human was far more studious and crafty in the arts than she, but he lacked what she possessed. He lacked the razor edge of conviction, a razor honed in flames.

Rivven caught herself musing about her younger life, before the dragonarmy, before Ariakas. He'd seen in her an obsessive nature that rivaled his, and a zealot's spirit. Unlike the dragon emperor, whose efforts were driven toward the acquisition of power and strength, Rivven focused on being where she needed to be. She could outlive all of the other highmasters and highlords. She knew it, and she knew Ariakas had known it. Leave the grandstanding and infamy to Kitiara or that general in the black army, Marcus Cadrio. Rivven could wait.

The highmaster stopped her pacing near the window and reclaimed her glass of wine. As Aubec began writing, she looked out again over steamy Wulfgar, the dragon-army banners hanging limp in the rain, and exhaled. "Six draconians vanquished, Cazuvel says. Make a note, Aubec, when you're finished."

She looked over at her scribe then into her glass. "I want to know who that swordsman is."

CHAPTER THREE

Before dawn Vanderjack woke with a grunt.

It was still dark. His room in the manor house was drafty and small, with only one window opposite the cramped bed he'd been given. Outside, the rain had stopped. The red and silver light from the two crescent moons let the sellsword see pink-edged silhouettes in the room but little else.

A mercenary lives his life in the dawn, one of his past associates had told him. Get up with the baker, gather your kit while the bread's in the oven, and be on the road while breakfast is still warm in your hand. Vanderjack didn't hold with every sellsword custom, but he had never been able to sleep in. He lived his life in the dawn.

He didn't know the manor house well enough to be used to its noises, to know if a creak in the floorboards was the shifting of the timbers or an intruder. But he had excellent hearing, and he could tell that an interesting conversation was going on elsewhere in the house. He heard voices that didn't belong to the baron, his aide, or the driver.

Vanderjack slipped out of his bed, pulled on his arming doublet, trousers, and boots, and strapped the baldric and scabbard for Lifecleaver around his waist. He pulled the sword an inch out of its scabbard and felt the Sword Chorus materialize around him.

"Enjoying the comforts of the wealthy, I see," said the Aristocrat.

"A little too much," said the Balladeer.

Vanderjack frowned. "You must be looking at a different room than I am." He approached the door and carefully opened it until a thin crack let him hear the voices more easily.

"Sneaking about is hardly honorable," said the Cavalier.

"Wait—there is danger," said the Hunter, and the ghost's insubstantial form disappeared through the wall.

The Hunter was often keenly aware of a problem without Vanderjack even having to mention it. Vanderjack could always count on the Sword Chorus for that kind of thing, especially when it catered to their individual roles. Some, like the Cavalier, were helpful in a fight. The Conjurer, alternately, had saved Vanderjack a number of times by identifying magic as it was being cast; could even allow the sellsword to react before a spell went off.

Vanderjack blocked out the comments of the other ghosts for a moment as they continued to discuss the audacity of standing quietly in the dark. He placed his ear close to the crack in door. He could definitely make out the baron's voice too.

". . . have no right to come in . . . time of night . . . "

A baritone voice, in response: ". . . causing us to pay a visit . . . highmaster never approved of the attack . . . "

The baron again: ". . . leave before I have you thrown out!"

". . . simply here to warn you to be careful . . . Ergothian mercenary . . . "

At that last, Vanderjack winced. The visitors must be from the dragonarmy. How brazen were they, first attacking the man on the road, then showing up at his very house?

The Hunter returned moments later. "Red Dragonarmy," he said, confirming the sellsword's suspicions. "Three draconians, one human officer. Two more draconians outside."

Vanderjack nodded. "You've been very helpful," he said, sliding the sword back into the scabbard. Alone again in the dark, he opened the door just enough to slip out into the hallway and closed it behind himself as he left.

He literally bumped into Gredchen as he turned a corner in the hallway. The baron's ugly aide was fully dressed in traveling leathers and had a satchel slung over her shoulder. Was she going somewhere?

"Idiot!" she hissed.

"I was about to say the same thing," whispered Vanderjack.

"What are you doing out here?"

Vanderjack pointed down the hallway, past Gredchen. "I heard voices. I'm assuming you did too?"

Gredchen sniffed. "Lord Glayward has visitors."

"From the Red Dragonarmy, I know. I, uh, was on my way to see if I could lend a hand."

"He's in no danger. It's Captain Annaud, from Pentar—one of the highmaster's officers. Apologizing for the attack today. Says that was a rogue group of draconians."

"Sure it was. Is he looking for me?"

"I'm afraid so. There's a price on your head."

"Well, then. I'd better be off to do my appointed job." Vanderjack grinned and started back in the opposite direction from the voices.

"You can't just leave!" said Gredchen, grabbing Vanderjack's bare arm. "You don't even know where the castle is. Have you ever been in the Sahket Jungle before? Or any further into Nordmaar than here?"

Vanderjack stopped, looking down at Gredchen's hand on his elbow. She withdrew it quickly. "Hmm, you're right," he said. "I should get a map."

"Maps are in the drawing room, which is where—"

"Which is where the baron and his visitors are talking. Of course." Vanderjack tapped his finger to his temple and showed his wide, white grin. "I guess you're coming with me, then."

"I am?"

Vanderjack grabbed her by the elbow, steering her alongside him as he continued walking. "As you say, I need a guide. You know the way. I'm sure the baron can take care of himself, and the driver knows how to use a crossbow. So come on and show me the back way out."

Gredchen sputtered. "But—"

Vanderjack turned. "Look. It's obvious that was what you had in mind. You're dressed for the road and that satchel probably has all the maps we need. Am I right?"

Gredchen said nothing, glaring at him.

"I thought so. So we're all square, then. And hey— maybe you can keep me honest!"

That was what she had been thinking, by the look on her face.

At the end of the hallway and through the kitchens, which would have been bustling with servants in a wealthier household, Vanderjack and Gredchen looked out a back entrance to survey their escape route. As the Hunter had said, there were two draconians patrolling the grounds—tall, hunched, scaly, with wings and tails in mockery of the dragons whose eggs they were created from.

"Those aren't baaz," Vanderjack whispered. "See the curving horns?"

Gredchen could barely see them in the poor light, let alone make out details. "No."

"You need to spend more time outside at night," said Vanderjack.

When Gredchen did nothing to respond, he continued. "Those are bozaks. Spellcasters, sometimes used as commanders of small units or religious functionaries. I knew one or two who were intelligence officers."

"So we have to worry about magic?" asked Gredchen.

"Ordinarily, yes," Vanderjack said with a glance around to scout the area and also to see if his ghosts were attendant. "But we should be fine. Come on. Wait until they're around front, and we'll make a break for it."

A stable, a barn, some outhouses, and a long, low-roofed building that might once have been kennels formed a roughly semicircular perimeter around the back of the manor house. The manor was on a lightly forested property that stretched for some considerable distance back from the buildings, sloping up toward a series of bluffs that looked out over the ocean to the north. Vanderjack could hear the sea perhaps a mile away. The road was to the southwest, but there were plenty of trees between their current position and there.

Once the draconians were out of sight, Vanderjack ran off the months of the year in his head, in Ergothian. It was an old mercenary trick to measure time. Once he reached the month of Phoenix, he tapped Gredchen on the arm and moved away from the kitchen door in a low crouch.

It was brighter than he had expected; he wasn't sure why, but he could see a lot better out of cover. That was a problem, since it meant he and Gredchen were just as visible to anybody else. As the sellsword approached the stables, he pressed close to the wooden wall, looking across the yard to the side of the manor house.

"Where are they?" Gredchen whispered.

"I don't see them. That's odd. They should—" He stopped and held his breath. The sound of chainmail links clinking alerted him to the presence of something close by. A breeze, probably from the coast, stirred the puddles of water in the yard and also brought a distinct smell to the sellsword's nose: dwarf spirits. It was the favorite vice of draconian soldiers.

Vanderjack drew Lifecleaver immediately, bringing it up in a defensive position in case of ambush. With his free hand, he pushed Gredchen down, hard, against the side of the stable door. "Stay there!" he hissed, ignoring her furious look.

A heavy curved weapon like a machete crossed with a scimitar took chunks of wood out of the wall where Gredchen used to be. It had appeared from nowhere, and it brought along with it one of the bozak draconians. He'd been invisible, but the spell had dropped once he'd made the attack. The other bozak was probably nearby.

"No good being invisible if you're going to smell like a Thorbardin brew house!" Vanderjack barked, bringing his sword up to shove the bozak's blade away. The Sword Chorus was with him, watching the battle. The bozaks and Gredchen, of course, had no idea the ghosts were even there.

"It is useless to resist!" the bozak said like a bad actor in a traveling minstrel show. It never ceased to amaze Vanderjack how such a dangerous and intelligent race as the bozaks could resort to such terrible dialogue.

"I've heard that before!"

Gredchen rolled away and got to her feet. "Leave him alone! He's under the baron's hospitality, you reptilian thug!"

"She's about to be grabbed from behind," said the Hunter from about ten feet away.

The other bozak, thought Vanderjack. Mortal eyes couldn't penetrate their magic, but ghosts could see right through it.

Vanderjack ducked a swing from the first bozak and launched himself away from the stable in Gredchen's direction. Startled, she dropped to the mud. Lifecleaver cut through thin air but left behind it a gout of draconian ichor. The second bozak materialized, his invisibility spell ruined, clutching at his scaly throat.

The first bozak raised a hand and uttered a string of words in the language of magic. Vanderjack had no fluency in it, of course, but he knew the spidery-sounding tongue when he heard it.

"Lightning bolt!" cried the Conjurer before the bozak could finish the incantation.

Vanderjack grabbed Gredchen and spun her out of the way, narrowly avoiding the hot white light of the bozak's bolt as it seared past him and into an outhouse. The outhouse exploded, the bozak cursed, and Vanderjack grinned in the Conjuror's direction.

The second bozak, unable to vocalize spells thanks to the wound to his larynx, drew his scimitar and charged at Vanderjack. Bozaks were stronger and quicker than the lesser baaz, but Vanderjack was stronger and quicker yet. Turning the oncoming blade to the side, the mercenary swung his sword around in a heavy riposte and took the bozak's arm off at the elbow.

Vanderjack readied for another swing. A warning from the Apothecary stayed his hand, however, for Gredchen had picked herself up and thrown herself at the armless bozak. She tackled the draconian around the legs, knocking both of them over.

"You really don't want to stay out of this, do you?" the sellsword grinned.

"Help me out here!" Gredchen yelled back, trying to force the bozak's clawed hand from her face. The draconian made a sort of gargled snarl in an effort to intimidate the woman, but Vanderjack didn't think it was having its intended effect.

"I'll be right with you," Vanderjack said mildly, turning to face off against the other bozak. Where was he? Another warning from the Conjuror allowed the mercenary to sidestep a fan-shaped gout of flames and close with the astonished draconian. Vanderjack drove his sword through the bozak's midsection before the draconian could bring its sword up to block the killing stroke. Remembering the way in which bozaks die, he leaped clear of his slain foe just as the creature's flesh shriveled away and its exposed skeleton began to smolder. Moments later, the bones exploded, flooding the courtyard with a monstrous green light.

A second explosion, just like the first, drew Vanderjack's attention back to Gredchen. She had managed to end the life of the bozak she'd been wrestling with, and the look of shock and soot on her face was evidence enough to Vanderjack that she hadn't faced a bozak's death throes before.

"Should have warned you about that," he said. "Nice work. Rolled over on its own sword, did it?"

Gredchen, who seemed mostly unhurt, though rattled from the blast, gave the sellsword a pained look. "Let's just get out of here," she said.

"You'll get no argument from me." He grinned and followed her through the trees toward the road to Pentar, quite aware that the noise they made in the courtyard would not have gone unnoticed.

******

Theodenes sat in a high-backed chair in his new office in the Monkey's Ear, going over a pile of paperwork. His poleaxe was within arm's reach, which for a gnome was about half the reach of the chair's former occupant. Theo was drawing up his to-do list.

After only one day of being the newest recruiter in Pentar, Theo was already starting to realize that the position called for a great deal of bookkeeping. His cousin Thermocouplet was the family accountant, and Theo considered sending for him. All gnomes knew something about numbers, but the gang's books were an order of difficulty higher than anything Theo had had to worry about before.

Unfortunately, Theo's family had largely disowned him, being a mad gnome and all.

"Sir," inquired a voice from the door. "I know it's early, but there's some recruits here for the muster."

"Yes, quite right. Send them in."

Theodenes knew he looked awkward in the overlarge chair, but he could manage a convincing enough look of professionalism when called to do so. As the three ne'er-do-wells came into the room, he lit a cigar and spun slowly around to face them.

The three men stared at the little cigar-smoking gnome seated behind the desk.

"Is there something the matter?" asked Theo, keeping his voice as deep and low as he could. "You look as if you've never seen a gnome in charge of an operation like this before."

"Begging your pardon, sir," said one. "I don't think we have."

Theo studied the recruits. The one who had spoken was an unshaven lout with a shock of dirty blond hair and sailor's trews. The man next to him had Nordmaaran blood, by the look of him, and if the barbarian leathers were any indication, he more than likely had just come off the plains. The last was a pale, pudgy, nondescript sort of character, the kind Theo used to see a lot back west—definitely not a local.

"Be that as it may, I am the new recruitment officer of this organization, owing to a recent change in leadership. My name is Theodenes. Learn it well!"

The blond sailor cracked a smile. Theo snapped his fingers, and one of the Seaguard loomed from out of the shadows. The blond sailor instantly regretted it.

"I'm sorry, sir, I didn't mean—"

"Cletus," said Theodenes. "This one isn't going to work out."

The Seaguard dragged the blond sailor from the room by another door. The two remaining recruits looked terrified.

"You," asked Theo, pointing at the Nordmaaran. "What skills can you bring this organization?"

"I rode with the Quetzal Raiders in the War, under Tlaloc of the Blade," said the Nordmaaran. "I slew twenty men. I tracked a manticore in the hills alone and brought it down. I climbed Mount Brego with my brothers to seek the oracles and brought wisdom back to my chieftain. I—"

Theo waved his cigar. "All very exciting," he said, "but not what we're looking for."

Cletus had stepped back into the room. Theo looked in his direction. "Cletus, this one's not working out either."

The Nordmaaran raised his hands. "I'll see myself out."

"An excellent decision." Theo nodded. He looked at the third and final recruit. "You there. Solamnic, I take it?"

"Yes, sir. From the Solanthus area."

"Marketable skills?"

The pudgy Solamnic cleared his throat. "Two seasons with the Third Crown Infantry, and one with the Eighth Sword Lancers."

Theodenes frowned. "Never heard of them."

"Not very active in these parts, sir."

"Well, I don't really need any more retired Solamnic soldiers. Can you do anything else?"

"Well, I . . . "

"How about cooking?"

The man coughed. "Cooking? Why, yes, sir."

"Really? You don't sound so sure."

"No, no. It takes me by surprise is all. Cook? Absolutely, sir."

Theo looked over at Cletus and back again to the Solamnic. "Do you handle poultry, pork, lamb, venison, beef, other meats?"

"Yes, sir. Of course."

"How about lizard?"

The man puffed his chest out. "If I can put it into a skillet or hold it over a fire, I can cook it, sir."

Theo grinned. "Perfect! You're hired. I assume you know your way around a sword and spear too?"

The Solamnic nodded. "You can't serve three tours with the Solamnic Army without knowing how to defend yourself, sir."

"Quite right. Now." Theodenes lifted his quill and turned to the first empty space in the ledger on the desk. "What is your name?"

There was a brief pause. The cook looked as if he hadn't been expecting that question. "Etharion, sir. Etharion Cordaric."

Theo thought the name sounded a little Ergothian, but then again the Solamnics were all descended from Ergothians anyway. "Welcome to the Monkey's Ear Company, Etharion. The kitchen's out back."

After the Solamnic had left, Theo sent Cletus out of the room and sat alone in his cigar smoke. With a cook on board, he had a full complement. All he needed was a job that paid, and things would really get moving.

It was dangerous work, he thought. But he'd seen the best in action before, the kind of man who left a lasting impression, the kind of man who inspired imitators in the profession, the kind of man who owed a gnome several hundred steel pieces and a new saber-toothed kitten.

"Vanderjack," said Theodenes to no one in particular.

CHAPTER FOUR

Vanderjack watched the sun going down over the Turbidus Ocean and thought of his mother.

There were hundreds of pirate kings in the Saifhumi shanty tales, but there had never been a pirate queen like her. Ireni Erj-Ackal was born on a ship and set foot on dry land only after she had first learned to climb rigging and walk along a spar. The Saifhumi made her their queen on the morning of her twentieth birthday, in the tradition of the sea nomads; she reigned for twenty more years before Mandracore the Reaver, a half-ogre, sank four of her ships and claimed her throne.

Ireni Erj-Ackal lived out the last three years of her life in forced retirement in Sea Reach, the capital of Saifhum, watching the minotaurs slowly take over the privateering around the island and hearing about rising stars such as Melas Kar-Thon and his daughter. Her own son watched her die, leaving thirty Ergothian brass coins on the side table where her sword once lay.

Vanderjack had never been back to Saifhum, nor spent another day on a sea nomad ship. The ubiquitous smells of patchai-ellai and curried fish sauces still made him sick to his stomach. He was no son of the sea. But he couldn't stop gazing at it, and that meant thinking of her.

"Well?"

The sellsword's thoughts came back to the present. Gredchen was standing there before him, and over her shoulder were the north gates of Pentar.

"Not until dark," he said.

The baron's aide exhaled and sat down next to him on the salt-worn rock. "Do you always walk into towns at night? They close the gates, you know."

Vanderjack scratched his chin. "It's the best time of the day to show up anywhere," he said. "And besides, closing the gates in Pentar doesn't mean anything. We'll go down along the wharves. You can walk around there"—he pointed at the westernmost end of the fifteen-foot stone wall surrounding the port town—"into the Temple District, where the Seaguard don't spend a lot of time, and these new priests are eager to be hospitable."

Gredchen frowned. "Waiting here means Annaud's men are going to catch up to us. You realize that, don't you?"

"I know what I'm doing."

"Uh-huh. Well, I certainly hope you do, for the baron's sake. He's paying you a lot of steel to sit around and wait until the sun goes down."

Vanderjack and Gredchen did just that for another hour until the sellsword was sure there wasn't any more light other than the slivers of the red and silver moons hanging above. Only then did he get up, stretch his legs, pick up his pack, and head toward the waterfront.

Pentar made its living as a trade port. During the

war, it had been occupied by the red dragonarmy, liberated by the Whitestone forces from Kalaman, then abandoned to its fate. That suited the Pentari folk just fine. It wasn't the melting pot that Palanthas or even Kalaman were. It wasn't a haven for pirates or wealthy merchants either. What it was, and had been for more than a hundred and fifty years, was home to a thriving import business. The red dragonarmy made heavy use of that business, even four years after they had been kicked out.

Such constant trade meant that the town was full of hired help or those who wanted to be hired. If you weren't a vendor or a sailor or a priest, you were a hireling, and that was exactly what Vanderjack wanted.

Vanderjack and Gredchen picked their way through a thicket of lobster pots and fishing huts before clambering up onto the Temple District wharf. Some of the locals were still perched on the edge of the wharf, muttering invocations to the gods—Habbakuk and Chislev and furious Zeboim. In the new age of godly reverence, the people of Pentar were keen to make as much use of the divine powers as they could to improve their lives . . . or their fishing.

Pentar had two small harbors, little more than niches in the coastline, which flanked a promontory that thrust out into the Turbidus Ocean between them. Upon that promontory rose the governor's palace, and between the palace and the town itself was a walled orchard whose redolent smells of citrus wafted across the water to the temple district. Vanderjack considered walking around to the orchard, if only to reacquaint himself with tangerines. Maybe later, he thought. No need to get too close to the governor.

The streets were dark; only the main thoroughfare

and the waterfront had lanterns. Gredchen walked close to Vanderjack; too close it seemed to him. Indeed she was always poking her bulbous nose into Vanderjack's face when talking to him. He wondered absently whether her sheer ugliness made her abandon most people's concept of personal space for lack of needing to concern herself with proprieties.

"Lots of temples," he said to break the silence as they walked. "Half of them don't even look open."

"Missionaries came here soon after the war," Gredchen said. "The baron had a priest of Paladine show up in person at his manor to welcome him into the faith if he so chose. He didn't. A lot of the locals, however, were really pleased with the idea."

Vanderjack stopped to look at one of the large, chunky idols set in front of a temple. It was a stylized striped and scaled cat of some kind, fashioned from brass and stacked on top of urns or amphorae or some kind of jug. It looked vaguely familiar.

"Isn't there one of these statues in Glayward's manor house?" he asked.

Gredchen nodded. "Very similar, yes. A big brass tiger icon given to Lord Gilbert's grandfather by the natives many years ago. I wasn't aware it had any religious association."

Vanderjack indicated the temple's dedication plaque. "Says this place is dedicated to a god of luck and the disenfranchised."

"Branchala," Gredchen said. "Usually a minstrel god, from what I've heard. But local religion always puts a new face on the gods. Supernatural mysticism and so on. It's been common in Nordmaar ever since the land rose out of the sea; the only difference now is that the gods are real."

Vanderjack snorted. "They're real, all right. They were behind all of that mess in the war too. I don't hold much store in that, although this luck god does sound interesting."

The baron's aide looked away, skimming the street with her eyes. "Are we done here, then?"

"Yeah, we're done. Next stop—an inn of some kind. We need sleep. Big day ahead of us, shopping around for henchmen." He patted the brass tiger statue on the head. "Good kitty."

As they walked away, Gredchen swore she heard a growl from the direction of the temple. Looking over her shoulder, she saw nothing but the brass tiger totem, grinning back at her. She reminded herself to cover the statue in Lord Gilbert's manor with a throw rug when she got back.

******

Rivven Cairn flew northwest with the sunset to her left and the jungle on her right, over the grasslands, toward the sea. Her red dragon, Cear, flew lazily, watching the grasses below for something edible.

"We don't have the time to hunt," the highmaster said, leaning a little forward in the ornate saddle so the dragon could hear her above the whipping wind.

"Why not?" replied the dragon. "I can do it easily from the air."

"Later," she said. Rivven wanted to be at the baron's manor before it grew too dark. The half-elf didn't like showing up when her hosts were sleeping. She preferred them to be awake, especially Lord Gilbert. She had a lot to talk to him about, and humans needed their sleep more than she did.

Above her, positioned between the thin crescents

of Lunitari and Solinari, the red and the silver moons, she could see the gibbous black orb of Nuitari shining its dark light upon the world. Nobody but wizards who had turned to black magic and creatures of ineffable evil could see Nuitari's moon. It was a beacon of wickedness, a constant reminder to her that her choices had opened a window into a sinister world few dared to glimpse.

Ariakas had tested her magical skills several years before, during the war. Curious of her talent, he had constructed a vivid yet entirely illusory proving ground on the borders of dream, a mindscape of meditation he himself used when calling upon the darkest of forces. She'd shown him all she knew, and he'd responded, and she realized how far along the path the emperor of Ansalon had already gone. Despite the fact that he had abandoned the black robes many years earlier in favor of the weapons of war, he had lost none of his arcane edge. Compared to him, she was a novice.

Rivven had used that experience to motivate herself into deeper study. Rather than embrace necromancy or the shadowy magic of guile and betrayal, as other evil wizards had, Rivven focused on fire. The constant flames of the outer dark flickered within her, just as they did within red dragons and fiery fiends and elementals. Her soul was a black candle, eternally lit. It drew her closer to Cear, who recognized within her a kindred spirit, and it fueled her magic as Ariakas's path of conquest fueled his.

In their last exchange, a week before the Whitestone Armies broke the defenses of Neraka and the Temple of Darkness was destroyed, Ariakas had asked Rivven of her progress in the magical arts. He said, "Have you found the thorn?" and she had understood what he meant. Ariakas did not draw upon Nuitari's power. He had found another path, under the guidance of his Dark Queen, a barb that bit deep within and pierced the heart of magic.

"I have," she had responded. Her thorn was blackened by fire, sterilized in the flames of ambition and evil, but it was there.

Ariakas was most pleased with her. He had arranged a place for her in his new Dragon Empire, at his side, once his mistress stepped through the portal and into the world.

So much for that, she thought. Ariakas's death almost put out those fires in her soul. Upon reflection, so much of it might just have been his charismatic personality, the same one he used to attract hundreds of other female conquests. She vowed not to let another man step so far within her boundaries again. He had shown her the Left Hand Path, away from that hungry black moon she was still capable of seeing, staring down upon her. There was nothing for it but to keep walking it . . . alone.

Cear flew a lazy arc over Lord Gilbert Glayward's estate, settling finally in the large open forecourt where perhaps a half dozen dragonarmy soldiers stood about, smoking and sharing a jug of ale. At the sight of Rivven's enormous dragon and the highmaster herself, they quickly stashed away the alcohol and dropped their still-smoldering cheroots to the gravel, grinding them out with their heels.

Rivven dismounted and strode over to the soldiers, furious. "What in the name of the Queen of Darkness are you idiots doing? Where is your captain? Wasn't there a full detachment sent here?"

One of the soldiers, a man with the rank of sergeant,

going by his poorly kept uniform, stepped forward. "Your Excellency, please accept our apologies, we—"

She slapped the man so hard, he almost fell over.

"Don't apologize! Just tell me where he is!"

Clutching his jaw, the sergeant continued. "We were told to stay here, Your Excellency. Captain Annaud took the rest of the unit south, to Pentar."

Rivven looked from the sergeant to the others, who were standing rigid with fear and shock. She knew it wasn't the dragon behind her that was responsible— it wasn't just the dragonfear. She'd made every effort to make her reputation as a fearsome governor as widespread as she could in the Red Wing. The soldiers were terrified of her.

"For what possible reason would Annaud have left you here to go to Pentar?"

"If it please, Your Excellency, he was pursuing the sellsword, who was here at the manor and killed two draconians on his way out."

Two more? The Ergothian was costing her a fortune in draconians, she thought. The ones she'd had Annaud take with him were bozaks. The man clearly had no problem dealing with spellcasters. Interesting.

"Is Cazuvel here? Or did he leave with Captain Annaud?" she asked, hoping to speak with the Black Robe before she sat down with the baron.

"The wizard would not say where he was going, Your Excellency," the sergeant said, flinching. She didn't strike him again, however. She just strode past him.

"Get your things together," she commanded, heading for the front doors. "I want all of you back at the outpost by morning. Anybody still here when I come back out gets fed to my dragon."

Cear showed an impressive set of teeth the size of

daggers. The soldiers scattered, running to pack their things and leave; Rivven left them to it and entered the manor. It was time to have another conversation with the baron.

CHAPTER FIVE

Vanderjack sat across the square from the Monkey's Ear Tavern, watching the front door and sipping a cup of tarbean tea.

The early-morning crowd was noisy, smelly, and constantly blocking his view, but he fixed his eyes on the doorway. Gredchen negotiated with a fish vendor somewhere in the throng, and the sellsword could hear her trying to take a forceful approach. She might be there all day if she didn't back off.

The Monkey's Ear was infamous for being a place to pick up paid help. He'd been there before, some years earlier, when the fires of war were still hot. He'd earned a purse full of steel from only a handful of jobs. With the sheer number of mercenaries in business nowadays, a man could barely squeeze in for a meeting with a patron. One had to get there first thing in the morning, as he and the baron's aide had.

That was more than an hour previous. Vanderjack tapped his fingers on the edge of his mug and watched as a trio of disgruntled axemen, probably Nerakans, left the Monkey's Ear and jostled their way out of the square toward the harbor. A gaunt face appeared in the doorway, called out "Thirteen!" and was gone again.

Vanderjack looked at the small wooden counter in his hand, the one with *13* carved into it, and got to his feet. Gredchen must have heard the announcement as well because she threw a handful of coins into the vendor's cup, picked up a wrapped bundle of salmon, and said a few choice words to the man.

"That's us?" Gredchen asked, stowing the fish in her satchel.

"Yeah," he said. "The three guys who had number twelve didn't leave happy. Could be a tough sell this morning."

"We're only looking to hire, correct?" she asked. "You're not signing on, so you don't have to be all that convincing."

Vanderjack shrugged, finishing off his tarbean tea and dropping the mug into a trough outside the Monkey's Ear. "You never know. Sometimes the patron's the one that needs to make the best impression."

The sellsword rapped on the front door. When a narrow window beside the door slid open and a pair of rheumy eyes looked out, Vanderjack waved the little wooden counter in front of them. Moments later the deadbolt slid back, and the door opened wide. The gaunt-faced man let Vanderjack and Gredchen in, impassive. Vanderjack wondered if the doorman was actually among the living. Maybe the Monkey's Ear was hiring on undead too.

Vanderjack had keen senses, and his eyes usually adjusted to bad light quickly, but in a place such as that he didn't want to take too many chances. As he passed under the eaves and inside the Monkey's Ear, he laid his hand on the hilt of Lifecleaver, summoning the Sword Chorus.

"Another bar!" exclaimed the Aristocrat.

"Here we are again," agreed the Apothecary.

"They all look the same to me," said the Conjurer.

The Hunter said nothing as he stepped through a wall and out of sight. Truth be told, the Hunter was the main reason Vanderjack put up with the ghosts recently. Too many ambushes, which meant the laconic ghost was supernatural insurance.

Gredchen noticed his hand, following him inside. "If they see you getting ready to use that . . . "

"Relax!" he said. "It's just a comfort tactic."

"The woman is right," said the Philosopher.

"As ugly as she is," added the Balladeer.

"We should be prepared for an ambush," said the Cavalier.

Vanderjack pinched the bridge of his nose in irritation. He didn't want to actually respond to the ghosts, not there in the middle of a tavern, not with Gredchen. The patrons wouldn't notice his hand; they were probably all drunk or asleep. With any luck, the Hunter would come back and report on what was happening in the rooms he couldn't see.

The common room itself was cramped and crowded with mercenaries, all of them recent hires. There was the usual mix of roughnecks and greenhorns, of fresh-faced youths just come into Pentar from some village along the coast and old-timers bearing the scars of former battles. Few of them even acknowledged Vanderjack and Gredchen's arrival.

Directly across from the entrance was a long table blocked from view by four men, all dressed in the uniforms of the Seaguard. Vanderjack knew they'd turned private, so it didn't surprise him. Who he saw when the marines stepped aside, on the other hand, sent his mind spinning.

"Theo?" he said incredulously, his body tensing.

The gnome, standing on his chair in order to get some height, pointed a finger at the sellsword and responded, "You! I knew it!"

Gredchen looked from the gnome to Vanderjack and back again. "You know each other?"

"I'll handle this," Vanderjack said under his breath and stepped forward. The Hunter materialized from the sellsword's left, stepping back into the room through the wall; Vanderjack looked at the ghost and did his best to silently impart the message, *Hold on a moment, I'm in the middle of something.* The Hunter, keen of eye and always an excellent judge of mood, simply waited.

"Theo! What a pleasant surprise. Imagine meeting you here, in a bar, surrounded by mercenaries."

The gnome went from standing on the chair to standing on the table. That gave him an extra foot of height advantage. He placed his fists on his hips. "Vanderjack. This is no coincidence, I assure you. Months of careful planning and expert tracking have led me here, knowing you would show up sooner or later. And so you have—soon enough!"

Vanderjack squinted. "Are you serious?"

"You doubt me? See how I have attained not only your location and details of your recent employment history, from Ergoth to Nordmaar." The gnome grabbed a handful of papers from a pile on the table and waved them furiously before him. "Also! I have secured the position of head of the only mercenary company in town, a town selected by forecasting algorithms you could not in your wildest dreams comprehend."

"You *are* serious."

The gnome grew pink in the face. "I am! I am indeed! Quite serious!" He indicated the room full of armed men. "I have a room full of armed men! That's how serious I am."

"Yes, I can see that. Actually, that's why we came, so if you have a moment—"

"Have you not been listening? *You* are why I am here, you imbecile!"

"Yes, I heard you loud and clear. And I'm very flattered, but I'm on a job right now and I'm fairly sure I have some disgruntled local occupying forces interested in my whereabouts too. So as long as you're running things, perhaps we'd better talk terms."

Some of the mercenaries in the room began to pay attention, since their diminutive new boss was engaged in a loud conversation with a tall bald black man with a sword. Several of them moved closer, making any exit from the room difficult. Gredchen decided to hover near the door just in case, but nobody was paying much attention to her. Being ugly meant more people looked away than not.

"Have you forgotten what you did to me? Where you left me? What happened to my . . . my"—the gnome was sputtering mad—"cat?"

"Right, the cat . . . "

"My precious Star, lost forever."

"I didn't really think gnomes had all that much affection for cats. And it was really a kitten, if you want to be precise."

"A saber-toothed kitten! One of a kind! Irreplaceable!"

"Yes, all the way from the Island of Gargath, you said. I am sorry about that. But you know, I don't think we established that it was my fault."

Theo grew livid. He was about to direct the entire room to grab Vanderjack and presumably tear him limb from limb when Gredchen screamed, "Stop!"

Everybody in the room looked at her.

The baron's aide ignored the filthy look from the gnome and the amused grin from Vanderjack and said, "Dragonarmy's here."

Theodenes leaped off the table as the room emptied—soldiers and sellswords disappeared through doors, out of back windows, and some even tumbled down into the wine cellar.

Vanderjack looked at his ghosts. The Hunter shrugged, "You seemed busy."

"I think I could have been disturbed for that," Vanderjack said, barely heard over the din.

"We must to arms!" shouted the Cavalier.

"Save the girl!" shouted the Aristocrat.

"Save the gnome!" shouted the Balladeer.

The ghosts fell to arguing with each other, so Vanderjack crossed in two steps, passed Gredchen and opened the door wide enough to look out. "Ackal's Teeth. There's a whole squad of them."

Theodenes joined them, staring out the door, then looked up at Vanderjack. "They're here because of you, aren't they? You're a wanted man!"

Vanderjack shrugged. "As ever. You didn't think you were the only one who was after me, did you? Can we hurry things up?"

Theo exploded. "Hurry things up? I have an operation here perfectly arranged for the purposes of hunting you down and bringing you and any of your associates to justice for the crimes you have committed to my person, my cat, and to all of the others you callously abandoned on Ergoth, and you still think we have any business matters to discuss?"

Vanderjack closed the door and smiled grimly. "In ten seconds, Theo, I don't think any of that's going to matter."

* * * * * *

The wizard Cazuvel stood at the threshold of the ancient door and spoke a single word of magic.

The door opened silently, and a whorl of escaping air stirred his black robes. Cazuvel looked behind him, out across the waters of the bay. Satisfied he wasn't being watched or followed, he passed through the door. It closed in his wake, sealing him off from the outside world.

The Lyceum was once a school of magic and a conservatory of learning for all three of the orders of High Sorcery. It had been built upon a promontory that extended out into Kalaman Bay but was little more than a sandspit covered in water when the tide was in. The building itself was a squat, featureless edifice that the locals ignored.

Cazuvel traveled the dark hallways of the Lyceum, gesturing and intoning more commands, opening doors and revealing passages hidden by sorcery. Finally, as a set of stone portals slid aside at a wave of his hand, the wizard arrived at his destination.

Cazuvel stood in the Grand Cloister, a circular chamber dedicated to conjuration and invocations. Hundreds of runes, sigils, and glyphs were carved or drawn upon the marble floor and walls. Encircling stone pillars divided the middle of the room from the curving walkway around it. Torch brackets mounted on each pillar shed light on the room's center and the elaborate major summoning circle boldly painted upon the floor at the room's very center.

There, inside the wards both physical and ephemeral, a mirror crafted from a single sheet of hammered steel mounted in an ironwood frame hung suspended in the air, anchored by invisible threads of magic. Cazuvel's reflection flickered within its lustrous polished surface—a white-blond albino, his violet eyes staring out from the mirror in the shadow of the black cowl of the robes.

"Here I stand again before you," said Cazuvel to the mirror. *"Cermindaya, cermindaya, saya memanggil anda dan mengikat anda."*

The image in the mirror—Cazuvel's image—writhed and grimaced. The mage watched as the Cazuvel in the mirror reached up his hands as if to grasp the frame surrounding him, and shook.

"Leave me alone, you bastard!" the image screamed. "You've taken enough! Let me out!"

Cazuvel smiled. His face was much whiter than his teeth.

"Not yet," he said. "It is necessary that I draw more power from you. The highmaster has a new problem."

The mirror Cazuvel seemed to press up against the glass. "By the Abyss, just let me out."

"By the Abyss indeed," said the first Cazuvel, extending his thin, white fingers in the mirror's direction. Arcs of blue and orange sprang from Cazuvel's hands, dancing upon the shocked image of the wizard; the lightning crackled for a heartbeat longer, then surged back to where it had come. Both Cazuvel and his image in the mirror jerked and shook with each sparking jolt, but while Cazuvel bore an expression of intense satisfaction, his image screamed.

When the lightning ceased, Cazuvel lowered his hands and smiled. The image in the mirror looked gaunt, haggard, the life drained from it. Cazuvel, on the other hand, seemed more vital and stronger than he had before he started. He turned and began walking to the doors.

"You'll never . . . " said the image, hunched over within the frame of the mirror.

Cazuvel drew his robed cowl over his head, hiding his violet eyes from view. "I'll never what? Get away with it? Why, of course I will."

"You'll be discovered. Found out. I'll get free."

Cazuvel laughed. "I think not. Remember how potent that spell you attempted was, my caged friend. Far beyond your own reach. You made a mistake, trying to cast it—incorrectly—and now here we are."

The image looked up and out, its sunken features tightening in anger. "She's no fool, you monster. She trained under Emperor Ariakas. She walks the Left Hand Path, as he did. Eventually she'll catch on to who you really are."

Cazuvel lifted his shoulders, shrugged. "Perhaps. But by then I will have already secured a permanent portal. I won't have any more need of you or the highmaster or any of the others in this careless game of souls you've all been playing."

The wizard spoke a single word, a word loaded with a violent finality. The image in the mirror flinched then vanished. The surface of the mirror grew dark, and Cazuvel left it there in the depths of the Lyceum.

As the wings of magic carried him across Kalaman Bay once more and to the east, toward Nordmaar, the wizard Cazuvel—or whoever he truly was—wondered whether the highmaster really would uncover all of his secrets. Was the armored, fire-loving Rivven Cairn truly that skilled in the art?

He would have to find out for himself.

CHAPTER SIX

Vanderjack poured himself a drink.

The bottle was just sitting there, and its owner was one of several mercenary barflies who had, upon hearing of the imminent arrival of the dragonarmy soldiers, vacated the premises. Not being the kind of man to let any alcohol go to waste and in need of some fortification in this time of stress, Vanderjack poured some of the bottle's contents into an empty tankard and looked around.

"Anybody else for a drink?" he asked cordially.

Gredchen and Theodenes were the only two left in the tavern, with even the cadaverous doorman having taken his leave. Neither of them responded positively.

"Are you insane?" asked Gredchen, shaking her head as Vanderjack held the bottle out toward her. "We need to be leaving, Vanderjack. I'm not the least bit interested in being thrown into a cell by the dragonarmy."

Theodenes looked out the window rather than take the proffered bottle. "Neither am I, frankly. In fact, I can think of nothing more insulting. In addition, I never consume wines, spirits, lagers, ports, or any other fermented beverage. Now is certainly not the time to start. Nor is it a good time for you to become inebriated."

Vanderjack took a long swallow from his tankard and wiped his lips with the back of his hand. "Ordinarily I would agree, but under the circumstances I think it could be a good thing. Besides," he looked at the bottle's faded label. "I think this is dwarf spirits. There's a bit of a kick."

Gredchen punched Vanderjack in the arm. "Put it down! They'll be bursting in here any moment. We have to leave."

The Sword Chorus was absent; Vanderjack had released his grip on the hilt in order to make use of the bar, and he knew he'd get no end of mocking from the ghosts at that point as it was. With the warm smoky feeling of the spirits collecting in his stomach, the sellsword set aside the tankard and slipped off the barstool.

"Right, then. Theo? Should I assume you're going to hold that Southern Ergoth thing over my head until I compensate you for it?"

The gnome sputtered. " 'Southern Ergoth thing'? "

Vanderjack nodded. "I can tell it's really bothering you. I mean, you went to all this trouble"—he motioned around to the bar and the empty seats formerly occupied by mercenaries—"came all this way, and so on."

"Single combat has crossed my mind," Theodenes said, moving back toward his big desk. "Given that monetary reparations don't appear to be something you are capable of."

Gredchen said, "Actually, Lord Glayward is paying him quite well."

Vanderjack watched as Theodenes reached behind the desk and brought forward a long pole with metal studs along one side near where a person would grip it.

"Yes," the sellsword agreed cheerfully. "And I'm sure to get a lot more too."

Theodenes brought the butt of the polearm down upon the wooden floorboards, as if to emphasize his ownership. "How much more?"

"Oh, enough to buy you passage to Gargath again to get a new cat."

Theodenes stroked his beard and considered.

Gredchen took another look out the window then called out, "They're checking all of the other shops in the square. I see eight soldiers and a captain. It's Captain Annaud, one of Highmaster Cairn's men."

"Oh, I'm sure we can handle nine little soldiers," said Vanderjack, his eyes on Theo and the polearm.

"Very well," Theodenes said. "I shall prepare a business contract stipulating transference of funds to me and attach it as a rider to your existing contract, with the unfortunate-looking woman as a witness." He looked up at Gredchen. "What do you say to that, who-ever you are?"

Gredchen grabbed her satchel and slung it over her shoulder. "I'd say the pot is calling the kettle black." She glared down at the gnome, who didn't flinch; he was a lot more intimidating than she would have given him credit for. "My name's Gredchen. I'm Lord Glay-ward's aide, and yes, I think that would be fine. Now really isn't the time to sit down and draw up a contract, though, so . . . "

Vanderjack adjusted one or two belt straps and clapped his hands together. "We can take care of the details later. Right now, I believe there's a gang of sol-diers preparing to break through the door and arrest us all. Why don't we go out through the kitchen? That's always popular."

There was a muffled exchange of words outside the door to the tavern and a stamping of feet. Theodenes and Gredchen both made for an exit at the rear of the common room, beside the bar. Vanderjack shoved a bench in front of the front door and ran after the others.

The three of them ran through the swinging wooden doors and into the kitchen, which was in a dreadful state of repair, and promptly fell over a man who had been standing immediately inside, apparently eavesdropping. Gredchen and Theodenes went sprawling, but Vanderjack, seconds behind them, remained on his feet.

"Cordaric!" shouted Theodenes. "Why haven't you left with all the others?"

"Who's this guy?" asked Vanderjack.

"Etharion Cordaric, my cook," said Theo. "Recent hire."

"Doesn't look as if he was cooking," said Gredchen, getting to her feet. "In fact, I would bet anything that he was listening at that door."

The cook looked as if he had had the wind knocked out of him, which wasn't far from the truth. Vanderjack found him completely nondescript, although he was vaguely Solamnic. "Not listening really," the cook said, catching his breath. "I was . . . worried about the commotion. I was just about to go out and investigate."

"Cordaric?" asked Vanderjack. "You don't look very Ergothian. I should know. My father—"

"My family were Solamnic exiles," stated the cook.

The sellsword looked the cook up and down. "The name Cordaric loosely translates to *recursive mistake* in Ergot. Your ancestors must have been very interesting people."

The cook rubbed at his head. "It does? Er . . . I mean . . . of course it does! It's inside humor in the family."

"Well, we're trying to leave, on account of the dragon-army soldiers," said Vanderjack, hooking a thumb back in the direction of the common room door.

"Yes, any time now," said the gnome impatiently.

There was a smash and the tumble of a wooden bench, followed by a series of curses and yells.

"That's our cue! Let's get out of here." The sellsword took hold of Gredchen's arm and raced past the ovens, pantry shelves, preparation areas, and sinks filled with soiled dishes. Theo and the cook ran after him.

The kitchen had a delivery entrance, which Vanderjack kicked out with his boot. Gredchen wrenched her arm free of the sellsword, but he kept going, ducking into the alley behind the Monkey's Ear and running along it. She and the other two followed, looking back over their shoulders to see if there was any pursuit.

There wasn't. Nobody seemed to be following them at all. Vanderjack stepped out of the alley and onto a street; he looked up and down the street before glancing over his shoulder and holding his finger up to his lips.

Theodenes frowned and looked around the corner. "I don't see anything."

"Trust me, Theo, any officer worth his salt's going to have the back watched. We need a distraction. They're probably only looking for me because I'm so infamous. I'll go out and draw their attention."

Gredchen rolled her eyes. "Bad idea. Lord Glayward needs you alive, not shot through with crossbow bolts. I'll go. I can steer them away."

Theodenes nodded in agreement. "Quite right. The woman is so monstrously unpleasant in appearance that the soldiers will have no choice but to look away."

"Monstrously unpleasant? Who in the Abyss are you to—"

Vanderjack held his hand up. "Quiet! Theo, we're mercenaries, not bards. We are expected to look fearsome."

Gredchen was about to say that she wasn't a mercenary and she didn't look fearsome either when Etharion cleared his throat. "Well, I suppose I could go."

"Great solution!" said Vanderjack. "We'll send the Ergothian with the strange name."

Theodenes frowned. "I would rather send out somebody I had no financial investment in."

Gredchen spoke up. "If Etharion wants to go, let him go. He can tell them he saw us running off in the other direction."

Etharion, who didn't in fact seem all that eager to follow through with his own suggestion, pushed past the others and out onto the street. Vanderjack watched as the cook loped along for a few yards, passed under a low-hanging canopy, rounded the street corner, and walked out of sight.

"So is he any good?" asked Vanderjack of the gnome.

"Actually, so far all he's made is cookies," said Theo. "Not bad, as cookies go."

"Cookies? Did you mean to hire a pastry chef?"

"He assures me he knows how to cook a wide range of dishes."

"Did he mean a wide range of cookies?"

Theo just shrugged.

There was a faint sound of a scuffle, a loud crash, then yelling. The cook came running around the corner, chased by dragonarmy soldiers, and straight into one of the canopy support poles. The canopy collapsed, enveloping the cook and the soldiers, and the entire affair slammed into a vegetable cart.

"Pretty good for a diversion," Vanderjack said. "Go! Go!"

The sellsword, the gnome, and the baron's aide ran across the street from the alley and away from the confusion. Crowds, attracted by the noise, milled into the area, creating further obstacles. Three streets later, Vanderjack called for the other two to stop and catch their breaths.

"Do you think Etharion will be all right?" asked Gredchen anxiously.

"I'm sure," Vanderjack said, not really caring. "This road here leads to the eastern gate, and we can take that out of town and be on our way. I really did want a little more help than just Theo, but beggars can't be choosers."

"But we can't just leave Etharion back there," said Gredchen.

"I agree," echoed Theo firmly.

"Besides, Lord Glayward's castle is at least six days from here and I could use some help in cooking this salmon." She patted her satchel.

"And there's my investment," added Theo. "I paid the cook two weeks in advance."

Vanderjack sighed. "All right. Stay here and I'll circle back around and see how he's doing. Keep out of sight."

Leaving the gnome and the aide hiding under the eaves of a clothier's shop, Vanderjack grabbed a plain-looking gray cloak, threw it over his shoulders, and sneaked back in the direction of the dragonarmy soldiers. Gredchen was right; they could use a good cook—assuming, of course, that Etharion knew how to make anything other than cookies.

* * * * * *

Highmaster Rivven Cairn stalked the halls of the governor's palace in Pentar, searching for the governor.

She had left Cear before sunrise in one of the sprawling courtyards on the palatial estate, telling him not to eat the gardeners, and then set off to find the man the red dragonarmy was paying chests full of steel each month to send reports. Yet almost four hours after her arrival, the governor still managed to elude her completely.

According to her sources, the real rulers of Pentar, the twin brothers Tochel and Tochi Pentar, were presently enjoying an extended vacation with Saifhumi pirates. After the fall of Neraka, the Red Highlord Rugoheras (Ariakas's immediate replacement, also dead) had informed Rivven that she was to install a governor in Pentar and lock up the brothers who had caused the Red Wing so much trouble during the war. Rivven didn't remember them causing any special trouble at all. In fact, she preferred the town before it was thrown into disarray, becoming a haven for mercenaries. Orders were orders, she reminded herself.

Rivven's first thought had been to give the town to Baron Glayward as yet another means of securing his cooperation, but the baron would have none of it. He said it would interrupt the flow of information from the west. He also said the Solamnic folk living in Nordmaar wouldn't enjoy having one of their lords govern a town full of ne'er-do-wells and rogues. She reluctantly agreed but had her men stationed on his grounds for two weeks to reflect her disappointment.

Rivven's next choice was the wizard Cazuvel, who had been her spy among the orders of High Sorcery and somebody she'd worked with closely near the end of the war. She needed Cazuvel to keep her apprised of the Tower mages' actions, especially those of the young mage Raistlin Majere, who many claimed had brought down the emperor—with Tanis Half-Elven's help. The irony of Ariakas's falling victim to the combined efforts of a wizard and a half-elf was not lost on Rivven, who was both.

Cazuvel had declined her offer, as she had half expected him to. The Black Robe liked his autonomy, and only Nuitari himself knew what the albino did when he wasn't assisting Rivven with one task or another. Black Robes nowadays were living under the constant shadow of the Majere wizard, and Cazuvel was no exception. If he had become governor, he wouldn't have had the time to plot his eventual mastery of all black magic, or whatever it was he was always so busy doing.

No, Rivven couldn't have either of her first choices. She was forced to recruit from outside her circle of contacts and informants, and so she had turned instead to the next most sensible pool of candidates—the family of the people who were really in charge.

Pentar had always been ruled by identical twins. They were traditionally male, but a hundred years earlier, the rulers had been two women, survivors of a generation of sickness and plague. The grandchildren of one of those women were Tochel and Tochi Pentar, but the brothers weren't the only family of twins in town.

Oxoloc Pentar was cousin to the brothers Tochel and Tochi, descendant of the other of the female rulers, and like his cousins, he was one of twins. Oxoloc, however, was alone; his brother had died at birth. Such a tragedy had far-reaching repercussions in Pentar. Although he was technically eligible to be the tribal chief of the Cuichtatl people, the circumstances of his birth were a shadow over his life. They were a dire omen, inescapable.

Oxoloc was, in many ways, only half a man because he was only one man.

Rivven Cairn had extended her reach through her usual local channels a year or so previous, when the Red Wing leadership had given her the command to eliminate Pentar's rightful rule. Those channels turned up Oxoloc, living a fairly depressing life in a luxurious yet tiny house near the palace. Shunned by his family, Oxoloc was more than willing to be placed in the role of governor. In return for his complicity and his almost completely hands-off approach to the problems of the town, the dragonarmy would support the leadership of the young Pentari man and maintain his opulent lifestyle.

Thus, in light of all of the history the governor had with Rivven's forces, and their deal, his not being available to the highmaster when she was in town was almost unforgivable. Rivven finally found him hiding in the orchards.

"Governor Oxoloc," she said, emerging from nowhere and blocking out the morning sunlight. A simple spell of concealment had allowed her to get close to the scruffy, dark-haired governor. She had been standing there, watching him eat from a basket of peaches until she was sure he wasn't actually waiting for somebody.

Oxoloc leaped to his feet, tossing his fruit to the side and trying to look aristocratic. He failed. He said, "My lady highmaster! What a . . . oh, *there* you are!"

"Here I am," she said. "Where were you?"

Oxoloc struggled to loosen the collar of his governor's robes. "Me? Ah, well, you see, I felt like taking a little morning walk through the orchards, in the fresh air. So stuffy and uncomfortable inside. Going to be another rainstorm, though. Can you feel it?"

"Governor, it's been over four hours since I arrived. Did you not see the enormous red dragon in the other courtyard? Whose did you think that was?"

"Ah. I confess to being a tad underinformed."

Rivven pinched the bridge of her nose with her hand. "You are one of the least informed men in all of Nordmaar. I thought perhaps you were avoiding me."

Oxoloc pulled on a cloak, a formal affair with gold lining and a clasp of ivory. "Ah, perhaps we should retire inside. I really do think there's going to be a rainstorm."

Rivven followed the governor inside the palace, through hallways she had grown quite familiar with. Sure enough, as they passed one line of stained-glass windows in a lengthy gallery, the heavy Nordmaaran rains started hammering against the glass. It was going to be another wet, humid day.

"So what may I help you with today, Lady High-master?" asked Oxoloc worriedly, settling into an over-stuffed chair in a drawing room.

Rivven didn't sit; instead she leaned against the garish white ivory carvings surrounding the windows. "I'm trying to protect some investments of mine. There's somebody in this town—your town, Oxoloc—who poses a threat to those investments. Now I know I could just send in my army, but they'd get in the way of everyday business, and I like to work in smaller ways. You know that, right?"

"Yes, yes, I know. I wouldn't want the people to be worried about armies and such. Terrible. So what would you like me to do about it?"

"You and I both know your Seaguard haven't been working for you for months."

Oxoloc wrung his hands. "Well now, I wouldn't go so far as to say that, necessarily—"

"They've become mercenaries, Governor."

"Ah. Mmm."

Rivven smiled. "Exactly. So this is how you can help. Who are they working for now? Who is the biggest employer in Pentar? I have been reliably informed that the threat to my investments will be looking to hire some muscle."

Oxoloc looked as if he had just won first prize in a kender-throwing contest. "Oh! Oh! I know of whom you're talking! Yes! The gnome!"

Rivven squinted. "The biggest mercenary boss is a *gnome?*"

"Yes, yes," Oxoloc said, grinning. "He really is very clever. He beat the last boss in a duel, my people tell me. Never heard of such a thing before, but that's Pentar for you. We get all kinds."

Rivven smiled again. "Yes, Governor. Yes, you do. Now tell me everything you know about this clever gnome."

CHAPTER SEVEN

Vanderjack stood in the pouring rain, watching as soldiers bullied the cook.

For the past ten minutes, he had watched from across the street as six soldiers harassed, mocked, intimidated, and jostled Etharion, presumably waiting for their captain to arrive. Captain Annaud was nowhere to be seen, nor were the two remaining soldiers, which the Hunter confirmed.

"Well, are you intending on saving him pretty soon?" asked the Cavalier.

"I am sure he is merely waiting for an opportune moment," responded the Balladeer.

"Likely so that he can miss that opportune moment and say that it wasn't one," added the Aristocrat.

"He's just a hired kitchen hand," Vanderjack said, wiping more rain from his face. "Bakes a lot of cookies." He looked above, noting the holes in the awning he was standing under. Water puddled around his boots and found a way down the back of his neck. "What I wonder is, what's so special about him, other than his ability to cook?"

"Answer unclear," said the Conjuror. "Ask again later."

"What does that mean?" Vanderjack demanded, turning to look at the ghost, hanging there, spectral and aloof. "Answer unclear?"

"He means that we can't tell you at the moment," said the Apothecary.

"You will have to trust our insight," said the Philosopher.

"Trust and act," said the Hunter, materializing from Vanderjack's left. The ghost lifted one semitransparent finger and indicated the approaching Captain Annaud, who was picking his way through the crowd farther up the street, making his way to rejoin his men.

From that distance, Annaud looked like any other dragonarmy officer. He was dressed head to foot in black scale armor, curved steel plates protecting his shoulders, lower arms, and shins, and a half helm that kept his face visible. Only the highlords and their highmasters were allowed to wear the full helms that obscured their features.

"Ackal's Teeth," muttered the sellsword, pulling his hood over his head and slipping out into the rain. "Why does it always have to rain when I'm rescuing somebody?"

With the Sword Chorus circling the area, Vanderjack headed straight for the soldiers. He estimated it would be less than a minute before Annaud reached them himself, so he didn't have much time.

The sellsword passed by a wagon filled with sacks of grain. He set a boot on the nearest wheel and used it to spring over the heads of a slow-moving cluster of onlookers. He landed on his feet, drew Lifecleaver all the way out of its scabbard, and dashed forward.

Bystanders scattered. Only Vanderjack, a half dozen heavily armored dragonarmy soldiers, and the cook remained in the courtyard. Etharion was sitting on a barrel, but as soon as he saw the sellsword charging at them, he fell backward onto the doorstep of a tea vendor. The soldiers all unsheathed their weapons, most of them armed with the curving Nerakan blades that Vanderjack knew all too well.

"By the Dark Queen!" one of them said. "That's the guy!"

"Get him!" yelled another.

Vanderjack and the closest soldier collided, their blades coming together with a loud ringing crash. Life-cleaver, crafted from meteoric iron, or "star metal," and further bolstered by magic, was almost impervious to harm; the dragonarmy soldier's scimitar was Nerakese iron folded hundreds of times upon itself. It was sharp but brittle. Vanderjack's blade shattered it, sending shards into the soldier's unprotected face.

The sellsword spun about on his heel as the soldier clutched at his ruined features. The Cavalier and the Hunter called out the positions of the other soldiers, as they always did. There was no comment from the Conjuror, which meant no spells were being prepared for casting, which was good. He sought out the next opponent, locked eyes with him, and said, "One down."

Etharion scrambled to a crouch and moved toward a stack of crates standing alongside the high brick walls of a scrivener's office. Vanderjack let the ghosts keep track of where the cook was, which meant he could worry more about the soldiers and getting rid of them before their captain reached the fight.

Three of the soldiers came at him at once; the first two cut at the rain to his left and right while the third went for where his head would have been had he not ducked. They pressed the attack, Vanderjack blocking each swing with Lifecleaver. The sellsword kicked one soldier's knee so hard he heard a sickening snap; that man was out. Slipping between the fallen soldier's companions, he found himself pressed against the crates. Rain pounded upon his head.

"Captain's almost here," the Hunter warned.

"Yeah, yeah," Vanderjack grunted. He had four opponents remaining. Two advanced, flourishing their scimitars. The others were off to the right and left, waiting. He was cornered. From behind, Vanderjack heard the cook stumbling over a crate and trying to stay out of sight.

"Come on!" shouted one of the two waiting soldiers. "Cut him down!"

Wet blades flashed; Vanderjack twisted, shifting Lifecleaver into a two-handed grip and disarming both soldiers. They stood there, mouths agape, looking at their empty hands. Vanderjack ran them both through, and they fell with a splash into the puddling rainwater.

With only two soldiers remaining and the cook nearby, Vanderjack chanced a call back to the man. "Etharion!" he shouted. "Can you possibly lend a hand?"

Etharion didn't have anything to say in response. He crouched down even lower behind a crate and watched over it as the last two soldiers cautiously approached Vanderjack.

"Last chance to run away," Vanderjack said with a smile he didn't really feel.

"Ergothian scum!" one of the soldiers said.

"Hey now," Vanderjack said, ducking to one side to avoid the sweeping cut of a scimitar. "I'm only half Ergothian. My mother was a Saifhumi pirate."

"Ergothian, Saifhumi, all the same," said the other soldier.

"Try telling that to the emperor of Ergoth," Vanderjack said. He feinted to the left, distracting the second soldier, and freed his right hand to strike out at the first. His balled fist connected squarely with the dragonarmy soldier's jaw, dropping him. It wouldn't keep him out for long, but the sellsword circled about, giving himself some room to move.

The last soldier backed off, looking around. All he had to do was distract the mercenary for a few more seconds and the captain would be on him. Vanderjack was keenly aware of that as he lunged. The soldier barely escaped a sword in the gut, throwing himself to one side and landing right beside the crates.

Seeing the opportunity, Vanderjack yelled, "Etharion! Push against the crates!" It seemed like a faint hope. But Vanderjack was pleasantly surprised when, with a grunt, the cook threw himself against the crates he'd been hiding behind.

There was a moment where it seemed nothing would happen; then wooden box after wooden box, filled with glass jars, small sacks of tarbeans, and the gods knew what else toppled and landed with a horrendous crash upon the last soldier and several of his incapacitated companions. The cook looked impressed with himself. "Huh," he said, grinning at Vanderjack.

The sellsword didn't have long to catch his breath. Just as the Cavalier shouted a warning, he whirled in time to duck a swift cut of the captain's blade. Captain Annaud had finally arrived on the scene, taken in the devastation, and charged Vanderjack.

Up close, the captain was somewhat more distinctive. His features were sharp and hawklike, with a narrow yet prominent nose, steel-gray hair with a widow's peak, and a raptor's eyes. He was Nerakan, probably from the eastern foothills of the Taman Busuk near Estwilde; Vanderjack recognized that predatory look from others he had served with in the Blue Wing, years before.

"Glad you could make it," Vanderjack said, glancing around to seek an advantage.

"Those men will cost you," Annaud replied, his voice thin and reedy, with a strong Nerakese accent. It sounded practiced to Vanderjack, though. Underneath the sinister tones the captain was affecting, the sellsword could detect the remnants of Estwilder vowels.

"I don't have much money on me at the moment," said Vanderjack, smoothly turning away the captain's sword strokes, wondering whether the captain was really trying. "Can you leave me with the bill, and—"

"Above you!" shouted the Hunter, cutting Vanderjack off. Vanderjack hadn't expected an attack from that direction, but he knew better than to question the ghost's warning. He bent low and spun away.

A hawk's talons narrowly missed Vanderjack's scalp. The bird was completely silent, highly trained. Annaud was laughing, still coming forward with the easily defended yet constant swing of his blade. "Impressive," he said, as Vanderjack rose again to fend off the attacks. "Most men don't hear Rajan coming."

The hawk had flown in swift and low but was wheeling around in the air above the street, clearly looking for another opening. Vanderjack spared Etharion a quick glance. The cook was once again hiding, then beside a pair of stacked wine barrels underneath a canvas canopy. Safe from marauding birds, Vanderjack thought. Unlike me.

"What can I say? I'm the best in the business," he offered, crossing right foot over left, keeping himself moving. The captain had taken a step back, his sword raised and pointed at the sellsword in a formal fighting stance Vanderjack had seen only once or twice before.

"I'm told you were one of ours," Annaud said. "Before you fled like a coward. Vingaard, wasn't it?"

Vanderjack shrugged, watching the ghosts for a signal. Both he and the captain were circling each other, a classic standoff. Vanderjack hated classic standoffs. "I don't remember," he called back. "It was all so long ago. Back when you guys were actually winning."

Annaud frowned and Vanderjack grinned. So the captain had a chink in his armor after all. "I am not the one scraping together his last steel pieces for a drink," said the captain, all humor gone from his voice. "Soon you will have nothing but a windowless cell in Wulfgar beneath the horse track, where I am told the highmaster keeps all of her favorite prisoners."

File that one away for later, Vanderjack thought: dungeons underneath the famous horse arena of Wulfgar. The constant drumming overhead of the races would drive a man mad, not to mention all of the dung and refuse that would drop on top of any poor soul unlucky enough to have a window. And the smell! He had heard the highmaster was a nasty piece of work, but he didn't know she was that nasty.

"It's nice to be so well thought of," Vanderjack beamed, switching styles gradually over the course of three sword strokes. He could tell Annaud was comfortable in at least four of the commonly practiced Nerakese martial disciplines, none of which were known for their finesse. He had to respond with just as much brute force as Annaud was dishing out.

Turning his side to Annaud, Vanderjack grasped the hilt of Lifecleaver at an odd angle with both hands, whirling it about in a crescent-moon cut. The captain flinched, snarled, and kicked outward. The two warriors resumed their exchanges, throwing more and more of their strength into the blows. Vanderjack felt that Annaud could put that curved blade through the neck of a horse without so much as a pause, and he had no desire to confirm his hunch.

"The hawk!" called out the Hunter.

"Move to the right! Quick!" said the Cavalier.

Vanderjack did as he was told, lurching sideways as Annaud's hawk screeched by his ear. Once again Annaud had that look of shock across his face, that look of mounting disbelief.

"The cook!" warned the Balladeer.

As he spun about, readying his blade for a chopping motion across Annaud's arms, Vanderjack scanned for Etharion. Incredibly, the stocky cook had stepped out of his place under the canopy, wielding a broom in both hands like a gigantic greatsword. Vanderjack watched as Etharion drew the broom back and swung it out in a fierce motion, swatting at Captain Annaud's hawk and, amazingly, knocking it out of the air. The hawk was rendered an unconscious pile of feathers.

The sellsword and the captain's dance of blades had brought them close to the canopy area where Etharion was standing; Captain Annaud, driven by anger at the incapacitation of his raptor, reached to grab the cook.

"His guard is down!" said the Cavalier, practically screaming in Vanderjack's ear.

"Here's your chance!" joined the Aristocrat.

They were right. Annaud had thrown open his defenses in order to clutch at Etharion, who was standing there, looking mighty pleased with himself. Vanderjack had to do something quickly; it was his chance.

At exactly the same moment, three things happened: Vanderjack tensed, then leaped forward, thrusting Lifecleaver out in a deadly lunge; Captain Annaud's mailed hand seized Etharion's collar and pulled him close and into a chokehold; and all seven ghosts wailed like banshees, a deafening keening sound of warning, shock, and grief.

Lifecleaver's star metal blade, sharper and stronger than any other sword, plunged right through Etharion's heart and into that of Captain Annaud.

The screaming of the ghosts stopped.

******

Theodenes paced back and forth in the sheltered courtyard, waiting.

He and Gredchen, who sat patiently on a bench beside Pentar's east-facing wall, had been there for more than fifteen minutes. If he had a chronospectus on his person, he'd know for sure how long. He could keep exact, precise account of how much time and money were being wasted on waiting for the sellsword to return. Then, he thought, he could enter the details into his ledger, tally the figures, and perhaps add a small percentage increase on account of the precipitation he was being forced to endure.

Theo's ledger, his accounting equipment, and his chronospectus were all back at the Monkey's Ear. Theo had no doubt that the forces of the Red Dragonarmy were poring over his meticulous records, trying to ascertain the reason for his association with the infamous mercenary. They would learn of the costs of running a mercenary enterprise (the overheads were really quite phenomenal), and they would perhaps find the itemized list of taverns, inns, bars, and public houses Theodenes had stayed in for the past year, stretching all the way back to Southern Ergoth. But none of that would tell them what they wanted to know.

Theodenes had first met Vand Erj-Ackal, son of a pirate queen, in the foothills of the Last Gaard Mountains. Vanderjack had been with another motley group of sellswords, hired killers, and soldiers at the time; Vanderjack's Band, the mercenary had called them, somewhat unoriginally. They were all searching for the Treasure of Huma, tipped off by the dragonarmies or the Solamnics or both; it didn't seem to matter to Vanderjack.

Back then, Theo had already been traveling for some time. He'd left Mount Nevermind, abandoning all of his research and his guild to pursue the ultimate of field tests—personal, singular, and decisive melee combat. As a young gnome, Theodenes had chosen a lifequest that made his entire family proud. "Buildtheperfecttool," his father had repeated rapidly when he'd told him. "Excellent! Yourmotherwouldbesoproudifshewerealiveandnoteatenbysharks." His mother, who had indeed been eaten by sharks, would probably have been just as pleased.

However, as he had grown older, "Build the Perfect Tool" had seemed too comprehensive, too broad. All of Theo's other siblings, friends, and associates had chosen highly specific and individualized lifequests, such as "Catalog the Ferro-Pervasive Nature of the Lesser Striped Rust Monster" or "Retroactively Establish a Connection between Two Points in Culinary Space-Time through Steady Application of Seafood and Dairy Products." Theo needed something more . . . *interesting.*

So as news of war on the continent had reached Mount Nevermind and visitors had started to arrive, bringing such things as dragon orbs and kender into the gnome homeland, Theodenes realized then that his lifequest ought to have some *relevancy* to the great struggle going on in the world outside. He had logged his changes with the Guild of Planning, Records, Patents, and Preliminary Schema, and they had approved it after much deliberation. "Build the Perfect Handheld Martial Weapon" was Theo's ultimate ambition in life, and he had the guild's thirteen stamps, certificates, and water-marked letters to prove it.

With his prototype in hand, Theodenes had per-formed some initial tests in-house, but the reluctance of any other gnomes to engage him in direct physical con-flict was a problem. He stumbled upon a gnome work crew, an expeditionary team bound for the legendary Isle of Gargath, far across the sea. They suggested that Theo accompany them in the almost-certain likelihood that there would be ferocious examples of wildlife to fend off, and what better test of his prototype than that?

So it had been that Theo and eighteen other gnomes piled into a corkscrew-propelled watercraft, rocketed across the waves for a week, and landed on a distant, jungle-covered island. The nautical charts claimed that it was Gargath, birthplace of the dwarves and kender and, according to legend, the site where gnome ingenuity had unleashed the potent power of the Graygem.

Why any gnome would want to travel all the way to a mythical land in order to poke about a ruined castle for clues about the use of a legendary magical rock was beyond Theo's comprehension. It didn't matter much to him. He quickly became used to driving off marauding beasts, some with more than the usual number of heads or limbs, others flapping and gurgling about, still more gnashing terrible teeth. At least, that's what Theodenes remembered.

It was on the island, somewhere in that primeval jungle, that Theo had stumbled upon the hunting grounds of a mighty saber-toothed cat. The animal was obviously a predator and clearly unhappy to have been found by a large group of gnomes. It attacked, killing at least half of the group and rendering many of the rest wounded or incapacitated before Theo defeated it. Despite the fact that his multipurpose hooked hammer, the prototype that he had brought from Mount Nevermind, had snapped in half delivering the final blow, Theodenes at least proved his initial hypothesis and saved the day.

With only a handful of gnomes remaining, the expeditionary force determined to return to the ship and limp back to Sancrist. Theo had cautioned them to make sure there were no more saber-toothed surprises waiting for them, so he scouted around the area, looking for the cat's lair. He found it, high on a rocky crag, and within the dark confines of the cave he discovered the only prize the cat had left behind—a small, fuzzy kitten with enormous canine teeth.

Theo named the kitten Star, after the star-shaped white patch on its forehead, and carried his new discovery back to the ship, where he hoped the other gnomes would be waiting. Unfortunately, in his search for the saber-toothed cat's lair, Theo had missed out on the rare opportunity to be eaten alive by a ferocious manticore. The other gnomes were all dead, and he had no idea how to pilot the corkscrew ship back home.

A gnome is never without a spot of ingenuity even if it falls outside of his field of expertise. Within twenty-four hours, and with Star helpfully fending off any further attacks by manticores (who would have guessed that manticores are terrified of saber-toothed kittens?) he was off again. The ship was incredibly complicated, in the gnome fashion, but Theo was determined. Weeks later, he reached what he hoped was the coast of Sancrist, just in time for the boat's corkscrew to grind out of its threading.

It wasn't Sancrist, of course. Theodenes had piloted the ship straight past Sancrist, through the western isles and right into the southeast coast of Southern Ergoth. He and Star escaped the vessel, which was hopelessly beached upon the sand, and subsequently managed to wander into ogre lands. The ogres, residents of the ruined city of Daltigoth, chased Theodenes and Star for days; the hill giant Thunderbane, son of the ogre city's dictator, Stormogre, made it his mission to destroy the gnome and his cat for any number of imagined crimes that Theo was never certain about.

When Theodenes finally ran into Vanderjack's Band, he was tired, hungry, exhausted from running, and desperate for help. Vanderjack offered his services, or rather, offered Theo a position in his band. That appealed to Theo, who was, after all, in the martial weapon business, and so began a three-month stint as a mercenary, scout, and freebooter.

It didn't matter that there didn't appear to be any Treasure of Huma or that, even if there had been, a band of heroes from the mainland had managed to do all the interesting things at Huma's Tomb instead. Theo was sure becoming a mercenary was going to lead to bigger and better things.

Theo began to get worried when, fleeing from more ogres and dragons, Vanderjack admitted he didn't have any money to pay Theo for his services. For added insult, Vanderjack was revealed to be a drunk, his entire band turned out to be shapeshifting sivak draconians, and Star was horribly murdered. Theo returned from a scouting trip to discover all of that. He had never known such bitterness, anger, and frustration in his entire life.

"Theo?" asked Gredchen, interrupting Theo's reverie.

"Yes?" he responded, blinking a couple of times to remember where he was.

"You've been amazingly quiet. What were you thinking about?"

Theodenes looked back at the ugly woman, marveling at how her hair did nothing at all for her. He wondered if she had any idea just how bad Vanderjack was and what he had done; trouble seemed to follow the sellsword everywhere he went.

"Nothing," he said. "Nothing whatsoever."

CHAPTER EIGHT

Vanderjack was surrounded by corpses.

It had stopped raining. Pentar's shocked residents stared at the bloody carnage in the street, at the dragon-army uniforms, and at the sellsword standing in the middle of it all. They didn't notice the dead cook lying at Vanderjack's feet, a nondescript and pale-featured, slightly overweight corpse that could have been anybody; they were all staring at the bodies of the officer and his men. Vanderjack, however, was staring at the body of Etharion Cordaric.

His sword had fallen from his hand shortly after he drew it out of Etharion and Captain Annaud. Both men had crumpled to the blood-soaked cobblestones, each with his own look of shock permanently fixed across his face. Without the sword, Vanderjack had no ghosts. He didn't notice.

The sellsword came to his senses when one of the onlookers came up to him and prodded his arm with a broom, perhaps to determine for himself if the man was actually alive and not a statue or merely an upright corpse. Vanderjack jerked away from the touch of the broom, spun about, and knocked it away with his mailed hand.

"Ackal's Teeth!" he cursed. "Back off and leave me alone!"

The other man held up his hands, backing slowly away. "Seaguard's going to be here soon, *hombo*," the man said, in the local Nordmaaran patois. "*Jamba* trouble you start. Nobody they like the Red Scale Men, but this mess . . . " He gestured around at the panorama of death. "Know what I mean, *gabeej?*"

Vanderjack rubbed at his bare scalp and recovered his breath. He was astounded that the man was so calm and full of sensible advice. It spoke much of Pentar that its folk were inured to the possibility of such violence and more concerned with keeping disturbances quiet.

"*Gabeej*," Vanderjack said, repeating the local word for understanding. "Sorry about this." He looked down at Etharion's body. It was a completely unintended development.

Sure that he would regret it, Vanderjack bent down and retrieved Lifecleaver from the ground. The moment his fingers wrapped around the hilt, the Sword Chorus materialized around him, filling his senses.

"You killed an innocent!" said the Apothecary.

"In all the time we have been with you, you've never been this reckless," said the Aristocrat.

"You are losing your edge," said the Cavalier.

"If he ever had it without us," said the Conjuror.

"Annaud was too quick. And you weren't fast enough," Vanderjack muttered. "Why pick this time to be so slow off the mark?"

"Don't place the blame on us!" the Cavalier said, angry.

"You were aware of Annaud's skill," the Hunter said.

"You knew how well he could fight," the Aristocrat added.

Vanderjack shoved the sword into its sheath, dismissing the ghosts. He briefly poked at the cook's body to see if there was anything to be salvaged from it then looked at the dead Captain Annaud.

A dragonarmy officer carries only enough on his person to get by, a testament to Ariakas's executive talents, but the heyday of the dragon emperor's influence was long gone. The remaining highmasters, flight marshals, and captains were swiftly becoming independent, following their greed or ambition without guidance. Captain Annaud seemed to be one of those, a self-styled celebrity in his part of the world. He was technically serving under Highmaster Cairn, which meant there was even more direct influence from the late Ariakas, but Rivven had a broad region to command, and Annaud was frequently out of her sight.

Annaud was wearing amazingly well-crafted armor, tooled leather and scale mail with no stains, signs of wear, or degradation. With the skill and speed of a seasoned looter, the sellsword drew Annaud's knife from the dead man's belt, cut a number of critical straps, and hauled the bulk of the armor from the body in less than a minute.

The people in the street, who had until that point stayed clear, seemed to be offended at his carefree looting of a dead body. Several of them ran off to call the Seaguard, while others rushed up to interfere with Vanderjack's actions. The sellsword looked up and brandished the knife threateningly, driving them off; when he was done gathering the armor together, he pushed his way out of the crowd without further trouble.

Vanderjack ducked down a side street and located a large sack on a pile outside the rear entrance to an off-street eating house that smelled strongly of hops and barley. He dumped the armor into the sack, tied the end with a length of cord he kept on his person, and left the alleyway with the sack over his shoulder as if nothing had happened. On the way, he wiped at his own armor and sleeves, cleaning off blood and grime; he doubted he would be stopped on the street, but it didn't hurt to present an innocent appearance.

Vanderjack thought about what the Sword Chorus had said to him, about his mistake, about the killing of an innocent. Etharion Cordaric couldn't really be considered an innocent, he thought. He was a member of Theo's company, wasn't he? He signed on knowing that was a dangerous business. Nobody volunteers to become a mercenary, even if it's just to bake cookies, without that understanding. But if that was true, why did Vanderjack feel so bad about it?

He saw a few members of the Seaguard running past him in the direction of the street where the cook and Annaud had been killed. They didn't spare him a glance. Apparently, his nondescript disguise was adequate for the situation. That or the Seaguard didn't really care about the perpetrator and wanted to get to the bodies in time to loot them themselves.

Killing people always brought out the worst in folks, he mused, including him. Vanderjack had stolen, broken into places, robbed people, even lied and cheated and beguiled his way toward riches before, all while acting as a soldier for hire. He wasn't a good man. He liked living well when he could get the money and the resources. It was all part of the lifestyle—kill people; take their stuff—wasn't it?

Vanderjack rounded the corner two streets away from the courtyard where he'd left the gnome and the baron's aide. Damn the cook, anyway. He'd never questioned his mistakes before. He didn't really care about the cook, but Theo evidently did, and right then he did actually need Theo not to be angry with him. Theo was good at what he did, and Vanderjack was sure that, sneaking into some castle behind enemy lines, he'd need those skills.

Sometimes sacrifices had to be made, he thought. The cook might not be the last one to die on his trip. Gredchen might not last it out ... or Theo himself. In that business you never could predict when somebody was going to get run through with a life-draining sword in the middle of a pitched battle with dragonarmy soldiers.

Vanderjack stopped just before the next corner, frowning. The ghosts had insisted he'd killed an innocent. What were the ramifications of that? He suddenly realized that if they were right, and Etharion's time to die was not in the middle of a pitched battle with dragonarmy soldiers, then the sword's curse might have been activated.

He drew the blade out from its sheath, feeling the power in the meteoric iron humming into his palm and up his arm as it always did, watched as the ghosts manifested around him, and counted.

There were eight of them.

"So you see," said the Philosopher. "Our number has grown by one."

"Your mistake has earned you another advisor," said the Conjuror.

"I hope you realize what you have done," asked the Aristocrat.

"So I have a cook's ghost now too? I suppose that will come in handy when I'm making dinner." Vanderjack tried to make a joke, peering at the eighth ghost, like all the others indistinct, spectral, and only semireal.

"On the contrary," said the Apothecary.

"He is not all that he appeared to be," said the Balladeer.

Then the eighth ghost spoke in a voice clearly different from the others, not as confident or loud or even as ghostly. He just sounded confused. "What happened?"

"Well," said Vanderjack. "What is he, then, if not a dead cook?"

"Give us time to let him become acquainted to his new state," said the Apothecary.

"You have other things to do," said the Aristocrat.

"Find the trail," said the Hunter. He and all of the others faded from sight.

Vanderjack looked down at the sword. He was still holding it, but the Sword Chorus had gone. That was the first time they had ever done that. Granted, it was the first time he'd actually killed any innocents with the magic sword. He slid it back into its scabbard and continued on.

He ducked under a low arch leading into the courtyard by the east wall, between a series of lean-tos, shanties, and other indications of those who live a life without a real home. Toward the gate itself, where the courtyard widened enough to admit the throngs of people, he could see the gnome and Gredchen sitting in a shaded spot.

"So," he said, walking over to them as bold as brass. "Do you want the good news or the bad news?"

* * * * * *

Highmaster Rivven Cairn gazed into a pool of water that had collected on the top of an ale barrel.

Rivven knew many divination spells, most of which she used to discern the nature or strength of her opponents or to communicate with her underlings. The latter was the chief purpose of the spell she had just invoked, conjuring a watery window onto a far place currently occupied by the wizard Cazuvel.

"So what news do you have for me?" she asked as she noted the locals keeping their distance from the exterior of the Monkey's Ear Tavern. Rivven had arrived there to find the place abandoned, and she was hearing news not only of a bloody duel elsewhere in Pentar but of disturbances to the east.

"My lady," Cazuvel spoke, his bone-white face swimming on the surface of the water. "I have arrived at Castle Glayward, though I believe it is North Keep that demands the most of our attention."

Rivven rubbed at the back of her neck, where sweat and leather had irritated the skin and where her great helm would usually keep the rain out. She'd left the helm on the saddle, and the saddle was on Cear. The dragon was presently perched on the roof of the tavern, another reason for the locals to stay the Abyss out of her way.

"Is that young idiot making public speeches again?" she asked the mage's image. "Doesn't he know we only let him out of his room if he promises not to rouse the rabble?"

"The king has indeed been making speeches, my lady," said Cazuvel, as smug as ever. "He forgets what that did to his father a decade ago."

King Huemac Kerian, the previous king of Nordmaar,

had refused to submit to the Red Wing when it had swept into Nordmaar. Proud and stubborn, his army had made its last stand at Qwes, a frontier keep on the edge of the khan's lands. The khan at the time, always one to throw his lot in with the winning team, joined the dragonarmy forces; without the support of the horse nomads, King Huemac couldn't hold the line, especially not against red dragons. Nordmaar fell before the Red Wing's assault, and Rivven had been there to enjoy the spectacle. Shredler Kerian had watched his father die at the end of Highlord Phair Caron's spear, and since that time the newly crowned king had remained sequestered at North Keep. It was the capital city of his inherited kingdom and his own personal prison.

"He is supposed to be watched at all hours by his personal guard," Rivven said, exhaling. "They are sivaks, second only in rank to the Red Watch that the highlord keeps with him in Kern. They're not blind idiots, are they?"

The mage betrayed no knowledge of the truth. "Not blind . . . perhaps idiots. I am but Your Ladyship's servant."

"Oh, that's enough of that nonsense," Rivven said. "Make sure the baron's . . . *property* is still at the castle, and stay there until I send more instructions." She dismissed the spell with a pass of her fingers through the water, and it was once more just a puddle on a barrel top.

"Cear!" she called out impatiently.

The dragon's neck craned down from the roof, lowering its head to level with Cairn's own. "You called?"

"Any sign of more disturbances?" she asked. "Do you see the sellsword walking about with the gnome I told you about?"

Cear bared a row of enormous ivory teeth. "Not as such," he responded, his hot breath washing over Rivven.

"Not as such?"

"What I mean is I don't usually pay much attention to gnomes. The human? Literally dozens of dark-skinned humans walking about the city, even now."

Pentar was a hotbed of piratical activity as well as being home to a diverse population, so Ergothians and Saifhumi weren't uncommon. Vanderjack was both, or so it was said, and thus, his ability to blend in there was to be expected. It was a fact that Vanderjack had become just famous enough to have a cult following almost the like of any Hero of the Lance. It was also a fact that Cear, like all red dragons, didn't really know how to tell one human from another until he'd roasted them with his breath.

"He may already have left Pentar," Rivven said, waving Cear away. The dragon's head rose up again, out of sight above her. "I'm tired of being one step behind this man, and if he's already hooked up with the gnome, then I can only imagine he's headed east."

Rivven pushed open the door to the Monkey's Ear. Inside, a handful of mercenaries who had been foolish enough to come back once Annaud and his men had gone off in search of Vanderjack were sitting around a table, plainly upset at being discovered by the highmaster.

Even without the great helm, she was a frightening woman when she wanted to be. "You men have a new employer," she said, stopping before them with her hands on her hips. "New contracts, new uniforms."

One of the mercenaries cleared his throat. "No disrespect, Highmaster, but we've got legally binding contracts with the gnome. Shinare's seal on them and all."

Rivven smiled, no trace of humor in it. "And you are signatories to those documents, correct?"

The men nodded.

"Then you should know that you can, under Shinarite code, voluntarily excuse yourself from such a contract citing irreconcilable differences."

The mercenary who had spoken first spoke again. "Begging your pardon, and I'm not sayin' you're wrong or anything, but what differences would those be?"

Rivven said, "Here's one," and with one swift, sure stroke, she drew the curved scimitar from her back and removed the first mercenary's head from his shoulders, sheathing the weapon again before it hit the floor.

The other mercenaries hurriedly searched through their pouches, knapsacks, and pockets for their contracts.

Rivven stalked off to the bar, helping herself to a drink while she waited for the collection of ragtag mercenaries to sort themselves out. The Ergothian had eliminated all of her current employees in the town, even Captain Annaud. She needed a fresh set of eyes, ears, and sword arms.

Turning around at the bar and leaning back, she pointed a thin finger at one of the more professional-looking hired swords before her. "You. Congratulations. You're my new captain. In a few minutes, some local people I paid well are going to show up here with a few . . . used dragonarmy uniforms. Put them on, pack up all of your gear, and get ready to head out."

The new captain saluted nervously and immediately started ordering the others around, going over travel details. Rivven smiled, looking at the headless body on the tavern's wooden floor. Discipline, she thought. It's all about discipline. She walked outside the tavern with her mug of beer and called up to her dragon.

"Give them another twenty minutes," she said. "Then set fire to the place."

Her business at the Monkey's Ear Tavern attended to, Rivven Cairn went off in search of a good fish vendor.

CHAPTER NINE

Vanderjack tightened the straps on his new magical armor and fastened his cloak around his shoulders.

Theo and Gredchen were poring over a map, practically fighting each other to see who would retain hold of the yellowed parchment. The baron's aide had the advantage of height, but Theo was quick and wily, and by the time Vanderjack walked back to them, the gnome had claimed more than two-thirds of the map.

"What do you think?" asked Vanderjack, showing off his new acquisition—the finely crafted scale mail, with its attached shoulder plates and leather accents. "I've worn dragonarmor before, but never as nice as this."

Gredchen looked at him with disgust. "I can't believe you actually took that from Captain Annaud's corpse," she said. "Besides, every suit of dragonarmor's made for a specific individual. It won't fit you properly."

Theodenes shrugged, looking up from his map. "The armor seems to have decided quite the opposite," he said.

"It's definitely magical," Vanderjack grinned. He shifted from one fighting stance to the other and ended with a little dance. "Snug as a glove and light as a feather! Worthy payment for having to fight the man."

"Not that fighting him accomplished anything more than attracting attention and killing that poor cook," Gredchen reminded him. "And if you haven't noticed, at least some of Pentar's been burning for the past eight hours."

Vanderjack looked back in the direction of Pentar, at least a dozen miles away at that point. A plume of black smoke was rising into the sky. He'd seen many of those before, during the war. It was the calling card of the red dragons.

"We've put plenty of distance between them and us," Vanderjack said. "And I've already said over and over I feel badly about the cook. Badly, I feel so badly. Theo, haven't I already said I feel so badly about him?"

"I don't believe you," Theo said sulkily. "And that's going to count against you when it's time to pay up. Now, if you don't mind, we have ascertained something of a route."

Gredchen didn't lose her disgusted expression as she exhaled and indicated a point on the map. "This is one of Baron Glayward's maps from about twenty years ago," she said. "Before a few places were established, or burnt to the ground by the dragonarmy. Here's where we are, a half day's journey from Pentar." She looked up and pointed past Vanderjack at the line of trees several hundred yards away. "And that's the edge of the Sahket Jungle."

"It's a mile away according to this," Vanderjack said, looking at the scrawled notes on the parchment. "Is it growing bigger or something?"

Theo rubbed his hands together. "Yes, it's quite fascinating," he said. "The Sahket Jungle is, by all accounts, growing at a steady rate. In the next few decades, it will meet the coastline and cover almost all of the northern regions of Nordmaar."

"Fantastic," said Vanderjack, lifting one eyebrow. "Even if the Red Wing's not gone by then, the rainforest will have taken over."

"According to the map," Gredchen continued, "the town of Willik's about twenty or thirty miles that way"—she pointed away from the setting sun—"which puts Castle Glayward roughly the same distance again afterward. We may just have enough supplies to get us to Willik."

Vanderjack frowned. "Isn't that Cheron Skerish's little town? It's bad enough he's an ogre, but I've heard he's also some kind of shaman. My vote's for Rangaar, *here.*" He pointed to a small dot about five miles east of where Willik was, deep in the jungle. "Nothing dangerous in Rangaar, I hear. Just a lot of spice merchants."

"You're afraid of ogres, Vanderjack?" Gredchen teased. Vanderjack observed that when she actually smiled, there was a faint hint that somewhere in her family tree there had to be somebody at least reasonably attractive. Of course, then she'd drop her smirk, and return to being one of the ugliest creatures, this side of a hobgoblin, that Vanderjack had ever traveled with.

Gredchen pointed once again at Willik. "Rangaar's fine, but it won't have what we need, and all of these towns are in red dragonarmy territory, so there's never a guarantee. Trust me; we should go to Skerish's town."

Theodenes snatched the map away a final time and held his face very close to it. "My estimate is that in our current position, it will take us five days to get there."

"That's factoring in the jungle?" Vanderjack asked.

"Quite," said Theodenes, "though there is a good road east. It leads through the Sahket Jungle, into Willik, continues past that town to Rangaar and, finally, North Keep."

"I like a good road," Vanderjack said. "That works for me. Let's go."

The three of them gathered their few belongings together and fell into line on the road leading into the Sahket Jungle. Theodenes walked ahead of Vanderjack and Gredchen, swifter than his little legs would suggest he could, his keen gnome eyes picking out potential problems in the dirt path such as quicksand puddles or the spoor of a dangerous animal.

Gredchen kept the maps and occasionally called out landmarks or an estimate of how far they had gone. They were the baron's maps, after all, and with some convincing, Theodenes stopped fighting Gredchen for them and let Gredchen manage them.

The sellsword came up behind the other two, his hand on Lifecleaver, waiting for the Sword Chorus to reappear. He hadn't fought a battle or engaged in any kind of violent encounter without them for many years. The thought of them vanishing forever made his nerves twitch.

The sellsword felt as if he were walking along a damp, green tunnel. Broad-leaved trees dominated the lower levels of the jungle, rising to about twice his height. Between them, enormous trunks, wide at the base and tapering upward, reached far above the smaller trees and formed the canopy above. Vines, creepers, and flowering plants clustered about the larger trees, and while the road was cleared of vegetation, those who maintained it hadn't bothered to keep the branches from knotting together overhead.

Several hours passed; daylight threatened to turn into night ahead of schedule. Theodenes would stop from time to time to pull a leaf from a creeper near the road or run his fingers through the packed mud and dirt below their feet or sniff at the air. The sellsword remembered Theo being an excellent tracker—for a gnome.

Had he not been ruminating idly, Vanderjack would have noticed the sudden emergence from the trees above of something large and hairy before whatever it was had scooped up Theodenes and swung away, screeching.

"Ackal's Teeth!" shouted Vanderjack, running up to Gredchen. "Get down, we're under attack!"

The baron's aide did as she was told, crouching low and off to the side, beside the base of one of the enormous banyan trees. Vanderjack stood over her, his sword drawn out—still no Sword Chorus. "To the Abyss with you, then!" he swore. "I'm still the best swordsman in Nordm—"

He was cut off as another large shape slammed into him, knocking him clear off his feet and on top of Gredchen. He fought for his breath, but it was just as elusive as the ghosts.

"Watch it!" shouted Gredchen. "Who were you talking to, anyway? Do you think those things are in a mood to negotiate?"

Two more shapes dropped from the trees. Vanderjack got a good look at them: apes, much bigger and larger than he was, with strong, muscular legs and two sets of arms. Their broad mouths were filled with teeth, trailing spittle. Their eyes were red and fixed on the sellsword and his erstwhile traveling companion.

"Girallons," muttered Vanderjack. "Perfect."

As the four-armed apes charged at him, Vanderjack decided that, magic armor or not, another blow like the last one would probably do more than knock the wind out of his lungs. Images of a disemboweled mercenary and his similarly eviscerated traveling companions danced in his mind. A reclaimed breath later, Vanderjack's world exploded in hair, claws, and a great deal of cursing.

* * * * * *

Theodenes flew through the trees.

One moment the gnome had been ascertaining the likelihood of a certain fruit-bearing vine to provide edible comestibles; the next he was whisked away in the hairy arms of a gigantic ape. The creature was unlike anything he'd seen before, or rather, it was very much like something he'd read of before but never dreamed of glimpsing in real life.

Girallons were enormous, four-armed simians written about in some of the bestiaries Theo's expedition had taken with them to the Isle of Gargath. The books had spoken of their wickedly sharp claws, huge fangs, formidable strength, and multiple arms, and that they were capable of lifting a gnome-sized object from the ground and carrying it off through an arboreal environment at great speed.

Well, thought Theodenes. That much is very true.

The expedition to Gargath had not come across any girallons, for which Theodenes had been grateful. Doing battle against such things as behirs and saber-toothed tigers was bad enough. At least then, thought the gnome, he'd had his weapon with him.

For Theodenes' multifunction polearm was missing. He knew he'd had it on him at the time he was taken, but in the rapid treetop transit that ensued, it had slipped out of his hands and tumbled into the darkness below. That presented the gnome with a problem of titanic proportions. He was going to have to deal with his girallon captor without the aid of any martial tool, and given the nature of his lifequest, that was quite a substantial setback.

The girallon swung and leaped and ducked and threw itself from branch to branch, all of its limbs in feverish use other than the one firmly grasping Theodenes. Every so often that limb would toss Theo ahead to free up the arm for complicated maneuvering as the girallon ducked under a low branch; then the limb caught the gnome on the other side.

After four such hair-raising toss-and-catch episodes, Theodenes resolved to make the best of an awkward situation and use the next instance to break free of the creature. He hadn't seen any other girallons, so it was possible the beast was alone. If it had friends, perhaps they were at that moment dealing with Vanderjack and Gredchen. Anyway, Theo was alone, so was the girallon, and it was time to act.

Dusk was swiftly approaching, so Theo was grateful that the next time the girallon threw him ahead through the trees came sooner than later. The creature swung Theo around and hurled him in a high arc across a wide gap between trees. That was the opportunity he was waiting for.

Spinning end over end, he gained his bearings, reached out for a hanging vine, and grasped onto it successfully before the curve of the arc headed downward. The force of the arrested movement almost tore his arm out of its socket, but he found himself whipping about and flung to the side, away from where the girallon was headed and into a thick mass of creepers and fronds.

Theodenes heard the raging bellow of the girallon as it landed on the far side of the space between the trees only to discover that the gnome was missing. Theo hurtled on the vine toward a broad expanse of tree trunk. At the last second, he let go of the vine and slammed into the tree, holding on for dear life. His ears rang and his vision blurred, but for the moment he was safe.

The sounds of the girallon's heavy weight landing on branches and crashing through leaves spurred Theodenes into action. He could see nothing around him but green and brown, but looking down, he spotted an opening in the jungle canopy and possibly a way to reach the ground without breaking his neck. With a grunt, the little gnome pushed away from the trunk, dropped about ten feet through the gap, and grabbed hold of a thick, ropy cluster of tendrils that had enveloped the banyan midway up.

He needed to clamber down the tree, keeping out of sight. That proved easy enough to do, with all of the foliage blocking him off from above. He finally set down on the jungle floor with only a few cuts and scrapes. He knew he'd evaded the girallon for the time being. The frustrated roaring of the creature up above was proof of that.

Theodenes tried to get a sense of where he was in relation to the road; he was at least a mile or more away from where he had been grabbed. Curse the woman for keeping all the maps! In his mind's eye, he conjured forth a vision of the map, with the symbols and markings he'd remembered. He thought to check the side of a tree for moss, but it was entirely the wrong sort of climate, for moss was all over it.

He had to take his chances. The best plan would be to strike out in a chosen direction and look for some kind of landmark. Picking a path completely at random, he hustled off, staying near trees and bushes, using the large leaves as cover.

Just when he thought he'd escaped the girallon completely, he heard more crashing and bellowing far above. He cursed his ignorance. The beasts lived in the jungle and must hunt small game all the time. The noise he had been making, if not his scent, had drawn the beast.

Darting through a wall of leaves and undergrowth, Theodenes emerged into empty space. He lost his footing, or rather, the ground simply disappeared beneath him, becoming a steep hillside that dropped down into darkness. Theo didn't have time to catch hold of anything. Luckily for him, neither did the girallon, which at that moment had burst from the trees above and swung down by one arm to snatch at him. All the girallon grabbed in its long claws was air. Theo slid rapidly down the slope and out of sight.

The slope formed one side of a narrow valley or ravine, slick with rainwater and slime. The ravine was sloped from end to end, so no sooner had Theo hit the end of the slide than he was borne immediately to the right and down a natural chute, cracking his head several times on thick roots. He was sore, covered in mud, and still being chased by the girallon when, finally, the ravine dumped him straight into a small lake.

Gnomes are not taught to swim as children, and indeed many gnomes never learn even as adults. Those gnomes who spend their entire lives in Mount Nevermind may never see a body of water larger than a bathtub unless they work in one of the many reservoirs. Even then the efficiency of the gnome city is such that the reservoirs are in well-maintained underground shelters out of harm's way. Theodenes, however, was a mad gnome, and capable of feats unforgivably alien to his kin. Swimming, or what passed for it, was well within his experience.

Theo broke the surface of the lake, underneath an overhang that sheltered him from any inquisitive four-armed apes lurking above. He continued to hear, at a moderate distance, the sounds of the beast searching for him. The water was very cold, and at some point Theo needed to decide whether he wanted to tread water some more or remain conscious.

In the middle of the lake, which was only about a hundred feet across, was a small island. The island's only distinctive feature was a totem or statue of what looked like some kind of winged, scaled cat; it was carved out of a single chunk of rock, polished smooth by time or uncanny skill. Theo figured that he could swim to the island without too much effort or noise, and the statue might provide some cover of its own.

Taking a deep breath, the gnome plunged his head below the surface of the lake again and swam toward the island. At the halfway point, he looked up; he could neither see nor hear anything of the girallon, so again he plunged below.

Gnomes are hardy individuals, despite their lean and wiry frames. Scholars claim that is strong evidence of their close relation to kender and dwarves. Theo, a paragon of gnome fitness, was able to reach the island with only the air he held in his lungs from the second time he submerged. Then, swimming around the island to the other side, away from the direction of the ravine, Theo pulled himself up onto the muddy bank and scrambled a few feet to the base of the statue. There was still no sign of the beast. Did girallons swim? The gnome made a mental note to look that up in a book, if he ever saw one again.

He allowed himself the luxury of a few deep breaths and checked himself for any major injuries.

That was when the girallon's bellowing roar announced its presence. So yes, girallons do swim, thought the gnome, peeking around the statue, which was about as big as an ox. Perched high in the trees was the very same beast, one clawed hand on either side holding onto branches while the other two beat upon its broad chest. Theo could see that those creatures were used to being the dominant predator in their part of the jungle and were far more intelligent than any other monster he'd had to confront. He racked his brain, trying to think of any way he could get out of his mess.

The bellowing suddenly stopped. Theo, who had slumped back behind the statue, felt the hairs on the back of his neck prickle alarmingly. Had the girallon moved on? The lake surface was still; the leaves were moving gently from the wind in the jungle, a light breeze carrying the heat of the day and making the lakeside area humid and warm. Theo chanced another look around the corner of the cat statue, peeking from below the large, scaly stone wings.

A pair of massive, prehensile feet appeared before him with a sudden smack of mud and a deep grunt. Theo jerked his head back in shock, then backpedaled around the statue as the girallon clambered over it to reach its long arms around to where Theo had been only seconds before. It roared, so close that Theo put his hands over his ears, realizing his foe was signaling the other girallons.

Theo ran through several scenarios in his head, but

all of them ended with him tossed about like a rag doll or torn to bits. He mentally shelved those ideas as interesting but ultimately fatal, and his body acted almost on instinct. He scooted around the statue, just managing to duck out of the way of the creature's grasping arms. Round and round the statue he and the grasping arms went, a dance that was doomed.

The gnome had nothing on his person to strike at the creature, no weapon or tool that wasn't already lost in the jungle. Theo halted, the merry-go-round ceased. Then he did what few gnomes would ever do; he did nothing.

Theo closed his eyes and waited. The girallon's breath was hot on his face. He felt the ape inhale, preparing to strike. He waited.

There was another roar, not at all like that of the girallons, and it sounded across the lake and into the thick jungle, carrying for miles. It was very loud. Theo felt the muddy bank hit him in the back and realized he'd fallen over.

When he opened his eyes, the girallon was gone. In its place, looking down at him from atop the statue, was a huge brass-scaled tiger with wings like that of a dragon and claws as sharp as knives. It bore an uncanny resemblance to the totem it was crouching on.

"Oh," said Theo. "Hello, kitty."

CHAPTER TEN

Vanderjack was surrounded by apes.

He was fifty feet up in the trees, his sword and dagger drawn, scratches all over his arms and legs, straddling two branches. His blades flashed about him, a whirling shield of steel that, for the time being, fended off the two mighty girallons. They roared, teeth bared, claws slashing. They had carried him up there, but they couldn't come near him anymore.

"Gredchen!" Vanderjack shouted. "How're you doing?"

Two trees away from Vanderjack, Gredchen was trying to wrench the gnome's polearm from the thick bark of the banyan tree. She had clambered up into the branches to hide, spotted the weapon embedded in the tree, and latched onto it as a means of helping the sellsword fight back. How it had come to be there was not readily apparent. "Still stuck!" she called back.

One of the two girallons attacking Vanderjack lunged suddenly, taking advantage of the sellsword's distraction. Together, man and ape fell from the branches and twenty feet down, crashing through the leaves and ending in a thick tangled net of vines. The girallon had an advantage over Vanderjack—the sellsword found himself on his back, under the ape's massive bulk, swinging wildly in the vines. The creature pounded on Vanderjack with its fists, three of them at a time; with each blow, the sellsword felt something break.

Gredchen gave the polearm a final tug and almost lost her footing on the branches she'd been balancing on as the weapon came free. The polearm had a single narrow spearhead at the moment. Looking around for the girallons, she gasped; one of them was heading straight for her.

The ape leaped, a howling thing with teeth bared like foam-covered daggers. The baron's aide had her weapon ready, however, and as the beast came for her, she raised it, closing her eyes against the sight. She felt the pole-arm twist in her hands and winced at the shock of the impact. The impossibly heavy mass of the girallon upon the spear jolted her arms and shoulders and forced her back into the tree behind her. When she opened her eyes, however, the creature was impaled through the stomach by the spear.

"A little help here!" she yelled, realizing that the girallon was not yet dead. Two of its clawed hands grasped at the shaft of the spear before it, trying to force its way backward. The other two snatched and clawed in Gredchen's direction. She saw red in the girallon's spittle and red in its eyes.

Meanwhile Vanderjack had kicked free of his attacker and shoved himself backward through the vines. When the girallon took a swipe at him, he fell onto another thick cluster of tendrils and creepers. "One moment," he shouted back, burrowing in and catching his breath. "Little busy."

Vanderjack's girallon leaped down through the gap in the vines above to follow its prey. The sellsword slid aside and watched it fall past, coming to a stop about ten feet below him. It snarled and looked around to find the human, but Vanderjack was pulling broad leaves over himself to hide.

They seemed hopelessly outmatched. Vanderjack looked over to where he thought Gredchen's voice was coming from and spotted one of the girallons with its back to him, a spear emerging from the matted fur. Well, he thought, she isn't doing too badly. His expression shifted when he saw the creature pull itself off the spear and toss it aside.

"Vanderjack!" Gredchen yelled, unarmed. "Any time now!"

The sellsword wiped the sweat from his face. No ghosts to be his eyes and ears meant that he was forced throughout the whole miserable fight to do all the work himself. It wasn't that he couldn't, but he realized he'd grown overly dependent on them.

"Ackal's Teeth, woman!" he called back, instantly regretting it. His girallon opponent whirled around and looked up, locking eyes with him. "Hold onto your skirts, can't you see I'm a little busy myself at the moment!"

With a high-pitched battle cry, Vanderjack gripped Lifecleaver in both hands and leaped from the trees, straight toward the girallon below him. The ape lifted its four arms before its face, but the sellsword's momentum propelled him heavily. Both boots struck the girallon's broad, muscular shoulders, forcing the beast back a step. Vanderjack brought the sword down as hard as he could, inflicting a vicious wound in the girallon's back. It screamed, arms shooting upward to dislodge the human who had brought it such pain, but Vanderjack had already let the leaping movement carry him past. Springing away, he landed a little more than a yard from Gredchen's foe.

"We're in big trouble," Vanderjack called to Gredchen, over the second girallon's shoulder.

"No kidding," Gredchen responded.

Gredchen's girallon spun around swiftly, knocking Vanderjack back and into the trunk of a banyan. Gredchen swore and stepped back around her own tree, roughly in the direction of where the girallon had thrown the gnome's polearm.

The first girallon swung across to where its companion had knocked Vanderjack. The leafy canopy and thick floor beneath them all shook with the added weight; trunks bowed inward. Both girallons, bleeding and frothing at the mouth, had somehow become even more terrifying and dangerous when wounded, than they were before they'd been hurt.

Gredchen glanced around but couldn't see the polearm anywhere. She guessed it had fallen below, somewhere in the darkness of the jungle floor. Rain began to filter through the upper canopies, making the dim light around them even greener. The girallons bellowed fiercely as they moved for a fresh attack.

Vanderjack's vision swam red before him, filled with motes of white light and pulsing with the blood in his temples. The fingers of one hand were still wrapped around the slick grip of his sword, despite the blow from the ape. All of his training as a mercenary and soldier kept him from fumbling the weapon, but he didn't have much strength left—a problem if the girallons carried on the way they were going. He closed his eyes, then opened them again.

The Hunter was standing there, ephemeral, translucent, the two girallons visible through his spectral body.

"Is that you, or me hallucinating?" he muttered, blood on his lips.

"Get to your feet," the Hunter said.

"You need to jump," said the Cavalier, materializing beside the Hunter.

"Help is coming," said the Apothecary, appearing on the other side, blue-white at the edge of Vanderjack's vision.

"Tell the woman," said the Aristocrat, heard more than seen, probably behind him.

"You need to jump," said the Philosopher, echoing the Cavalier.

Vanderjack reached out his free hand, wrapped it around a thick, ropy vine, and slowly pulled himself up. He felt as if he might black out with the effort. The girallons were advancing methodically, spending more of their time screaming and roaring at him than actually lifting a claw in his direction. They must have known he was near unconsciousness; they were playing with him.

"I'm . . . trying," he said.

"Vanderjack! Get up!" he heard Gredchen call out.

"I'm . . . trying!" he repeated. He got to one knee and felt the tremors beneath.

"You need to jump," said the Conjurer from off to the left or the right.

The girallons tensed, their muscles twitching, bunching up to leap at Vanderjack and tear him to pieces.

The Balladeer hovered nearby, in front of a dense wall of vegetation and foliage. "Help is coming," the ghost said.

Vanderjack found his footing. The eyes of the girallons

were locked on his, their fangs and teeth slick with their own ravening. Vanderjack could smell their rancid breath from where he stood. It smelled like rotting meat.

"You need to jump," said the new voice of the Cook, right beside him.

In that last second, the girallons pounced, Gredchen finally succumbed to a scream, and the leaves and trees and thick, twisting vines all around them flew apart as if released from years of wound-up tension. Something even larger than the girallons tore through the wall of leaves behind the Balladeer. It flew straight through the ghost as if he weren't there; a huge brass cat with wings furled close to its body, tiger-striped all over where the scales did not reach. On its back rode a gnome, clutching a familiar polearm under one arm like a lance, the other arm holding tightly to the fur at the back of the creature's neck.

"You got it, fella," Vanderjack responded to Etharion's ghost and threw himself sideways, toward the gnome and his scaly mount. The girallons landed right where he had been, smashing through the foliage. More leaves filled the air. Gredchen lunged and grabbed the cat from the other side as the gnome cried, "Go, Star, go!"

Another heartbeat later and the green hell that was the Sahket Jungle exploded in sound and noise, the tiger roaring a pure and triumphant note, carrying its passengers high above the highest canopy and skyward.

The Sword Chorus faded again from sight, but Vanderjack, lying across the back of the dragon-tiger, didn't care. He was blissfully, finally, unconscious.

******

Highmaster Rivven Cairn stood nose to belly with an ogre, but onlookers would have sworn later that they were the same height.

The fully armored and helmed half-elf, sword on her back and gauntlets firmly pressed against her hips, was always an intimidating sight. The ogres, half-ogres, and ogre kin presently dominating Willik weren't smart, and they weren't accustomed to seeing their spiritual leader challenged. In the case of a high-ranking dragon-army officer, however, they were smart enough and wise enough to know that creating trouble for the highmaster was like poking a stick into a basilisk's nest. That was doubly true in the case of Highmaster Cairn, for Rivven had been there many times before. It was Rivven who had overthrown the large town for the spiritual leader she was presently holding her own against, a fact she never let him forget. At the moment, though, she needed him out of there.

Cheron Skerish was a veritable giant. He was nine feet tall and thick around the shoulders and arms, though stooped and bent with age. The ogre must have been in whatever passed for middle age in an ogre, with a mane of greasy, gray hair surrounding a shiny bald pate covered in age spots and warts. Some ogres couldn't grow beards, but Skerish sported a long, droopy mustache and a forest of spiky hair at his chin, making him look wizened. As a shaman, Skerish affected numerous trinkets, talismans, and grisly amulets crafted from the body parts of animals and worse. Tattoos and scarification covered his bare arms, symbols of his dedication to his mighty god, Sargonnas.

"Yes, you heard me correctly, Skerish," Rivven said in a clear and ringing alto voice. "I'm temporarily relieving you of command. Go. Go now."

"You have idea how long I work to make town right?" Skerish grunted in response.

"I do," Rivven said. "I know that you and your god

are very popular here. It's done wonders. The highlord is very impressed, all the way back in Kern, and he wonders if at some point you might care to visit him there. I was thinking now would be an excellent time."

"Gonnas speak not to I," said Skerish, using the ogre name for the god of vengeance and spite. "Last I know, Gonnas want I stay here. Highlord or no highlord."

Rivven looked aside. The other ogres and all of their human slaves stood in a huge group around the shaman and the highmaster. Skerish's confidence must be at a very high level, Rivven thought. Or maybe it was just his stupidity.

"We get our orders from Her Dark Majesty," said Rivven, lying. She'd never been given direct instructions from Takhisis, of course, but the shaman claimed all kinds of things from Sargonnas, so perhaps he'd allow her that little exaggeration without examining it closely. "I assume you—and your god—are not so proud as to countermand a request from the Queen of Darkness."

The shaman frowned, looking around him at his followers, some of them several degrees human as well as ogre, one of them a trusted lieutenant willing to risk death fighting the highmaster for Skerish if he was asked. None of them looked happy or pleasant. "Gonnas no like I leave Willik. Gonnas want proof highmaster make speak with Darklady."

Now who's making things up, thought Rivven. She was convinced that Sargonnas didn't give a gully dwarf's nose what she or Cheron Skerish wanted. She had to make the ogres believe her, however; she needed a little demonstration.

"You can tell your god that his mistress, the Queen of Darkness, speaks through dragons, and her dragons speak to me. I have a red dragon just outside the town walls waiting to burn this place down if you won't relinquish control immediately."

That caused a number of frightened and angry grunts and growls from the ogres and ogre kin. Rivven knew Skerish didn't have any dragons of his own, despite being the shaman of Sargonnas. Skerish wasn't an officer in the dragonarmies, merely an infamous ogre shaman with good connections. If Black Dragon Highlord Lucien of Takar were there, or even that Green Dragon Highlord Hullek Skullsmasher in the south, both of whom were half ogre and half human, that might be a problem. Rivven was half-elf, and they wouldn't overlook that. But, of course, she had Cear at the ready, and the black and green highlords weren't there.

"Gonnas say highmaster do his worst," said the mule-headed Skerish, apparently assuming Rivven was male. Or maybe that was how ogres spoke of all highmasters. "Gonnas is fire god. Gonnas is vengeance god. Highmaster try burn down Willik, maybe find Willik no burn so good."

The shaman was irritating Rivven, calling the highmaster out like that before his loyal ogre lackeys. It was the sneering that really got to her. She poked the shaman hard in the chest with one gauntleted finger.

"Listen up, Skerish," she snapped. "I'm not going to stand here all day arguing with you. Either you go on a short vacation to Kern with all of your friends, or you're going on a very long and extended vacation in the Abyss with your god."

That was clearly the wrong thing to say.

Cheron Skerish drew back his big, meaty hand and brought it forward, catching Rivven full on the side of her helm, knocking her sideways with a blow that would have stunned an ox. She staggered, feeling a concussion blossom like an angry purple flower within her head.

"Nobody threaten I without back up threats!" yelled Skerish, his voice echoing around the dirt streets and wattle-and-daub houses of Willik. His followers muttered approvingly. "Gonnas! Bring wrath on heathen who speak for Darklady! If heathen speak true, Darklady protect! *Ogflamgoddag!*"

Rivven spoke only a little Ogre, and his last statement wasn't part of her vocabulary. Her magical training told her that it was probably an incantation or evocation of the shaman's god, however, so she didn't want to stand around and see what was going to happen. Pridefully shaking off the ogre's blow, she fell back two steps and swiftly whispered the words of her own magic in response.

Wizards did not wear armor, typically, nor carry weapons. The gods of magic were said to allow the use of a dagger in honor of the wizard Magius, who had reportedly died doing something noble involving a big knife. But Rivven spared little thought for magic's history or its traditions. Emperor Ariakas had taught her to eschew those petty restrictions, to walk the Left Hand Path that he followed, the one that Takhisis offered him and he had, in turn, offered her. With training, therefore, armor had become no hindrance.

Skerish's invocation manifested itself moments later as a column of roaring, twisting, black flames, thundering upward from around Rivven like a fountain of incandescent darkness. Rivven had spoken the words to a protection spell, however, which deflected some of the shaman's fiery magic; she laughed aloud at the irony of using fire on a red dragonarmy highmaster. Rivven's armor was magically enhanced with protections against fire and heat, in part because the red dragons the Red Wing made use of were prone to turning on their masters. With her magic and her armor combined, all Rivven felt was a light scalding around her legs. Skerish had done his best. She'd had worse.

"Was that it?" she taunted, drawing her sword smoothly from her back.

The other ogres backed off, widening the circle around the shaman and the highmaster. Skerish wasn't easily cowed, however. It was obvious that he was expecting a battle, and might even have decided that before his pathetic magical outburst. He reached out one big hand, as if asking somebody to place something in it. From somewhere over the heads of the ogres in that direction, an enormous blackened warhammer—a weapon almost as big as Rivven herself—flew toward the shaman. He grasped it and brought it down, sending up clods of earth inches away from where Rivven was standing.

Not bad, thought Rivven. Skerish really did have powers that would impress any other opponent. She didn't really want to kill him; he was too useful in Nordmaar, keeping his ogres in line. She had often used ogres in her efforts to quell rebellion among the Nordmaaran towns, but if Skerish was going to refuse her orders, Rivven regretted she might have to get rid of him.

Darting forward, Rivven Cairn launched into a routine that she'd practiced often. Her blade came low; the style allowed her some footwork options, a number of defensive positions, and so forth. All very academic, she thought, but when you have to fight an ogre, having something up your sleeve was key

Skerish watched Rivven approach and simply brought

the warhammer down again, pounding the ground. When that didn't work, and he'd taken three or four cuts to his arms from Rivven's sword, he tried swinging the warhammer from left to right, hoping to knock her over. One swing almost caught the highmaster on her side, but she evaded it. Even though he wasn't able to land a hit, however, he was making it very hard for her to get close enough to score a decent wound.

The shaman's ogres stood back and watched patiently. A duel in ogre society was always left to play out its course, never interfered with. Ogres feared the reprisal of a superior officer or a chief, and especially the reprisal of a shaman. Getting involved was a bad idea, so they didn't. Rivven knew, however, that if she beat Skerish in a duel, she was likely to be dog-piled by ogres soon after.

The highmaster knew that if she called Cear, the dragon would arrive and belch flames all over the crowd, finishing them off. That was appealing in some ways, but she didn't want to kill all of her potential ogre allies. It was far more important to show Cheron Skerish that she was in charge, show him where she stood on the ladder of power.

"You may not believe me," she said, ducking out of the way of another swing of the shaman's warhammer. "But the Queen of Darkness is very much on my side. I can tell your shamanic powers are good enough for this crowd, and the highlord in Kern is going to miss having you around, but I'm not going to put up with insurrection."

"So far you not show any sign to I that Darklady is with you," Skerish grunted, taking another superficial cut from Rivven's blades. "Magic armor save you from Gonnas' spell. Not save you from Gonnas' hammer."

All right, then, Rivven thought. She needed something flashy to prove that she was in Takhisis's good graces. Stepping back in time to avoid a brutal crash of the hammer, she sheathed the sword, lifted her hands, and called upon her magic once again. As she always did, she felt the hot prickling of power deep within her soul, that rush of energy filling the hollow left behind by her commitment to Takhisis's path. She never heard the mages of the Towers speak of magic in such a way, as an injury that the use of magic temporarily eased. But they did speak of an almost addictive quality to the art, and there was nothing more addictive than the feeling of relief from such an abiding inner pain.

As the words of her spell seized hold of that well of power and brought it forth, her body became ghostlike and insubstantial, almost vanishing from sight. Before Skerish could react, she stepped forward, forcing her spectral hand through the wall of the ogre shaman's chest and into his massive heart.

Skerish shuddered and stiffened, his eyes rolling back into his head. The ogres in his retinue watched him collapse backward, landing heavily in the damp earth. Three of them called obscenities in Ogre and charged Rivven, but her spell was still active. They ran right through her, tripping and falling over each other.

"Cease this!" she cried, her voice eerie and chill. "I am the Darklady's servant! She is displeased with you and Gonnas, her consort! Your shaman is not dead, but he walks the paths of the spirits as we speak. No doubt Gonnas will protect him, but even the god of vengeance cannot deny the will of the Dragon Queen."

The ogres muttered and growled, and the lieutenant who Rivven had noticed earlier stepped forward. Rivven stood before him, wavering, an ethereal mist coiling from her incorporeal body. She had to admit to herself she looked good. "Are you the second in command?" she asked the lieutenant.

"Yes," he said. He had some human blood, she noticed, wasn't as tall as the shaman, and probably had more education. "I am the shaman's half-brother, Trom."

"Are you through with opposing me?" she asked him, wondering whether the rotten apple had fallen far from the tree.

"Yes," he said. "My brother is proud. He is a good leader, and Gonnas favors him, but he forgets that we all serve Darklady, shaman or not."

Rivven breathed a sigh of relief, masked by her helm. "That shows wisdom," she said. "Listen, Trom. I'm going to set up my base of operations here for the time being. I'm expecting somebody to come along this way in a day or two, and I plan on being here when he does. Take the shaman and your war band south to Kern, and report to the highlord's camp. You'll be told when you can return."

More than likely, Red Highlord Karelas would refuse to see the ogres and have them sent off to some guard post or another. Karelas was happiest being left alone. Still, Kern was an ogre nation, and Trom and his brother would find welcome somewhere.

Trom bowed then gestured at the prone figure of Cheron Skerish. "How long will he be like that?" he asked.

Rivven shrugged. Her body grew more substantial as she released the spell, returning to normal. "About an hour. Give him a lot of water and make sure he eats enough meat." She smiled to herself. It was like leaving care instructions for a pet animal with a family member. Leaving Trom to organize the exodus of ogres from Willik, Rivven walked off in search of some home or building suitable for her temporary quarters.

At the end of one street, near the gates to the town, she saw four figures standing in wait for her.

"Ah, there you are," she said. They looked like ordinary peasants or common folk, but there was something predatory about their eyes. "I've just made an arrangement with the shaman. He's leaving."

"That is good news, Excellency," the first peasant said. "You will not be needing our services?"

She shook her head. "No, not at the moment. Proceed on ahead to Castle Glayward. I want you to attend to the wizard Cazuvel there, in case the Ergothian decides not to show up here in Willik."

"In which form shall we attend the wizard's needs, Excellency?" asked the man.

Rivven considered. "May as well drop the disguises," she said. "Cazuvel knows what you look like. If I have any further instructions, I'll send them along to him."

"As you wish, Excellency," said the man. Before Rivven's eyes, the four peasants began to swell in size, their features distorting, growing more and more metallic and scaled, their clothing melding into their bodies and being replaced by thick plates of armor. When the transformation was complete, four sivak draconians—as large as ogres, and capable of winged flight as well as being able to take on the forms of those they kill—stood before her.

The four sivaks bore the markings and insignia of the infamous Red Watch, indicating they belonged to the elite forces that once served Emperor Ariakas when he was alive. They were a parting gift of his, before the end of the war and his death at the hands of the Whitestone Forces. She hoped those in front of her performed better than the others she'd left watching King Shredler in North Keep.

As the sivaks took wing, Rivven chose an empty building in sight of the main gates as her own. As always, she was being forced to move pieces around on the khas board that was Nordmaar. With the information she had gained from her sources, Rivven felt she'd covered all possible moves on the part of the Ergothian.

All she had to do was wait. That, and get somebody to wash away the stink of ogre.

CHAPTER ELEVEN

$\mathbf{V}$anderjack was soaring above the early-morning jungle.

Technically, he thought, it's this creature that's doing all the work. Theo's new friend, who bore an uncanny resemblance to that totem Gredchen had identified back in Pentar, was a powerful flier. With the wings of a dragon and the strength of a great cat, the dragonne—or so Theo had identified it—could carry the gnome, the sellsword, and the baron's aide without affecting its ability to fly.

Theodenes had named it Star, but it was not a saber-toothed tiger kitten. Granted, the whole mess with the original Star and the circumstances of Vanderjack's parting of ways with Theo was half a decade gone, and had Star survived, she could have grown since then. But it was very unlikely that Star could have sprouted wings and acquired the scales of a dragon. And besides, though the dragonne's jaws were filled with razor-sharp teeth, none of them were as long as knives and permanently hanging out of the creature's mouth.

For the past few hours, Vanderjack and Gredchen

had been slumped on the back of the beast, attempting to recover somewhat from the fight with the girallons as the sun rose in the east. Theodenes regaled them of the importance of ambush detection, the value of his multi-function polearm in today's economic and military climate, how much the two of them were in his debt, and so forth. Gredchen had been initially grateful and apologetic, but that soon wore off. Vanderjack did the usual and appropriate thing and pretended to be unconscious. Given his broken ribs and numerous bruises, pretending to be unconscious wasn't difficult.

They were swiftly approaching the town of Willik, which would have taken them another day by foot but was merely a handful of hours by dragonne. The sellsword had to at least go through the motions of waking up and acting surprised and astonished at Theo's victory over his four-armed pursuer. While he did that, he took hold of the pommel of his sword, waiting for the ghosts to arrive.

"You have escaped the apes," said the Aristocrat.

"You almost didn't," said the Cavalier.

"Didn't we say jump often enough?" asked the Balladeer.

"You need to see a healer," said the Apothecary.

Vanderjack, at the rear of the dragonne's back, listened to the ghosts harangue him for a few minutes. The Cook hovered there among them, not saying anything, but the sellsword was admittedly glad to hear their heckling voices.

". . . which is why you cannot ignore us," the Philosopher was saying.

"You know," Vanderjack said, under his breath. "I've missed this. I'm sure I'll be sick of it again soon, but I've missed it."

The Sword Chorus responded with more comments and opinions. Vanderjack focused on the Cook. He said, "Etharion?"

"Vanderjack," the Cook responded.

"I, uh."

"Now probably isn't the time," said the Balladeer.

"Right," said the sellsword. "Probably not. But we have things to, uh, discuss."

"I'll be around," the Cook said. "I have some questions for you too. You see, I'm not—"

"Later," said the Aristocrat, cutting Etharion off. "They are descending."

Vanderjack looked over the side of the dragonne, who was apparently conversing with Theodenes and Gredchen while Vanderjack spoke with the Sword Chorus. He wondered if he'd been overheard talking with the unseen ghosts. "We're there?" he asked loudly.

Gredchen looked back over his shoulder. "Oh, you're awake. Were you talking in your sleep?"

Vanderjack shrugged. "Maybe."

"Weak comeback," chided the Balladeer.

Vanderjack added, "Or maybe my unconscious self provides me with more enlightening conversation than you and the gnome." He winked at her, letting go of the sword's pommel.

Gredchen colored and said, "Fine. Be like that. Yes, we're here."

Vanderjack stretched then winced as pain shot through his chest. "Theo. Tell . . . Star to put us down outside Willik, about a half mile. If this town's under the thumb of that ogre shaman, he's going to have a lot of ogre friends with him, and we don't want to just land in the middle of that."

The gnome stroked his short, pointed beard briefly

then nodded. "A wise choice of action," he said. "Rare as that is."

Vanderjack rolled his eyes and turned back to Gredchen. "Has your employer had dealings with this Skerish character before?"

She shook her head. "An ogre? Unlikely. Willik is fully within the territory claimed by Highlord Karelas and overseen by Rivven Cairn. They wouldn't allow it."

"If he's a shaman, what power do they have over him? I would have thought he'd be claiming independence to do the work of the Dark Queen or somebody like that."

"I heard that Rivven Cairn opened up Willik for him," she said. "Before she arrived in Nordmaar a decade ago, Willik was a spice merchant's town on the King's Road to the west. I suppose she thought he'd make a good governor."

Vanderjack frowned. "Cairn's the one in charge of Captain Annaud's little faction, isn't she?"

Gredchen nodded. "Yes. She occasionally visits Lord Glayward to remind him where he is, put him in his place. The baron is far too proud to let that worry him."

It dawned on Vanderjack that Annaud's group may have had survivors, and they would be telling the highmaster all kinds of things about him. "It might be a mistake for me to go into Willik," he said.

"Who said that you were going to go in?" Gredchen said with a smile, which came off more like a grimace. "No offense, Vanderjack, but you're one of the most recognizable mercenaries in the region."

"You might say that. But on the other hand I'm really in need of a healer, in case you hadn't noticed."

Gredchen paused while Star dropped below the trees,

tucking his wings in and landing with barely a thump on a dense mat of vegetation some distance away from a crop of carved boulders. She slid off the dragonne's back and continued. "Listen, I know you're hurt, but you're under contract with the baron. I'm his agent, and the reason I'm along with you is because I need to make sure his wishes are being carried out. Best if you stay behind and rest up.

"So I'm going in myself and you're staying here. You've been in military service long enough to be able to do your own field dressing, haven't you? We can bring healing tools and supplies back with us."

Vanderjack pointed at Theodenes the gnome, who was talking quietly with his new friend. Star's voice was deep and resonant, and at the moment the strange creature was speaking in a language Vanderjack had never managed to pick up—the language of dragons. "What about Theo?"

"He can come with me."

"So I'm staying here alone in the jungle?"

Gredchen smiled again. "You won't be lonely. Star's here!"

Vanderjack exhaled. "I think I'll try to sleep my injuries off," he said and started looking around the clearing for a likely spot to sit.

"So we're to visit the town?" Theodenes asked, coming over. "Star has agreed to stay with us for the time being."

"Star can stay with Vanderjack," Gredchen told the gnome. "They can get acquainted."

Theodenes stiffened slightly. Vanderjack noticed, and shook his head. "What now?"

"The last time I gave a feline companion of mine named Star over to your safekeeping, I never saw her alive again."

Vanderjack indicated the dragonne. "Does he look like a saber-toothed kitten to you?"

Theodenes jabbed a finger in the sellsword's direction and said, "Just watch yourself."

"Watch myself," muttered Vanderjack, turning away.

After sorting through their rucksacks, pouches, and pockets, Theodenes and Gredchen set off for Willik. Vanderjack found a place against a banyan, with a bedroll for support, and drew Lifecleaver from its scabbard. He laid the weapon across his knees and watched as the Sword Chorus appeared around him.

"Wise of you to remain here," said the Philosopher.

"You'll need some agaric, the root of the summerfoster plant, and some weak tarbean tea," said the Apothecary.

"What for?" Vanderjack asked, making a face. "Scouring out the inside of a cast-iron pot?"

"A simple healing salve," said the Hunter.

"Any mercenary should know that," said the Cavalier.

"Not this one," said Vanderjack. "Besides, I have you lot around to remind me."

"I think that's the root of your problems," said the Cook, stepping forward. Etharion somehow looked less spectral and indistinct than the other seven ghosts. He appeared much as he had in life, although as a ghost he was bleached of all color and partly transparent.

"Hmm?" Vanderjack rose and began poking about in the edges of the jungle clearing for the herbs and ingredients the Apothecary was directing him to find.

"Look how much trouble you were getting in when the Sword Chorus wasn't here to help you."

The sellsword turned back to the Cook's ghost. "I'm always in trouble. It has nothing to do with you and your ghostly friends."

The Cook shrugged. "Have you ever thought about whether you're becoming too dependent on them?"

"It may be dependence, but it could just be good advice," countered the Aristocrat.

"Indeed. Advice taken well is a boon," said the Conjuror.

"But nobody should be this reliant—" began the Cook, but mysterious looks from the other ghosts cut him off.

Vanderjack shook his head and looked over at the dragonne. It was looking back at him. After a second or two, the sellsword realized that Star's eyes were following the movement of the ghosts as well.

"That dragonne can see you all!" he said. "Did you know that?"

"They have a heritage of magic and heightened awareness," said the Conjurer.

The Cook turned and beckoned toward the dragonne. It got up from its scaly haunches and stalked over, stopping a few feet from where the Balladeer floated.

"He's right. It can see us," the Cook said warily.

"I can hear you too," said the dragonne in an accented Ergothian dialect.

The other ghosts seemed unsurprised. The Cook, on the other hand, seemed to be fascinated. "Hmm, that's an unrecorded quality of dragonnes," he said. "We knew they hailed from the Dragon Isles, and were once the guardians of the good dragon eggs. . . . " His voice trailed off.

"Mind what you say, Etharion," said the Aristocrat.

"How do you come to know of my kind?" asked the dragonne, clearly talking to the Cook.

Vanderjack looked between the ghost and the beast and said, "That's a good question. Etharion, when did you turn into a librarian?"

The Cook shook his head. "Uh, just something I picked up from my years in mercenary camps."

"Right. All those years cooking." Vanderjack lifted an eyebrow.

"Yes. Cooking."

"Anything other than cookies?"

"Another time," advised the Cavalier sternly.

Etharion looked somewhat apologetic and drifted away from Vanderjack to join the other ghosts.

"Star's not your real name, I take it?" Vanderjack asked the dragonne with what he hoped was a tone of polite inquiry. "Theo can't be *that* cursed."

"The gnome likes the name, and so I honor the memory of his companion and bear it with pride," Star said.

"Whatever he told you about that, don't believe all of it," Vanderjack said, once again selecting herbs from the undergrowth. "These ones?"

"Yes," the Apothecary said. "Not the ones to the left; those will poison you."

"Oh. Nice of you to mention it," he said, tossing the poison aside and stuffing the tonic herbs into his fist. He returned to the banyan tree. The dragonne moved closer and seated himself in the clearing, watching him.

"Perhaps you should tell me about my predecessor," said Star. "Why is Theodenes upset with you?"

Vanderjack, with the Apothecary's continued guidance, crushed the herbs together, set up a small traveling sellsword's stove, and started a pot of tarbean tea brewing. "That's quite a story, long in the past, and I really don't think too much about the past. That was during the war."

"I was in the war," the dragonne said with enthusiasm. "I joined with the good dragons."

"Really? I have to admit never seeing one of your kind before."

"Many of us resemble lions. One or two of us are cougars."

Vanderjack stirred the herbs into the tea, watching it thicken. "Hmm. Well, like I said, you're the first I've seen. Has all this been happening here in Nordmaar?"

"In various places."

"Like here in Nordmaar?"

The dragonne growled, but the sellsword shrugged, feigning indifference to Star's apparent annoyance. "Yes," the dragonne said finally. "Here in Nordmaar."

Vanderjack grinned. "How's that working out for you?"

"As you can tell, it isn't."

"Mmm. Well, you're welcome to come along with us for a while. I'm being paid to rescue a beautiful girl for that ugly woman's employer, a nobleman who for some reason hasn't been kicked out of a dragonarmy-occupied region."

"She isn't ugly," said Star.

"Are you serious? I don't know about you and your magical eyes, Star, but I don't think I've seen a person more likely to crack a mirror if she looked at it."

"As you like."

"I know what I see."

The tea seemed to have thickened completely. The Apothecary directed Vanderjack to soak a bandage in the salve. He wrapped his chest in the bandages, wincing as his ribs ached. He also hoped the Apothecary wasn't setting him up for yet another stinking poultice that put him to sleep or threw his nerves off. With the other ghosts quiet and the Apothecary's advice done, the sellsword set aside Lifecleaver and started another pot of tarbean tea.

"I have been asked to remain with you, at least for part of your journey," said Star.

Vanderjack grunted, raising an eyebrow. "What do you mean, you've been asked to remain with us?"

"That is my purpose for the moment."

"Who asked you?"

Star's tigerlike features formed a curious expression of shame or discomfort. "It isn't important. There are powers involved in the outcome of events here in Nord-maar that wish to see you succeed."

"Ho! Wait a minute," Vanderjack said accusingly. "What powers? And since when has this been about anything more than a rescue mission for some noble's daughter?"

Star shifted his wings and settled them against his flanks. "That is all I will say."

" 'That is all I will say,' " Vanderjack echoed mockingly. "It better be because I've had enough of your mysterious blather."

There was an awkward silence for about ten minutes. Vanderjack lay back against the overgrown roots of the banyan, muttering, "Powers. Powers wish for me to succeed. Hah!" Star sat there in the clearing, watching the trees, ignoring the sellsword. Finally, Vanderjack broke the silence and said, "So you can see the ghosts."

Star looked up, his massive chin resting between his forepaws. "Yes."

"The others can't. You realize that, right?"

Star shook his head negatively.

"Nobody else does. It's just me. The Sword Chorus is pretty much a secret. If you could keep that secret, at least until it no longer matters, I'd appreciate it."

"The Cook is right, isn't he? You *are* dependent on them."

Vanderjack pointed at the dragonne. "That's enough of that!"

Vanderjack closed his eyes and leaned back again. This is a sign of just how far things have come, he thought. I'm talking about my feelings with a big scaly flying tiger. Vanderjack resolved to stop talking about his feelings in the future, whether the other individual in the conversation was a dragonne or not. People would start thinking he was crazy.

If they didn't already.

******

Theodenes and Gredchen walked the quiet, early-morning streets of Willik, wondering where all the people had gone.

Willik was supposed to be a fairly prosperous town, founded by a small cabal of spice merchants who felt that its central location would help them make a fortune selling spices all around Ansalon. That was in the first century after the Cataclysm, when the world was in disarray. Nordmaar had risen from the ocean floor, transforming itself from a small archipelago of islands to a single region of tropical jungle, grasslands, and swamp. It was the ideal sort of climate for spices, and the natives were more than happy to help the merchants with their business.

With the invasion of the dragonarmies, Willik and other merchant-driven settlements in the region experienced a sharp decline, as might be expected. However, the canny highlords and highmasters found a way to make use of the already-established trade routes. Red Highlord Phair Caron made sure her officers, including

Rivven Cairn kept the steel and goods flowing in and out of Nordmaar, Kern, and the other territories she conquered. Even after Phair Caron's death in Silvanesti, her orders were upheld, and under Rivven Cairn the spice business had flourished.

It was, therefore, a surprise to Theo and Gredchen that Willik seemed barely occupied. They saw one or two people, peering out of windows; there was no shortage of houses or shop fronts or trade buildings. The merchants' hall was standing where it was most appropriate, in the center of the town, and tools and belongings were strewn about. But it was as if the residents themselves had simply vanished, without taking anything with them, and leaving behind only a handful of citizens to maintain an illusion of daily life.

"This doesn't seem right," Gredchen said in a low voice. "I was told there were many ogres here."

"I see ogre-sized implements," Theodenes said. "These houses along this row here have even been renovated in the past few months to incorporate individuals of a larger size."

"So there were ogres here recently. And where there are ogres, there are slaves, and occasionally goblins and hobgoblins. I don't see any. Maybe we should ask one of those people down there."

In front of the spice merchants' hall was a low area, probably originally meant as a gathering place with built-in seating. About a dozen humans, male and female, sat watching the large brick building expectantly. There was no sign of life within the hall, but the people seemed content to just wait patiently as Theo and Gredchen approached. All along one side of the area, mounds of fresh dirt were piled up. What the dirt was doing there or where it had come from was unclear.

Gredchen tapped one of the nearest people on the shoulder. "Excuse me."

The woman turned around slowly, lifting her head toward Gredchen. Gredchen gasped and took a step back. The woman's eyes were black—no white or colored iris, just empty black orbs. Others nearby seemed to notice the two outsiders as they also turned to look. All had the same black stare.

"By the gods, look at them," Gredchen said, moving a little closer to Theo. The gnome had his polearm at the ready, currently configured as an axe at the end with a vicious-looking barb behind it. He boldly flourished the weapon before him.

"Fascinating," said Theo. "Some kind of enchantment, perhaps. No doubt the work of the ogre shaman."

Neither of them were very experienced with the supernatural, not even Theo, who had let that side of his broad underpinning of scholarly research subside in his lifelong pursuit of weaponsmithing. As they watched, the woman whom Gredchen had touched rose from her bench and stood to face the new arrivals.

"I've never seen anything like this before," Gredchen whispered to Theo. "Are they ogre slaves? Are they dangerous?"

As if in answer, the closest woman's face twisted into a hideous, snarling mask. She no longer looked human. The other townsfolk curled their fingers into clawlike shapes, hunched themselves over, and leaped up onto the benches. As Gredchen and Theo backed away, the first woman opened her mouth, and her tongue extended out, long and barbed and monstrous.

"It would seem they are very dangerous indeed!" said Theo, pulling the polearm back for a swing. "In fact, I would wager that they intend our immediate harm."

The woman-creature sprang, propelled by strength that her slight frame gave no impression of having, hissing like an angry snake. Her fingernails were chipped and broken but long, and once Gredchen had a better look at them, she saw that dirt, or worse, was heavily crusted underneath them. The other black-eyed strangers leaped through the air and landed close by Theo and Gredchen, bent over, some on all fours.

Theo let the closest one have it. He took a step forward to give himself additional leverage and swung the axe head of his polearm straight at the torso of the fiend. It crouched low, barely evading the swing, then jumped right for Theo. The gnome was able to bring the polearm around and up just in time to knock the creature to one side. He let out a grunt and prepared to defend himself against another, a female, edging forward.

Gredchen, unarmed but for her satchel, looked about for something handy to wield as a weapon. She spied a long-handled shovel thrust into the closest pile of dirt, about ten feet away. Breaking from Theo, she made a dash for the shovel as two barb-tongued men scampered toward her on all fours. She reached the shovel, grasped the handle with both hands, and used her forward momentum to pull it out of the dirt and leap over the pile at the same time.

The two barb-tongued men followed her over the dirt mound, but she was waiting for them. The first one she cracked across the side of the head with the flat blade of the shovel. It tumbled away, leaving the second one to hiss wickedly at Gredchen and her makeshift but effective weapon.

Theo was trying to strike at the female creature, which leaped from side to side, successfully keeping out of his way. He finally caught her thigh with the hook on the axe head, snagging the point in her dress and knocking her flat to the packed earth. With a couple of twists and a press of a button, the barbed hook extended out a foot, with the axe head collapsing into the shaft of the weapon. Theo effectively held a scythe and was able to pin his opponent down quite handily.

As more creatures closed in, however, Theo backed away until he stood next to Gredchen, who was busy fending off her own handful of foes. They stood back-to-back on Willik's main street, knocking back the foul and ravenous former residents of the town and occasionally severing a limb or two. Theo even lopped the head off one of them, but its body continued to claw its way in his direction as the head lay on the ground, tongue whipping in and out of its toothy mouth.

"I wager these people have been waiting for visitors," called Theo above the din of hissing and rasping. "Indeed, I'd guess that the ogre shaman left them here just for us."

"I can't have Skerish take the credit," declared a woman's voice, resonant and ringing clear across the main square. Looking up, Theo and Gredchen saw a woman in red and black dragonarmor, no helmet, standing astride the upper-level balcony of the spice merchants' hall. Her hair was thick and blonde, falling just below her pointed ears in waves, and her features were ruddy and tight, like somebody whose favorite emotion was anger. "He was going to have the ghouls buried, but I decided to make use of them."

Gredchen paled. "That's Highmaster Rivven Cairn," she hissed to Theo, just before driving her shovel into the neck of an attacking ghoul. "She's a mage. She's used magic to bind these creatures to her!"

Rivven floated from the balcony, borne by unseen forces and drifting over the top of the hissing, clawing creatures. "I have to say I wasn't expecting you specifically, dear Gredchen," Rivven said. "Nor you, gnome, although I was aware you were caught up in this adventure."

"I'm surprised you gave me a moment's thought at all," replied Gredchen through clenched teeth. "And this is no form of hospitality I'm familiar with." Another pair of ghouls leaped at her, but Theo's scythe cut them down.

"I'm looking for somebody your employer paid to work for him, Gredchen," Rivven said, her black cloak fluttering in the morning breeze that carried the stench of rot to the gnome and the baron's aide. Many things had died in Willik. "If you're here, then you must have come with him—I should have guessed as much. And Theodenes is apparently the new mercenary boss in Pentar. So that explains why he is here too."

"I don't know what you're talking about," yelled Gredchen. She noted that Theo had kept his mouth shut the entire time. "We're just passing through these parts, taking a little sightseeing trip, my boyfriend Theo and I."

Theo winced but still bit his tongue.

"Why yes, a little sightseeing with your boyfriend," the highmaster smirked. "I can send even more of the ghouls at you, if you're inclined to keep this ruse up. Then when you and your *boyfriend* are dead, you can join their ranks."

"This is pointless, Highmaster," Gredchen yelled. "We're under highlord protection, bearing the seal of Baron Glayward and a legal and binding contract of mercenary activity for Nordmaar and Estwilde."

"Who do you think gives that seal any degree of legit-imacy?" responded Rivven. She waved a hand, and the two remaining ghouls fell backward as if tugged on a leash. They scrambled, a male and a female, eventually clambering onto a pile of dirt and watching eagerly.

"All right, he's not my boyfriend, but we're only here for supplies," Gredchen said as innocently as she could. "I'm on my way to North Keep. It's that time of the year. I insist that you let us pass without further threat."

The highmaster drifted slowly to the ground and swept her cloak behind her in a functional manner. "I'm amused that you think you've got any room for nego-tiation or threats, Gredchen," she smiled. "I have spies and agents everywhere. There's no other reason for you to be so far within the Sahket Jungle, which you know quite well is firmly in my territory, unless it's got some-thing to do with the Ergothian."

She looked down at Theo, who still held his scythe in front of him. "And I can't so much as spit in Pentar right now without hitting some minor sellsword or freebooter who would rat you out, Theodenes. Espe-cially since the Monkey's Ear burned to the ground. They're talking about rebuilding it in the Floating Marketplace. Isn't that clever? Right above the water, in case of future fires."

Theodenes finally spoke. "I have relinquished my position as boss," he declared haughtily. "I am presently under independent contract, and by Shinare's seal, I am under no obligation to reveal any information not perti-nent to the proper completion of the contract."

Rivven tapped her foot angrily, glaring at the two irritants—bugs she would prefer to squash. "The God-dess of Oaths and Contracts has nothing to do with your mischief."

"Are we under arrest?" Gredchen asked indignantly. "I'm asking because if not, I really would like to carry on my way. Legally. As I said."

Rivven paused. "You really do have guts, don't you? I would slap you if I didn't think it might somehow improve your looks. Here's what I'm going to do. I'm going to let you go. I'm pretty sure you're going to hook up again with the Ergothian at some point, despite what you claim, and when you do, you can tell him for me that he owes me for significant damages—some expensive draconian troops, some soldiers, and a valuable officer. Tell him that I got the ogres out of the way here, just for him. He might elude me today, but when he gets where he's going, I'm going to be there waiting for him. And I'm going to collect."

Gredchen frowned. "You sent Skerish away? Why would you do that?"

Rivven smiled. "I don't like interference with my plans. Just tell him that it appears I have a vested interest in his career and that he's going to have to either settle up with me or deal with the consequences."

"I'll tell him, but I don't think he's going to be any more trusting of you than I am."

Rivven lifted her shoulder plates in a shrug. "I really don't care. I'll be in touch. And Gredchen?"

The baron's aide and the gnome had begun to back slowly away, keeping the highmaster and her two ghouls in sight. Gredchen said, "What now?"

"Say hello to the baron's beautiful daughter for me when you see her."

Gredchen let out a small gasp but quickly recovered enough to furrow her brow. She didn't say another word, instead turning and walking forcefully down the street and away from the highmaster. Theodenes, glancing warily over his shoulder, trailed behind, stopping only long enough to grab a handful of items from abandoned shop front carts and windowsills.

The highmaster watched them leave, then turned to the two remaining ghouls. "What are you two monsters looking at? Pick up a shovel. There are bodies lying all over this street." She walked off, leaving the ghouls to clean up the mess.

CHAPTER TWELVE

Vanderjack was dreaming.

He was back on the island of Southern Ergoth, in the lands of the refugee elves during the war. Winter had claimed so much of the region, frosting the evergreens and encrusting the grassy foothills of the Last Gaard Mountains with ice. It could be overwhelming, the cold, and more bitter and pervasive than anything he'd felt in the north.

He was in his old mercenary outfit, with his old mercenary buddies: the kender, Danilo Findabuck; the men from Coastlund, Antor and Claustin, with their stolen Solamnic swords; Agate Splintergem, the dwarf outcast from Kayolin who'd killed his own father for selling out to the dragonarmies. He vividly remembered asking Agate if it was still fratricide if you were already regarded as a fatherless dwarf, and Agate had just glowered and told him to watch his lousy human mouth. Those were the days.

In his dream, they were with him again, just as they were for three years, in and out of service with the Solamnics and the dragonarmies. They were the band he'd been traveling with when he met Theo. That was the place where it had all started. Or rather, that was where it ended.

Vanderjack never found the Treasure of Huma. He'd gone looking for it and signed on with the elf refugee kingdom—some old regent named Belthanos had actually paid his band steel coins to help them kill ogres and track down a missing Kagonesti elf woman—just as an excuse to get closer to the legendary tomb in which the knight was said to be buried. He'd combed the foothills and mountain passes looking for the right place, somewhere known as Foghaven Vale if his sources were right. He'd never made it.

Theodenes had fallen into some trouble near Daltigoth, and being as Vanderjack was supposed to be fighting ogres (it was in his contract, after all) and was in the area at the time, it wasn't hard to convince his band to help the poor gnome out. The gnome had some strange cat with him, a kitten he said, although it was about as big as a large dog. No problem, said the band. Can't go wrong with a kitten as big as a dog and teeth as long as steak knives.

Then everything went south. After they saved the gnome, they'd all been drinking ale and telling stories around the campfire. Next morning, they did the usual scouting of the area, with Vanderjack and Theo getting acquainted and sharing theories about the location of the tomb. When everybody got back together, something was amiss. None of them talked about the Treasure of Huma or even about the Kagonesti woman they were on the lookout for.

It happened again the following day and the next. In his dream Vanderjack relived that lack of caution, the almost constant drinking. He had the Sword Chorus to help him in a fight, so he always sent the others off to scout around, poke their noses into avenues of interest. His dreaming mind saw the change coming over his companions and how it hadn't even registered with him. He dreamed of telling Theodenes that it was all right, he'd watch Star for a few hours while Theo scaled a cliff face and examined the signs of possible ancient ruins. He saw himself simply wander off, a flask in hand, whistling merrily. He saw himself not anticipating what happened next.

The others had returned. Theodenes was a hundred feet up, and Star was at the base of the cliff, and there were Danilo and Claustin and Antor. Agate came up the rear. Vanderjack's dreaming self saw them, even as he saw himself sprawled somewhere not far away, draining the last of his drink and ignoring the Sword Chorus's warnings. He saw them shift and change and grow in height. He saw the sivak draconians, for that was what they were, closing on Star. Red markings on their armor, wickedly serrated swords, and—

Vanderjack awoke with a start. Daylight still washed the clearing in radiant green, stirring up the humidity of the jungle, reflecting on the brass scales of the dragonne not twenty feet away. "Ackal's Teeth," he said, shaking himself out of the daze.

The dragonne was awake too. "You made a lot of oaths to the founder of Ergoth," Star said in his deep voice, "when you were dreaming."

"I never dream," the sellsword said, pulling himself into a sitting position. He felt his ribs gingerly. The pain had substantially subsided. The poultice and bandages seemed to have worked miracles, at least as an anesthetic. "Almost never. I think I had a dream last year when I ate some bad goulash in Kalaman, but this was different."

Star rumbled. "Omens, perhaps."

"I don't get omens."

"You are having a lot of first-time experiences," said the dragonne. "Change is part of life."

"Are the others back yet?"

Star looked in the general direction of where they had gone. "No. But it has only been two hours. What was your dream about?"

"I told you, I don't dream," Vanderjack said.

"As you wish," the dragonne replied. "But don't expect this to be your last dream. On the Dragon Isles, the dragons of Light dreamed for a thousand years, and great magic worked its way into the world as a result. Your dreams, Vanderjack, may be important too."

"No offense," the sellsword said, standing. "But I think all that dreaming was the reason they had their nests ransacked by the Queen of Darkness's dragons. I don't think that's the kind of magic they wanted."

Star growled. "Never speak ill of the Children of Paladine. My brothers fought and died to protect them as they slumbered, defending their nests. Had they the power to waken, they would have. We bear their sorrows for them to this day."

Vanderjack raised his hands. "Hey now. Look. I'm just a human, I don't know from dragons other than the ones I met working for both sides a few years ago. I'm sure you did your best and all."

Vanderjack shook his head. That was smart. Get the dragon-tiger good and mad; that'll help matters.

The sound of somebody approaching proved a welcome distraction. Vanderjack pulled on his sword belt, and in so doing he grasped Lifecleaver's pommel. The Sword Chorus appeared around him, the Hunter already setting off in the direction of the noise.

"Sleep well?" asked the Apothecary.

"You know how I slept," said Vanderjack. "Did you have anything to do with that?"

"Lucid dreaming is a possible side effect of that compound," the Philosopher said.

"Indeed," said the Apothecary. "The swifter the healing, the more intense the dreams."

"They aren't saying it," said the Cook, stepping forward. "But we all saw the dream ourselves. While you slept, you had your hand on the sword."

Star watched but stayed out of the conversation. The sellsword, however, shot the Cook a look. "You mean they had something to do with the dream?"

"We merely observed," said the Aristocrat.

"Quite an eye-opener, though," said the Balladeer.

"Had you known your fellow mercenaries were sivak draconians?" asked the Conjurer.

"Of course I didn't bloody well know they were sivaks," said Vanderjack.

"You were drunk," said the Cavalier.

"And soon after that, Theodenes returned and there was only the remains of the cat," said the Balladeer. "Sad. Worthy of a ballad, if I say so myself."

Vanderjack rolled his eyes. "I had already left," he said. "I could hear Theo screaming for help a mile away. There was such a mess. I didn't want to deal with it, so I took off."

"And your mercenary band?" asked the Cook. "What happened then?"

"I found them—the real them—all dead, a couple of miles away. They had been dead for days."

The ghosts fell quiet, as if to let that sink in. Star still watched and still said nothing.

The Hunter appeared through the trees and broke

the silence. "They are approaching. The gnome and the woman."

"Well, thank the Abyss for that," Vanderjack swore. "I can tell the gnome all about what happened—in the past, in the dream—and we can all stop talking about spilt milk."

"I wouldn't bring it up," said the Balladeer.

"Don't open an old wound," said the Apothecary.

Theodenes and Gredchen walked out into the clearing, the gnome hefting a sack of acquired goods over his shoulder. Vanderjack released his hand from Life-cleaver, and the ghosts winked out of sight.

"You took your time," he said, walking up to meet them. "How are the ogres? Did you run into any trouble?"

"You could say that," muttered Gredchen.

"Star!" Theodenes cried warmly and went over to update the dragonne on the events in Willik. Vanderjack wiped his brow with a sleeve and felt as if everything had grown a few degrees warmer. Damn that nagging guilt.

"What do you mean? Did they pick a fight with you?" Vanderjack indicated the sack the gnome had set down to the right. "I can tell you didn't come back empty-handed."

"The ogres are gone," Gredchen said. "Willik's been emptied out by the highmaster. She was there and told us to pass along to you her interest in your future."

Vanderjack narrowed his eyes. "Ackal's Teeth!" he swore. "Rivven Cairn was there? What in the Abyss for? Just waiting for me to happen by?"

"I don't get it either," Gredchen said. "She and the baron have always had an understanding. She leaves him alone, and he doesn't interfere with politics in Nord-maar. Now she tells me that she's keeping tabs on what you do and that you owe her."

"Hmm. Well, I did kill one of her officers," Vander-jack said, rubbing his jaw. "But if that was such a big deal to her, why didn't she just come out here and get me? Doesn't she have a dragon of her own that she can sic on me?"

"The red dragon Cear. We didn't see him. But it hardly matters. Now that we know she's watching us, we need to be sure to go straight to Castle Glayward as soon as possible."

Theo came over. "Right," he chimed in. "I've told Star, and the dragonne has agreed to carry us to the castle."

"When we get there, there's a good chance it's been overrun by red dragonarmy forces, and this daughter of the baron's is there as some kind of collateral," said Vanderjack. He turned to Gredchen. "Is that how it is?"

"That's what the baron has been led to believe. I've not visited the castle recently. But on those rare occasions when the highmaster has visited the baron's manor, he's pleaded with her to bring his daughter back to him."

"Let me guess," said Vanderjack. "She said no."

Gredchen pointed at the sellsword. "Are you fit enough to keep going?"

Vanderjack coughed. "Of course I am."

"Excellent," said Theo. "We fly now to liberate the baron's daughter. Once we have her, we can leave Nord-Omaar and take our earnings with us."

One by one, they climbed onto Star's back. Vanderjack looked back over his shoulder in the direction of Willik as they lifted off from the ground and flew due east.

A dragon highmaster had rid a whole town of ogres just to let him know she was watching him. Powers taking an interest in him! Something very curious was going on, Vanderjack thought. And eventually, he reflected with a silent groan, he was going to learn what it was.

******

Cazuvel stood on the battlements of Castle Glayward, surveying the wet jungle vista.

The highmaster had sent him four sivak draconians, under orders to serve and assist him. Of course, she was still unaware that he wasn't the real Cazuvel, who was trapped inside a mirror deep within the Lyceum. The creature wearing Cazuvel's form suspected that the sivaks, who were themselves shapeshifters, might guess something was amiss if they spent too much time in his presence. Cazuvel had given them orders to leave him alone and gone up to the roof of the castle.

There, he could see the single road leading through the rainforest, a wide and once-paved road that wound south to North Keep. Cazuvel preferred to use magic to get from place to place, but he could appreciate the effort once taken to make the road passable. Nobody had lived in Castle Glayward for a decade, however, so nobody had cared enough to maintain the road's state. The Sahket Jungle had encroached upon it, vines and creepers forming a latticework of pale green above the tumbled paving stones. Cazuvel briefly felt a sense of wonder at the power of nature, which he supposed was all a reflection of the goddess Chislev. The feeling quickly passed, however; Cazuvel was not a part of that world and sought no solace in it.

Cazuvel had been told that the sellsword was on his way. He spent a few minutes sketching out a pattern of magic in the air with his dagger, as an artist might use a pencil, gestures invisible to eyes not sensitive to such things. The delicate threads of magic crisscrossed the roof, hanging there in space, waiting for him to flood them with his arcane power. Instead of completing the spells, however, the mage conjured forth a series of invisible energy receptacles, fist-sized constructs of magic, and stored a considerable amount of his personal energy within them. He linked those receptacles to the patterns with a sliver of power, just enough to keep them active and aware. The patterns were traps, primed with sorcery, and once he was done with them, Cazuvel would be instantly alerted to the presence of any intruders as their proximity closed the magical circuit and released the stored power into the traps.

Cazuvel would need to set up more patterns, also connected to storehouses of power. They would be located on the grounds of the castle and perhaps surrounding several windows. To do that, he had to go to those places.

The wizard took a step off the battlements, dropping softly from them toward the ground a hundred feet below, robes fluttering. His descent frightened off the brightly colored birds that found their usual perches along the lower crenellations. Animals sensed the creature he truly was. He needed to be more cautious if it came to being in the presence of horses or other trained animals, for he did not want to alert anyone to his fundamental nature just yet.

Walking around the base of the castle, Cazuvel set up more of his wards and enchantments, poised for activation, strung together like chains of anemones, beautiful and alien. It was a shame they weren't visible to the uninitiated. Cazuvel had developed a sense of vanity since he had assumed the mage's form. The transformation was deep, and Cazuvel's personality had crossed over to some extent; the creature felt emotions, passions, desires, and other weaknesses of mortality. It wouldn't be long, however. Soon he would shed all of those. For the time being, the creature decided he would enjoy them all, the taste of flesh-and-blood frailty that his dark kind could not ordinarily possess.

Once his work was complete, Cazuvel transported himself into the castle's great hall, appearing before a huge rectangular arrangement of tables. In the center of the arrangement, a fire pit filled with coals and covered by an elaborate iron grate gave light to the chamber. Tapestries of Solamnic heraldry and symbols of the Knights covered the otherwise bare gray walls of stone. Even with the dragonarmy's occupation of Nordmaar, and the baron's forced departure from his ancestral home, the trappings of Solamnic nobility remained behind. Cazuvel wondered why Rivven Cairn allowed that to be so.

The sivaks weren't in there, so Cazuvel made use of the time to sit on one of the two high-backed chairs that rose above the others on a dais. A part of the true Cazuvel's mental imprint that had come with the body filled the creature with pride, a sense of achievement. The mage had been ambitious, Cazuvel thought. That was a large part of his undoing, of course. It was another flaw of mortal character, but particularly among Black Robes. The true Cazuvel dwelled in the shadow of Raistlin Majere, Fistandantilus, even Ladonna, Black Robes all, and could not help but aspire to those worthies. Unfortunately for the hapless sorcerer, aspirations were no substitute for true power.

Power was something Highmaster Rivven Cairn had,

Cazuvel reflected. She was not a dedicated wizard; she had undertaken the Test, yes, but she hadn't taken up the robes as her brother and sister mages had. She wore armor and bore that elven sword. Still, it was a common rumor among the Tower wizards that Rivven had been a student of Emperor Duulket Ariakas himself. Neither the true Cazuvel nor the creature that wore his likeness had ever met Ariakas, but the emperor's might had extended into realms beyond this one, enough that the Abyss rippled with the aftershocks when he was assassinated. With such a master, Rivven must know secrets Cazuvel must have longed to attain for himself. Since the creature boasted Cazuvel's psyche, those desires were his as well.

"Honored master," called a voice from the hall's entrance. It was one of the sivaks, filling the doorway with his great silvery bulk. Cazuvel twirled a finger, temporarily channeling some of his power from the arcane structures filling the castle and strengthening the magic that maintained his appearance. With any luck, the sivak wouldn't suspect a thing.

"Enter," the mage said. The sivak, who went by the name of Aggurat, was the Red Watch commander. His three subordinate officers were probably stationed elsewhere on that floor, maybe even standing motionless like statues in mockery of the empty suits of armor that Baron Glayward kept there. Cazuvel had spoken only once or twice with Aggurat, and he didn't know the other three sivaks' names. It was normal not to, Aggurat had told him. The mage had no need to ever address the others, in accordance with dragonarmy protocol.

Aggurat marched up and around the tables, standing before Cazuvel's chair. The sivak was so tall that he and the mage met at eye level. Cazuvel admired the strength and power in those creatures. The Red Watch were the elite; he hoped he would not need to test that strength and skill personally. "Honored master," Aggurat said, "our scouts have reported no sign of the sellsword, nor any evidence of a traveling gnome and an ugly human female companion."

"The highmaster says we are to expect them. How reliable are your scouts?"

"Master, they are kapak scouts who have worked for us for some time," Aggurat said. "They were hand-picked by the upper echelons of the Red Watch and by Emperor Ariakas himself."

Cazuvel doubted that. Ariakas rarely deigned to speak to his draconian servants, let alone personally select a few lowly kapak draconian sneaks to serve as scouts or rangers. Aggurat must be embellishing the matter.

"I see," said the wizard. "Am I to understand, however, that your scouts are limited to ground-based reconnaissance? None of them are capable of flight, as are you and your sivak brothers."

"That is correct, master. Do you suspect the sellsword and his allies of approaching from the air? I cannot imagine how—"

Cazuvel waved a hand. "I trust the highmaster," he said. "If she says they approach, then they approach. If your kapaks have seen no evidence by the roads and jungle paths, then they must look to the skies."

"Regrettably, master, the skies are unreachable to the kapaks, and we have no fliers."

"On the contrary," Cazuvel said. "You have yourselves."

Aggurat stiffened. The draconian's deep and sibilant

voice rose an octave. "But, master, we were given strict instructions to aid and protect you here."

"I am well protected. The castle is well protected. Indeed, the lands immediately around the walls of the castle are well protected. Your instructions were to serve at my pleasure, were they not?"

"Yes, honored master."

Cazuvel smiled and leaned back in the chair, letting its wooden confines surround him. "Excellent. Then do as I have commanded. Take wing and patrol the skies above the jungle. Maintain a perimeter of at least a mile, and if you see the sellsword and his companions advancing by air, engage them at your earliest opportunity."

Aggurat saluted. "As you wish, honored master."

"You are dismissed."

Cazuvel watched as the draconian turned and marched out of the room in rigid and disciplined steps. With the Red Watch out from under his feet and the sellsword likely defeated before he and his companions could even arrive at the castle, he could progress with his plans unhindered.

"But first," he said to himself. "First, I must pay another visit to my dear friend in the mirror."

CHAPTER THIRTEEN

Vanderjack was staring at the mountains.

He had seen mountains before, of course. Every mercenary in the last war had seen mountains: the frigid peaks of the Last Gaard Mountains in Ergoth, the barren altitudes of the Khalkist Mountains in Neraka, or the windswept towers of the Kharolis Mountains in Abanasinia. Ansalon was a continent of mountains, forged in the birth of the world, or thrust up from the earth during the Cataclysm. But the Emerald Peaks of Nordmaar were like no other mountains the sellsword had ever seen.

The Sahket Jungle could be described most accurately as a broad, green swath across three different topographical regions. In the east, near the ruined city of Valkinord and the Blood Sea of Istar, the jungle crept across swampy lowland, eventually receding and becoming the Great Moors. In the west, from where the sellsword and his companions had come, the rainforest rose from the plains, descending for a time into the Yehudia Valley but for the most part remaining level and even. In the north and central Sahket, however, the tropical vegetation surged up into the dizzying heights of the Emerald Peaks, eventually giving way to the knifelike obsidian and towering basalt columns that formed the last northern ridge before the sea.

Before the Cataclysm, the Emerald Peaks had been islands in the Courrain Ocean, inhabited by what would later become the native peoples of Nordmaar. Temples, shrines, and ancient tribal structures lined gentle slopes. Wide shelves devoted to the growing of rice and other grains were marvels to the seafaring peoples of Istar and Ergoth. Nordmaar's islands were a fantastical and mysterious land of opportunity rarely visited, for it was alleged that dangerous and savage creatures dwelled there. That, of course, was folklore and rumor swollen beyond reason by sailors. Mighty Istar considered the islands beneath its notice; the Kingpriests barely recognized them at all, in fact, and those few priests who visited them returned with fanciful tales of converting hundreds of natives to the True Faith of Paladine and left it at that.

Nordmaar survived Istar but fell to the same punishment as that holy city more than three hundred years before Vanderjack was born. Whether that was because they failed to observe the gods or simply because they were destined to change remained a subject of controversy among the Aesthetics, but after the fiery mountain smote the Kingpriest and his empire, bringing about the Cataclysm, Nordmaar's mysterious islands were gone.

The seafloor rose sharply as the continental plates buckled and shifted. The waters receded, leaving behind the plains and swamps that the Solamnics would eventually discover; the islands lifted skyward. Volcanic forces pierced the islands from below, shattering the terraces and tossing aside the temples like so many tiny pebbles. In their place stood colossal pillars of rock, hung with the remains of the islands like bejeweled fingers reaching up through the earth. When the Sahket Jungle raced like green fire across Nordmaar in the coming decades, it laced those fragments with vines and creepers as it did the rest of the land. The result was a wall of trees and rock that had no equal elsewhere on Krynn.

Theodenes leaned across the dragonne's back, breaking into the sellsword's reverie. "Quite magnificent, are they not?" the gnome said, shouting over the beating of the dragonne's wings.

"This close, I suppose they are," Vanderjack shouted back. "You can see them from the west, but you can't really make out any details. It's just a wall of green and brown. How do the trees get so far up?"

"It's the heat," said Theodenes. "The tree line is much farther up the mountains because of the elevated temperature here in Nordmaar, as opposed to the Kharolis or Khalkists."

"Are you making that up, or do you actually know what you're talking about?"

"He's a gnome," interjected Gredchen, just as loud as the other two. "Even a gnome warrior knows more about this kind of thing than most of us humans."

"Quite so," said Theodenes. "In fact, gnome education is far superior to that of any other race on Krynn, even that of the elves. It comes of not busying ourselves with world conquest, frivolous fancies, or magic."

"I thought it was because you were cursed by the Smith God to be obsessed with everything from waterwheels to tinderboxes," Vanderjack said.

"While it is true that many of my kinsgnomes are considerably more attuned to the scientific qualities and properties of the world, I would not call it a curse," Theodenes replied. "Theological experts within Mount Nevermind have attributed this belief to ignorance on the part of the other peoples. That, or pathological envy."

"Right," said Vanderjack, grinning. "We're all jealous of you."

"As you should be," said Theodenes, ignoring the sarcasm in Vanderjack's voice.

"All right," Gredchen said, lifting a hand. "I think we're closing in on where the castle's located. It's in the foothills of the Emerald Peaks and rests upon a solid base of bedrock. Baron Glayward's family chose it hundreds of years ago for its defensive advantages."

"I do not wish to interrupt your fascinating conversation," said Star, his voice loud and resonant. "But we are about to be engaged by the enemy."

The sellsword, the baron's aide, and the gnome all looked around, shielding their eyes from the afternoon sun and scanning the horizon to catch sight of what the dragonne was warning them about. Vanderjack was the first to spot them, flying low over the trees to the southeast, in the general direction of where Gredchen said Castle Glayward was.

"Draconians!" he called out, pointing at them. "Sivaks, by the size of them. Ackal's Teeth, that's all we need."

"The highmaster is said to have a small cadre of sivaks as part of a gift from the emperor," said Gredchen. "Red Watch sivaks, hailing from the City of Darkness itself."

"Red Watch?" Vanderjack asked.

"Red Watch!" repeated Theodenes.

Vanderjack thought back to his dream and to his recollection of the shapeshifting draconians who had replaced his war band back in Southern Ergoth. They, too, bore red dragonarmy insignia. Theo must have known that the Red Watch sivaks were the emperor's elite, but he probably didn't know they were responsible for the death of his beloved saber-toothed tiger kitten. It might not be the time to impart that information. On the other hand . . .

"Theo," Vanderjack shouted, drawing his sword in a swift motion and readying it for when the sivaks came close enough. "There's something I needed to tell you."

"I cannot possibly imagine what that would be," Theodenes replied, gripping his polearm tightly, his thumb pressing a button that added a foot of razor sharp steel to the end of the weapon. "We are about to engage in battle with draconians, so idle conversation is most likely nonefficacious."

"Forget that," Vanderjack said as the Sword Chorus manifested around him. They had a marvelous ability to keep up with the swift speed of the dragonne, who had angled himself into an interception trajectory with the approaching sivaks. "I had a dream," he shouted to Theodenes, "about the job we were on during the war. About you and Star. I think Red Watch sivaks killed my men and replaced them and then killed your cat."

Theodenes spun about, staring straight at the sellsword, his already-tanned face darkening. "What in the name of the Great Engine would possess you to tell me that now?" he shrieked.

Vanderjack shrugged. "I don't know. Better now than never, right?"

The gnome turned away. "We will talk more about this," he called back, lifting his polearm-turned-spear in readiness.

"That was hardly fair," said the Aristocrat, finally voicing his opinion.

"A most unusual and unorthodox strategy to engender fury in the gnome against the enemy," said the Cavalier.

"It has a good chance of backfiring," said the Balladeer.

The Cook was close by, spectral features blurring and shifting as if his ethereal form were affected by the wind. "Vanderjack. I have a suspicion about those sivaks."

"Perhaps you suspect that they're going to attack us," Vanderjack said, out of earshot of the others. "Because I think I figured that out myself."

"I shall find out if the Cook is right," said the Hunter peremptorily. Heedless of the altitude or gravity, the Hunter's spirit raced away through the air, away from Star and toward the sivaks. Vanderjack watched with a frown as the ghost flew unseen around the draconians, who were less than a hundred yards from the dragonne, and a heartbeat later was back among the others in the Chorus.

"I'm right, aren't I?" the Cook said.

"Right about what? What are you talking about?" said Vanderjack. He estimated that they had about thirty seconds before the draconians would be in striking range.

"They are the same draconians," said the Hunter.

Vanderjack narrowed his eyes. "What?"

"Those four are the Red Watch draconians who killed your mercenary friends," explained the Cook.

"Well, then," said Vanderjack. "This should be entertaining on all kinds of levels."

He was aware then of Gredchen crying out, "Here they come!" and the gnome responding with "Strike from above!" As he turned Lifecleaver around in his right hand, letting the years of martial training bound tightly within his muscle memory take control, Vanderjack also heard the mighty roar of Star. It was a paean of grief forged from the failure of the great cats of the Dragon Isles, Star's ancestors, to defend the eggs of the metallic dragons. It was a soul-wrenching scream that immediately preceded the loud, violent collision between the sivaks and the dragonne's passengers.

Two of the sivaks were sent reeling backward by the shock of Star's roar. The other two, one of whom was a very large and physically impressive specimen with the markings of a draconian commander, shrugged it off and swung upward with their huge serrated greatswords. Star evaded those weapons, but in doing so had to twist sideways. Gredchen had to seize hold of Star's fur to keep from flying off his back. Theo, who had his polearm braced for the engagement, thrust it forward and let Star's motion and the sivak's attack keep him in place. The spearhead caught the sivak commander's wingman in the shoulder, right beneath the curving metal plate that protected that part of his body. Black blood splashed forth along the length of the polearm, whisked into a froth by the velocity of the combatants; Vanderjack turned his head away to avoid befouling his eyes.

"Now!" said the Cavalier.

Still looking away, Vanderjack lifted himself into a straddling position on the dragonne's broad back and thrust his sword downward, into the space between Star's wing and his head, right where the sivak commander had appeared. Their swords clashed together. The serrated edges of the sivak's weapon caught Lifecleaver, the force of the collision carrying upward into

Vanderjack's arms. Lifecleaver, forged from star metal, was not so easily pinned; Lifecleaver continued through the serrations and severed them from the sivak's blade. The triangular remnants were sent up and away, one of them catching Gredchen in the thigh. The sivak flew right over the dragonne's neck. Just as quickly as they had come together, they were all separated again, and Star flew down and down.

"Ready for the next strike!" Vanderjack yelled. He spared a moment to look over at Theo, who still held the polearm, slick with draconian ichor. Star was unharmed. Gredchen was binding her leg with a strip of cloth.

Vanderjack's mind was racing. If they were the same draconians who had, years earlier, brought death to his band and killed Theodenes' feline companion, what kind of forces were at work to bring them into contact again, so far from Ergoth?

"Why now?" he found himself saying to the Sword Chorus. "What's going on?"

"Prepare yourself," said the Cavalier.

"Set aside your concerns, and trust to your sword arm," said the Philosopher.

"It does seem a little strange," said the Cook, but the other ghosts glared at him. Vanderjack shook his head and gritted his teeth. Star had flown in an upward-curving arc, soaring around to intercept the sivaks yet again.

"Sound your roar again!" shouted Theo above the whistling gale. "It's already taken out two of them!"

Sure enough, the two sivaks who had been sent spiraling away from the battle by the dragonne's roar had not yet managed to regain control of their flight. They were plummeting toward the jungle along the slopes of the Emerald Peaks. There was a good chance that when they hit the upper canopy of the rainforest, their bones would be pulverized and they would become part of the landscape.

The sivak commander and his wounded companion were not yet out of the fight, however. Star's next roar was deafening, but they were ready for it, so when Theo, Vanderjack, Gredchen, and the dragonne charged them again, it was all they could do to avoid being struck by the sivaks' wickedly serrated blades.

The sivak commander's weapon caught Star across his front flank, cleaving through his brass scales and opening a horrible wound. Star screamed, jerking upward. Gredchen couldn't hold on, and the momentum of the upward flight sent her end over end into the sky above the conflict. Theo had both hands on his pole-arm, striving to bury the spearhead in the same sivak as before. The draconian reached out a clawed hand and grasped the shaft of the weapon, using it as a lever to flip the gnome off the back of the dragonne and into the open void.

Vanderjack's ghosts were calling out a number of options for him, all of them conservative. He was alone on the back of a wounded dragon-tiger, his two companions falling to their deaths. There were two sivak draconians, easily more adept in the air than he was, and likely the same draconians who had once destroyed his mercenary company in Southern Ergoth and were responsible for years of division between the sellsword and Theodenes. Vanderjack didn't really want to hear conservative options.

As Star fought to remain upright, bleeding and beating at the air with his draconic wings, Vanderjack gripped the hilt of Lifecleaver with both hands, shouted

"For Southern Ergoth, you scaly bastards!" and leaped at the sivak commander.

Somewhere between leaving Star's back and cutting the arm off the sivak, Vanderjack's head exploded with a thundering wave of darkness.

******

Highmaster Rivven Cairn watched the evening rain wash away the blood on the clay surface of Wulfgar's Horseman's Arena.

She and Cear had returned only a few hours earlier, southwest of Willik, which she had left to the ghouls. After reporting the passage of Gredchen and Theodenes to her Black Robe agent, the highmaster decided to return to her base of operations. Wulfgar was, for all intents and purposes, home; even Cear appreciated the place. Perhaps the dragon liked it because he'd already staked his claim with fire and claw back when Rivven had flown in with her forces, driving the famous Feathered Plumes of Wulfgar into the jungle and overwhelming the city.

Another reason she had returned was to watch the fighting in the arena. There, steel and iron were set against claw and horn as humans and other races engaged in life-and-death battle with all manner of monstrous opponents. Many of the inhuman gladiators were chained and bound, in part to prevent them from leaping into the stands and tearing the spectators to pieces, but also to limit their movement and give the slave combatants a sporting chance.

It was the day before the chariot races; Rivven enjoyed the spectacle every year. They combined all the thrill of competitive racing with the brutality of gladiator combat. Weeks of bloodthirsty conflict led up to it, with the victors earning the chance to take part in the chariot race and perhaps win their freedom.

Rivven grew up alongside gladiators. Before she became an apprentice mage, she was entertainment, a token half-breed in a pit fighter's house in Lemish. Her owner was a thick-necked human with a wispy excuse for a beard, a man she later killed in the course of her escape. He would force her to take on one opponent after the other, sometimes in the dark of night, sometimes under the hot light of day. She learned to kill with a knife, with a sword, with her own fists. She made no friends, saw no future, until the day she understood her owner's weakness.

Yasmut Shaad had a thing for meek and shy girls. Rivven was anything but. For twelve years, years that most humans would have grown too old for the kind of blood sport her master was making money from, her elf blood kept her body young and undeveloped. Her time in the pit hardened her, made her lean and wiry. Then she realized that her only way out would be to get close enough to Shaad to kill him. Rivven knew that she would have to feign weakness while remaining alive just long enough to use her anger.

The rain grew stronger, pounding on her helmet, collecting in bloody puddles around her boots. She was taken back to the Shaad's pit again by the *thum-thum-thum* of the rain, which in her mind became the percussion of bucketfuls of water dumped on her from above. The blood at her feet was the blood of her last opponent, a pale human body on the ground before her with her knife in his chest. Her own chest heaved, lungs burning, and she looked up and saw the man she hated more than anything else.

Engorged with the food and wine that her killing had

bought him, Yasmut Shaad did not spare his champion even a glance. He was fawned over by a trio of curvy girls, Lemishites with rich fathers who curried favor with Shaad and his men. Rivven's vision was blurry, a cut across her forehead bleeding into her eyes and making her face ache, as the girls draped themselves across Shaad's lap, fed him dates and figs and other luxuries brought in across the mountains from the east. She saw how close they were to him.

Rivven knew that later that evening Shaad would come by her cell to inspect her for injuries and remind her how easily she could be replaced if she disappointed him. As Shaad's burly thugs dragged her out of the pit and toward that cell, she fought away the fire within her heart, forced it down into a tight knot in her stomach, allowed her body to relax and subside. By the time Shaad came by, still popping figs into his mouth but alone, she was curled up in the corner of the cell, small and white.

The slave owner was visibly astonished at first. He yelled at her to get up, which normally would have provoked an angry outburst from Rivven. He would then berate her and call her names, and that would be the end of it. But that night his yelling provoked no response. His eyebrow lifted with curiosity, and he stood there for some time, watching her.

Eventually, Shaad beckoned her over, using a softer voice, perhaps to test her reaction. She knew exactly what she needed to do; she meekly looked away then slowly crawled over to the bars. In her stomach the knot of fire grew more intense, but outwardly she was cold, shivering. Shaad's questions and inquiries were all responded to with shrugs and shakes of her head. He grinned toothlessly, an expression that sent her mind spinning into a whorl of rage. All Shaad saw was a young girl responding to his clumsy attempts at sooth-ing utterances with fragile acceptance.

Shaad opened the cell door and drew Rivven to him. As he sought what his base instincts demanded, Rivven saw to hers. She took the curved paring knife from his belt, the knife she'd seen him use hundreds of times to peel Haltigothian citrus fruits, and drove it into his brain.

Rivven left Yasmut Shaad twitching there in the hall-way of the dungeon and ran. She didn't stop running until she had fled Lemish, making it all the way into Estwilde. She left slavery behind, but she carried the fiery spark within her and her memory of using decep-tion and guile to get ahead. It was that same deception and that same fire that laid the path toward her arcane studies and from there to Ariakas.

Rivven opened her eyes. She was back in Wulfgar, soaked to the bone. The arena was empty. Somebody had come and taken away all the corpses, patched up all of the living. Maybe they had seen her standing there the whole time, her helm hiding any indication that her mind had been back in Lemish. Wisely, they had left her alone.

She turned, looked up at the stands, and saw a single figure moving at a brisk pace down the central stairs to the arena floor. As he approached, she lifted her hands, palms upward, and spoke a word of magic. The arcane power rippled within her, bright and hot, and the water on her body and armor boiled away into steam. It was easy to keep dry when you were a pyromancer.

"Hello, Aubec," Rivven said to the man.

"My lady," the Nordmaaran aide-de-camp said, out of breath. "A message for you."

Rivven took the folded note from Aubec, who stood

in the downpour as his mistress's spell continued to keep the rain off her. Opening it, she looked over the contents then handed it back to him.

"We've got him," she said and smiled widely behind the mask.

CHAPTER FOURTEEN

Vanderjack opened his eyes, seeing nothing but black.

He had a ferocious headache. He felt his neck and the back of his shaved head, felt the telltale lump, and knew that the sivak's wingman had probably smacked him with the flat of the sword. He didn't feel the wetness of blood, only the damp floor beneath him, which smelled like urine and rotting straw.

"Gredchen?" he said, speaking into the dark. No response. He felt around, hoping to rest his hand on something he recognized. "Theo?"

There was a moan off to his right. He couldn't tell if it was the girl or the gnome. Then he remembered his sword.

It was gone—no scabbard, no Lifecleaver. In fact, all of his gear was stripped from him. He had the arming doublet but not Captain Annaud's dragonarmor. He had no knife, nothing. Combined with the darkness and the horrid smell, he realized that he'd been captured and tossed in a cell.

"Gredchen? Theo?"

"Vanderjack?" came the gnome's voice. "I might have known. Star? Star?"

"It's good to hear your voice too, shorty," Vanderjack said stoically. "We're in the clink. Somehow I don't think the big brass tiger's with us."

Theodenes sighed. The moan came again too, and Vanderjack knew it was Gredchen. Shifting position, he rose to kneeling, and tried to use the wall beside him to get up.

He almost collapsed from the rush of blood to his brain. "Sivaks got me in the head," he said. "Are you all right?"

"Well, I daresay I have had better days," Theodenes replied. "Also, I have deduced we're in separate cells."

"So gnomes *can* see in the dark!"

"Of course not. Don't believe the rumors. I have deduced this because right now I am holding bars in between myself and your voice."

Vanderjack rubbed at the short stubble where the lump on his head was. "Gredchen? You conscious?"

A weak and annoyed voice said in response, "Only just."

"Theo and I are both here. I think we're in the dungeons underneath Castle Glayward."

"What makes you so sure?" Theodenes replied. "We could be anywhere."

"I know, but based on what you two were told by Rivven Cairn, that sadistic cow's probably got us set up for an extended stay in the baron's castle. I know these highmasters and highlords. They like the drama."

"If this is the dungeon," said Gredchen, "then my memory tells me there are six cells. Three on either side of a hallway, with iron bars between each."

"It's a good thing I have my people's expert senses,"

said Theodenes.

"You have big noses, if that's what you're talking about," said Vanderjack.

"Extraordinary senses of smell, yes," grumbled Theo. "But hearing, too—unless you're in the Guild of Resonant Sonics, perhaps—which I have been employing as we talked."

"Congratulations are in order, then?" Vanderjack said, groping his way to the bars near where he thought Theodenes' voice was coming from.

Theo ignored him. "Gredchen and yourself are linearly arranged about me," he said. "Which means that I am in the middle cell of a group of three."

"If we're lucky," said Gredchen, "the current occupants of the castle don't know about the loose slate in the floor near one of the cell doors. If you're where I think you are, Vanderjack, then feel around underneath the door to your cell."

Vanderjack did so. The floor was covered in fitted stones, the slates Gredchen had spoken of. Most of them were stuck fast, caked in foulness and a kind of mucilage produced from years and years of straw breaking down in the muck of vermin droppings. One, however, shifted slightly when he pressed it.

"Got it," he said.

"Great," Gredchen said, relief in her voice. "Then the door to the dungeon's next to my cell. See if you can pull that slate up."

"While I'm doing this, I don't suppose these bars are wide enough for Theo to squeeze through, are they?" Vanderjack dug his nails into the muck around the slate and tried to get enough purchase to lever it up.

"The baron was plagued by kender for a while," Gredchen said. "He made sure the cells were designed with that in mind."

"Typical," Theodenes said. "Once again, gnomes are lumped in with kender. As if we shared anything in common beyond stature."

"I think I have it," Vanderjack said. He gave the slate a final tug, and it came free from the floor with a thick squelch.

He heard Gredchen move around in her cell, coming as close to the bars as she could. "All right. Now you should be able to slide the vertical iron bar immediately above where you removed the slate down and out of the socket, and then lift it free from the other bars."

"You've given this a lot of thought, haven't you?" he said. He wiggled the bar she had described; it was definitely loose.

"Of course. It's one of my duties as the baron's aide to oversee the security of his person."

"Not doing a lot of that at the moment, though," Vanderjack said and pulled on the iron bar. With a creak of metal, it came free, and Vanderjack almost tumbled backward into the darkness.

"Was that it?" asked Theo from nearby.

"Pretty much, yes," Vanderjack said. "Now what?"

"In an ideal world, Theo would be in that cell, not you," said Gredchen. "However, as ample proof has already indicated, this is not an ideal world. Pass the bar through to Theo. If you work together, you should be able to lever it horizontally through the bars on the front of his cell and pop a couple of them out. Then he can squeeze through."

"This isn't a very secure dungeon," Vanderjack noted.

"The baron didn't anticipate a lot of residents," Gredchen said.

After a few minutes of blind fumbling around, the

banging of iron against iron, and some curses from both the gnome and the sellsword, the plan went into action.

"Ready, Theo? Pull!" Vanderjack threw his weight into the effort. He heard the gnome do the same, which only reminded him of just how strong the little gnome was in proportion to his size. He'd seen Theo wrestle with Star the saber-toothed cat many years before. Although Star was twice Theodenes' size, and probably three or four times his weight, Theo had been an equal match for the cat.

The bars of the cell creaked and groaned, grinding together with a rasping sound that might have been heard all the way up the stairs into the castle. Vanderjack didn't want to waste any time, so with one final shove, he pulled on the iron bar and heard the loud *tang-tang* of two bars ripping away from their sockets. The clattering of the bars rang more loudly than ever.

"Theo!" shouted Gredchen, trying to be heard over the clatter. "It's up to you! Get through the bars and then up to your left at the end of the hallway is the door out, which should be unlocked. Once you open that, there will probably be a torch or lantern or something lighting the stairway up."

Vanderjack heard Theodenes moving around in the darkness, then a deep creaking of wood shed light into the dungeon. Vanderjack squinted as his eyes readjusted; he saw for the first time what the cells around him looked like and just how fetid and awful they were. He wouldn't even keep a gully dwarf down there. Though a gully dwarf might like it.

Theo stood silhouetted in the warm, orange glow of the doorway. Gredchen had been right. There was a torch mounted in a bracket outside, close to expiring but still serviceable.

"Great, Theo," said Gredchen, who was covered in muck herself. Not all of it looked like it came from the cell. She looked as if she'd fallen into a pig's pen face-first. "The next thing to do is open the cell doors. There should be a series of—"

Theodenes made a sound of excitement. "By the Great Engine! Levers!"

"Yes," continued Gredchen. "Those. Another of the baron's design specifications. He thought keys would only get lost."

Theodenes manipulated a few of the large brass levers by the door. The sound of more metal against metal echoed around the room, and the cell doors in their group of cells swung open.

"That was easy," Vanderjack said, frowning suspiciously. "In fact, too easy. I have to say I don't think I've ever escaped from a cell as easily as that since the time I was locked up in a Qualinesti elf hut and got out through the hole in the roof where the smoke went up."

Theodenes waited by the door as Gredchen and Vanderjack stepped out of their cells. "Nonsense," Theo said. "I was present at that great escape, in case you had forgotten. We were freed because one of your companions lowered a rope down into the hut. And this only after a long, argumentative conversation about how you could just force yourself out because you were a mighty sellsword who could take on as many elves as the Speaker could throw at you."

"Now why do you have to go and ruin a perfectly good anecdote like that with the truth?" Vanderjack said, grinning, and looked around for his sword. Finding it absent, he cursed and scanned the dungeon hallway for something that he might use instead. There wasn't a scrap of wood or metal anywhere, other than one of the long iron bars, so he picked that up and motioned for the others to follow him up the stairs.

The dungeon stairs led up in a spiral, the stones slick with moisture. Building a castle in the middle of a rainforest wasn't the most sensible of ideas, Vanderjack thought. His head was feeling somewhat better, but he felt something deep in the pit of his stomach that wouldn't go away. It was like being hungry for a side of beef at a Majerean monastery in Khur, where they ate only rice and the shoots of plants.

"Where are we headed?" Vanderjack asked over his shoulder.

"This comes up where the stables once were, but shortly before the dragonarmies invaded, the baron sealed those up and turned them over to storage," Gredchen said. "Even the windows were bricked up. It smelled like horse for such a long time . . . " Her voice trailed off.

Theodenes came up near Vanderjack and sniffed at the air. He was also carrying the torch, so Vanderjack had to lean out of the way to avoid being singed. "Watch where you put that!" he said, putting his back against the wall of the stairs. "Are your amazing gnome senses telling you anything?"

"Still smells like horse," the gnome said and fell back in line.

At the top of the stairs, the trio stepped into the rear of a large stone area lined with many stalls. In many of the stalls were wooden crates filled with dry goods, bundles of woven cloth, casks of Southlund wine and Palanthian brandy, and what appeared to be a set of four earth-filled wooden troughs. Each of those was more than six feet long, set two abreast within a pair of horse stalls just to the left of what Vanderjack thought was the stable entrance.

"Mushroom gardens?" Theodenes asked, pointing at the troughs.

"I have no idea what those are," Gredchen said, "other than horse troughs filled with soil. I can't think of any reason to do that."

"There's plenty of wine at least!" Vanderjack grinned, fetching up a wineskin and filling it from one of the barrels. Gredchen made no move to stop him, so halfway through the process, he looked over his shoulder and said, "You don't mind?"

"Those aren't the baron's," Gredchen said simply.

"Ah. Must be the spoils of war for our friend Rivven Cairn and her highlord masters. Theo, maybe you should poke your head around the corner of that entrance and see what's what."

Theodenes gave the sellsword a scathing look. He placed his torch into a bracket on a nearby horse stall and strolled over to the large wooden gates. He pushed one of them just slightly ajar, enough to stick his nose through and get a good look at the hallway outside.

Gredchen cried, "Watch out!" and Vanderjack spun around, almost dropping the wineskin. He followed her pointing finger toward the dirt-filled troughs, which were only about a dozen feet away from the gnome. Bodies, still somewhat caked with soil and dirt, had sat up from underneath a cover of earth with their pasty white features bearing expressions of utmost malice.

Vanderjack's hands gripped the iron bar tightly. It was about seven feet long, so it would make a handy quarterstaff, but it wasn't Lifecleaver. That knot in his stomach turned and throbbed. He looked around and saw only the gnome, the baron's aide, and the four figures pulling themselves into standing positions from their troughs—no ghosts, no Sword Chorus.

The gnome dropped into a rudimentary fighting stance of his own. With no weapon, he raised his fists in a show of bravado, but Vanderjack had the feeling that anything that had at one time been dead and was moving around would not be intimidated by a gnome. Theo needed help.

Vanderjack sprang forward, charging across the stable's main floor toward the stalls that housed the troughs. But he didn't feel strong, he felt overwhelmed by the smell and the odds. He thought he might throw up.

The corpses, exposed once they had climbed fully out of the dirt, were remarkably well preserved. These weren't mindless undead, the kind of thing a necromancer animates to perform his household chores. They were definitely intelligent, with empty eyes that seemed to emanate wickedness and tongues that slavered from their rictus grins, barbed and wormlike.

"Ghouls!" screamed Gredchen. "Like those in Willik!"

"Why didn't you mention ghouls before?" Vanderjack said, choking down the rising bile and bringing the iron bar around in a wide swing. He aimed it at the nearest ghouls' legs.

"Back then I had a shovel, and Theo had his multipurpose polearm," she said, climbing up onto a crate and looking for something to use as a weapon herself. "And I didn't think it was going to be a trend."

"Seriously, no mention at all?" Vanderjack knocked the ghoul off its perch on the edge of the trough, but it tumbled over and over in the air and landed on the balls of its feet, hunched over like a gargoyle or a feral cat.

Theodenes threw a couple of experimental punches at the ghoul that had closed on him. His first left hook was cautious. The follow-up right into the ghoul's midsection was more confident. That punch set the ghoul back a step, more surprised than anything else, and it hissed.

"Just a quick 'Rivven had some ghouls' . . . something like that would have been fine." Vanderjack raised the iron bar to fend off the ghoul's nails as it lunged forward to scratch at his face. He withdrew one or two steps and looked quickly to his left, then his right. He knew there were at least two other ghouls somewhere in the stables. They had leaped away from their troughs. Not knowing where everything was made sweat bead across his back, his face, and on his forearms.

Gredchen leaped upward, grabbed one of the long wooden beams that crossed the room, and pulled up onto it. There she found a loose board hanging from the sloping wooden roof of a horse's stall and grabbed it up, eyeing the room below warily.

"Really, I could have used a little warning about the ghouls," Vanderjack muttered, spinning the iron bar in his hands. He aimed one end fiercely at the ghoul before him, driving it into the creature's face. It left a nasty dent, and the ghoul hissed and rasped, twitching.

The gnome shot the sellsword an exasperated look but was busy trying to lay blows upon the ghoul, which was equally busy scratching and raking at Theo's face. Theodenes was an excellent pole fighter but a poor pugilist. The diseased scratch of a ghoul often sent the ghoul's victim into shock or paralysis; Theo's arms and legs looked as if they were already becoming stiff and ungainly.

Thinking quickly, Vanderjack shouted, "Heads up, Theo!" and threw the iron bar in the gnome's direction. Theodenes nimbly caught the bar and immediately pushed his opponent back, extending the distance between them and delivering a series of well-placed blows to the ghoul's head.

Of course, that left Vanderjack needing another weapon of his own. Spying the still-burning torch Theo had left behind, the sellsword darted over to the horse stall it was mounted on and tore it from the bracket. His ghoul opponent was still jerking spasmodically where he'd left it.

"Ackal's Teeth," Vanderjack cursed. "Where are the others?" He waved the torch in front of him, unable to see any of the other creatures. He glanced up at Gredchen, who shrugged, just as mystified as he was. Then at the same moment, one ghoul leaped from behind a stack of crates at him as its companion scaled the wall and jumped across to the wooden beam Gredchen was standing on. Both ghouls hissed, their long barbed tongues snaking out to taste the air, as they advanced.

"So why is Rivven Cairn keeping these things here?" Vanderjack called. "Ghouls hang around necromancers. Isn't fire her thing?" He lunged forth with the torch, searing ghoul-flesh and causing the creature to recoil.

"My guess is she inherited them from the ogre shaman in Willik," Gredchen called back, swinging the wooden board at her own ghoulish opponent. The ghoul crawled up onto the ceiling, claws allowing it to cling to the wood as if it were an insect. It grasped and reached toward the baron's aide in an effort to knock her from her perch.

Meanwhile, Theo had delivered a final crushing blow to his ghoul, but the paralyzing toxin in the creature's claws finally overcame him. His muscles had grown rigid, and his fingers were stuck as if in a rictus; the iron bar dropped to the floor, and he followed soon after.

Vanderjack cursed to see the gnome topple and drove the burning brand into his ghoul opponent's face. It screamed, darted forward with its head smoking, and knocked Vanderjack over onto his back. The sellsword turned away his own face as the ghoul smoldered and expired on top of him. If that didn't make him throw up, nothing would.

"Are you quite done with that one?" Gredchen yelled at the top of her lungs. "Because I could use a little help!" Vanderjack pushed the ghoul aside and looked up to see the baron's aide clinging to the beam by one hand. The last remaining ghoul was tugging at the wooden board in her other hand, shrieking.

"Let go!" Vanderjack said, climbing to his feet. His head was hurting again; he must have hit it again, reopened the old wound. "Just drop!"

Gredchen did so. She fell to the floor of the stable, landing with a heavy thump on a pile of old horse blankets stacked on a crate. The crate flew apart with the sudden weight; the wind was knocked out of Gredchen's lungs.

With nobody on the other end of the wooden board, the ghoul fell backward, dropping from the support beams and smashing through the rotting wooden roof of the horse stall below. As it fell out of sight, Vanderjack heard a disquieting crunch.

The sellsword staggered over to help Gredchen up, and as she dusted herself off, he went to investigate what had happened to the last ghoul. Opening the stall door, he saw that it had fallen on the rusty prongs of a hay fork, carelessly left point up within the stall.

"Couldn't happen to a better undead," Vanderjack muttered and let the stall doors swing back shut.

"He's completely immobile," Gredchen said as the sellsword came back over to where the baron's aide was cradling the little gnome in her arms. "I don't know anything about ghoul paralysis. Is it permanent?"

Vanderjack shook his head. "No. It should wear off in a couple of hours. The only problem is we can't exactly stay in here. If all the noise in the dungeon didn't alert the master of the castle, crashing about in here fighting ghouls would have done so, no question."

"So we take him with us?"

"Unfortunately, yes. Now if you'll excuse me just a moment, I'm going to be sick."

******

Cazuvel sat patiently in the high-backed wooden chair in the great hall of Castle Glayward.

For the past hour, he had waited for the arrival of Highmaster Rivven Cairn. A few hours before that, he'd sent word to her in Wulfgar, telling her of his remarkable luck in capturing not only the sellsword Vanderjack, but his gnome companion and the aide to Baron Glayward himself. Even more remarkable, he'd captured a living dragonne, which he'd fully sedated by the powerful threads of magic the wizard strung about it.

He watched the great beast sleeping fitfully within the enormous iron cage in the center of the great hall. All of the tables had been shoved back and stacked up by the sivaks to line the walls, crumpling the tapestries.

Aggurat was there too, also studying the cage. The sivak commander, missing his left arm, stood silently near the huge, ironbound doors at the hall's entrance. He wore the guise of a minor Nordmaaran official he had killed the previous week: tanned, hair cut short, purple tunic and the arms of King Shredler Kerian emblazoned on his chest. He had said nothing in the past hour.

"My lords!" said the sivak, in his natural draconian form and thus bulky, winged, and silver-scaled. "The prisoners are escaping!"

"I know," said Cazuvel. Aggurat looked over at him, raised one eyebrow, but said nothing.

"Should I take the others downstairs and stop them?"

"Not at all," said Cazuvel. "I expect the highmaster here any moment. Besides, I have something the sellsword wants. He's not going to leave here without it. Nor, indeed, is he going to leave here without that which the baron has sent him to collect, nor without this great beast slumbering in front of us. I am not concerned."

The sivak looked at Aggurat, who shrugged. Confused, the draconian turned and left the room.

Aggurat finally spoke. "If he comes in here, do I kill him?"

"All I need you to do is protect me in the event of any assault on my person," Cazuvel said, stretching his arms and relaxing back into the chair. "I shall be drawing upon magic you could not possibly comprehend, and it is very focused work. Keep the sellsword and his friends from interrupting the magic, and it will all be over quickly."

"I shall do my best," Aggurat said. "One last thing, honored master."

"Yes, Aggurat?"

"What did you do with the real Cazuvel?"

CHAPTER FIFTEEN

Vanderjack carried the gnome up a flight of stairs.

Castle Glayward was awkwardly laid out. It had been built upon a broad, flat mesa of basalt, a much smaller cousin of the impressive towers of stone that composed the highest reaches of the Emerald Peaks. During construction, the rear half of the mesa had cracked and dropped twenty feet, prompting the inclusion of the dungeon rooms, a guard post, and a stable before the main part of the castle was added. Buttresses and support columns were later added for the mezzanine levels that helped keep the main tower level. When Castle Glayward was finally done, it was a maze of hallways, rooms, secret passages, and staircases.

Somewhere along the way, they had acquired a lantern with just enough lamp oil in it to push away the darkness for about six hours. Two of those hours were already up.

"Do you need me to take over?" asked Gredchen, stopping in front of him and looking down.

"I'm fine. Keep on going."

"It's been a long time since I've seen anybody throw up that much," she said. "Was it the ghoul fever?"

Vanderjack paused. "Yes. Ghoul fever. I'm fine now, though. I've had worse."

Gredchen climbed a few more stairs and onto a landing. She waved the lantern off to one side, revealing a simple, ironclad wood door. "Through here is the east ballroom."

"Did gnomes build this place?" Vanderjack asked. Theo didn't flinch in his arms, though the sellsword entertained the thought that the unconscious gnome could hear all of their talk.

"Baron Glayward comes from an eccentric family," she replied. "It's . . . complicated. His ancestor, having fled Solamnia, was thought in later life to have been afflicted by madness."

"Nice. So where's his daughter most likely to be locked up? She wasn't in the dungeon."

Gredchen coughed. "Right."

"Oh, don't tell me. She's not really here as a prisoner; she's been married off to some dragonarmy officer, and they're living happily ever after upstairs with ghouls in the basement."

"This is no joking matter," the baron's aide cautioned briskly. "Anyway, if we pass through the east ballroom and the lower residence suite, we'll get to where we are headed, the grand stair, right beside the great hall."

"And up the grand stair is . . . ?"

"A gallery."

"She's locked up in a gallery?"

Gredchen put her ear to the door and raised a hand to quiet Vanderjack. He shut his mouth and waited. When she looked back at him, she gave the sign for all clear and opened the door.

Thankfully, the door didn't squeak or groan. Beyond, an impressive vaulted chamber waited. A mosaic covered the floor, and seven narrow stained-glass windows lined one wall. Vanderjack followed Gredchen in and gave a low, impressed whistle that echoed throughout the ballroom. Gredchen glared at him.

"Sorry," he whispered. He looked around for somewhere to lay Theodenes down and settled on a long bench underneath one of the windows. He took a moment to look up at the stained glass, which featured a stylized harp surrounded by stars and rays of light, all fashioned from pieces of amber, crimson, and emerald.

"Looks like you've found more Branchala," said Gredchen, standing beside him. "It's traditional in old Solamnic castles to not only represent the standard symbols—kingfisher, crown, rose, and sword—but also all of the religious iconography of the old gods."

She indicated the other stained-glass panels. "I used to know all of them, from stories I heard as a child. The new clerics are bringing those stories to life, I suppose, with the return of true believers and so on. But of course, as I said back in Pentar, the baron wouldn't have any of it."

"Not the religious type?"

"No. Not for lack of missionaries trying."

Vanderjack sat on the bench beside the rigid body of Theodenes. "How about yourself?"

Gredchen looked nervously over at the doors out of the ballroom but sat down on the other side of Theo. "It hasn't been that long since the war," she said.

"You said a priest of Paladine came by once. Lord Gilbert sent him off, but you weren't tempted?"

Gredchen shrugged. "I suppose. But I have my place in the baron's manor, and if he's not going to join the club of the faithful, who am I to take the other option?"

She grinned. Vanderjack had to admit that, despite

the heavy brow, the big nose, and the lopsided cheek-bones, she had a smile you could warm up to. "Your turn," Gredchen said, pointing at him.

"Oh no. Not a chance. I think the closest I've ever come to following a god is when one of my commanders told me to go to the Abyss."

"Not even Shinare? I hear she's a popular mercenary goddess in the south."

"Most of the Shinarites I've met have been money-lenders hoping to score a few more steel coins by quoting scripture. And their scripture was probably made up first thing in the morning before breakfast." Vanderjack shrugged. "I'm not swayed by religious talk. I have my sword, and—" He reached for his belt again, remembering he didn't have his sword anymore and feeling suddenly vulnerable.

"I think it's time we pushed on, don't you?" The sellsword took a breath, steeled himself, and stood up wobbly. "The baron's daughter is surely sick and tired of being locked up in her makeshift prison."

Gredchen cleared her throat and nodded. She waited for Vanderjack to pick up the gnome, then followed him across the ballroom and through the doors.

The residential suite Gredchen had spoken of was really nothing more than a handful of rooms leading off a central curving corridor, ending with a sitting room. More windows, set with latticework, allowed the light from outside to illuminate the passage. Vanderjack put his face close to the glass to try and see outside, but it was milky-white with age.

"I have no idea what time of day it is," he said, stepping back from the windows. "This could be daylight, but then again, Solinari's in High Sanction at the moment, and it could just as well be moonlight."

"Once we pass through these doors we'll be near the balcony overlooking the entrance hall," whispered Gredchen. "There's a really large rose window, and you can see the Emerald Peaks through them if the weather's cooperating."

"Lovely," Vanderjack said. "But I'd bet that balcony's guarded." He felt the absence of the Hunter, who would ordinarily be coming back to him at such a time to tell him all about the armed forces in the castle—where they were, what they looked like.

"Of course. Hand Theodenes to me, and you take a first look." Gredchen held out her arms.

Vanderjack handed the gnome over as if he were a bundle of hearth logs and crept to the doors. He threw the latch and opened one door a crack.

Through the narrow gap, he could see the wide curve of the balcony sweeping around an open space. A flight of marble stairs led upward from a landing in the middle of the curve, and Vanderjack caught movement just out of sight: something large, silver, and dressed in red.

"Ackal's Teeth," he muttered.

"What is it?" asked Gredchen.

"Sivaks."

"We can't take on sivaks," hissed Gredchen.

Vanderjack looked at Theo then at Gredchen, silently agreeing with her. "But I think I have an interesting idea," he whispered, grinning.

"Not Theo!" she said, aghast, reading his mind.

"Why not? He'll be useful. He likes being useful."

"Absolutely not!"

Vanderjack looked at the door then back at her. "Well, if you'd prefer charging on out there and taking our chances with the sivaks . . . "

Lord Gilbert's aide exhaled. "All right. What's your plan?"

A few minutes later, after some poking around in the bedrooms in the residence suite, Vanderjack and Gredchen had gathered together an old footlocker, a child's wagon with four wheels and a handle, several linen sheets, a length of thick silk cord from the curtains around a bed, and a three-pronged candelabra. The two of them carefully stood the gnome up on the footlocker, set it atop the wagon, threw a sheet over his head, and tied the candelabra in place on top of everything with the cord.

"This is never going to work," said Gredchen, looking over the gnome.

"Sivaks, even the ones from the Red Watch, aren't that smart," said Vanderjack. "They may be tactical geniuses, masters at deception and infiltration, but drop something on them they weren't expecting and most of the time, you've got the advantage."

On the count of three, Gredchen pulled the door open all the way. Vanderjack gave the wagon-footlocker-gnome a mighty shove and it raced out across the balcony, banged twice on the railings, and slammed into the sivak standing on the central landing.

The draconian, as Vanderjack predicted, reacted with startlement. Leaping backward, the creature spread its wings outward to steady its balance and prevent it from falling down the staircase. The gnome ricocheted off the sivak and careened against the railing, sending it speeding off around the other side of the balcony area.

Vanderjack raced in while the draconian had his back to him. The horseshoe-shaped balcony allowed him to use the railing to gain altitude and leap toward the Sivak. Unfortunately he didn't have a sword. All he had were his wiry, outstretched arms and what he hoped was a fearsome look on his face.

Gredchen, following hurriedly, watched as the sellsword tackled the sivak around the neck, pinning the draconian's enormous silver wings against his body. Already unbalanced, the sivak dropped immediately to the top three or four stairs of the grand stair.

Vanderjack hoped that surprising the bigger and stronger draconian would keep it from simply flexing its muscles and throwing him off. And it worked. The sivak flailed uselessly. Tightening the grip around the sivak's neck, Vanderjack gave a mighty heave and felt the draconian's neck snap.

Gredchen skirted the melee and ran to recover Theodenes, who was lying facedown under the sheet and candelabra on the far side of the balcony. She turned him over, dusted him off, and picked him up.

Vanderjack watched, amazed, as the body of the sivak shrank and shifted. Silver scales blended, darkened, and retreated in places. Where moments before had been a sivak draconian there lay a perfect copy of Vanderjack.

"Ackal's Teeth," the real Vanderjack said. "I never will get used to that."

"Will it stay that way forever?" asked Gredchen, coming back around with Theo's immobile body. "Cute. It looks just like you."

He gave her a pained look. "After a long while, it'll burn up and turn into ash. Meantime," Vanderjack added, arranging the position of his doppelganger on the stairs, "the sight of my dead body should slow down anything that comes up from down there." He pointed down the stairs to the entrance hall below, a marble and granite chamber dominated by the wide staircase and, as Gredchen had said, an enormous rose-shaped stained-glass window. "Come on. We'd better get moving."

Gredchen handed Theodenes back to Vanderjack. The gnome twitched, once, and Vanderjack saw the bushy white eyebrows moving just a little, as if Theo were trying to form an angry expression and only his eyebrows would cooperate.

"The paralysis is starting to wear off," he said, hefting the gnome over one shoulder and taking the stairs two at a time.

The stairs rose up into a small semicircular area, an anteroom or waiting room of some kind, at the far end of which was a pair of huge, ironbound wooden doors. To the left of them was a spiral staircase that continued upward. Suits of Solamnic plate armor stood on either side of the doors, bearing halberds. The armor looked purely decorative, but the halberds seemed very real.

"I sure need one of those," Vanderjack said, indicating a halberd. "But how much do you want to bet that those suits of armor are ensorcelled? Odds are we'll walk by them and they'll animate and attack us viciously with polearms."

Gredchen stared at him but couldn't tell if he was kidding. "Impossible."

Theodenes jerked again, and his eyelids closed and opened. Vanderjack suspected the gnome would go limp soon, then start to experience feeling in his limbs and extremities. The sellsword hadn't been paralyzed by ghouls before, but he'd seen it often enough in the service of the dragonarmies.

"So up the stairs again, one more time," he said.

Vanderjack shifted his hold on Theo so he could fit on the spiral staircase and went up. Gredchen took the rear, watching the ironbound doors as they ascended, but nothing burst forth or even so much as whispered from them.

At the top of the spiral stairs, the entrance hall and stained-glass windows were left behind. All that Vanderjack could see was a long hallway lined with rugs and animal skins, and bare white walls with unlit torches at regular intervals. At the far end, in total darkness, a single large, rectangular shape was dimly visible.

"There it is," said Gredchen, fatigue and perspiration showing on her face.

"There's what? I can't see a thing. This gallery has no pictures in it at all."

"They're all in the baron's manor now," she replied. "All except one." She crossed over to a large silk bellpull hanging from the ceiling. "Here, look."

Gredchen gave the bellpull a tug. There was a faint hissing sound, and instantly the torches lining the walls flared into life, shedding a brilliant light. The light extended even into the corners of the room, and especially the darkness at the back.

The single painting hanging on the wall at the rear of the gallery was of a young woman, barely in her twenties, breathtakingly attractive, with long honey-brown hair and features so perfect that Vanderjack simply marveled at the skill and talent of the artist.

"Lord Gilbert Glayward's beautiful daughter," said Gredchen.

"She's beautiful all right, but where's the real one? She's not in here, that's for sure."

Gredchen looked at him, nodding her head. "Yes, she is."

"What are you saying?"

Gredchen looked away. "I'm saying the object of

your mission, the baron's beautiful daughter, *is this painting.*"

"You mean. . . . "

"Yes," she said. "Now all we have to do is get it back to the baron's manor."

Theo dropped to the rug from Vanderjack's arms, suddenly forgotten.

"Ackal's bloody Teeth," swore the sellsword.

******

Highmaster Rivven Cairn alighted from the back of her red dragon and removed her horned great helm.

She let the winds up on the tower roof of Castle Glayward buffet her hair, then strode over to the opening in the roof that led to the stairs down. A sivak officer of the Red Watch was waiting alongside the opening for her.

Stopping long enough to look back at Cear, who had flown her directly from Wulfgar, she waved a hand, which told the dragon, "I have no immediate use for you," and also, "Go burn something for a while."

"Your Excellency," said the sivak.

"Lieutenant," Rivven said, correctly deducing the draconian's rank from his insignia. "Walk with me."

"How was your flight?" he asked, stepping aside to let her start down the staircase. He followed immediately after, matching steps with her despite his much greater stride. Rivven noticed he was extremely well trained . . . for a draconian.

"Always a pleasure," she said formally. "How are matters being taken care of here? What is the status of our prisoners?"

"They have escaped, Excellency."

Rivven almost choked. She stopped and looked up at the sivak, who remained expressionless. *"Escaped?"*

"Yes, Excellency. Master Cazuvel said for us not to be concerned, that he has matters under control."

"Under control? How in the Abyss did they escape?"

The sivak said nothing.

"What does he intend to do? There's just you and your fellow sivaks, Captain Aggurat, and whatever staff he held onto for the kitchens. Blast him. Where is Cazuvel at present?"

The sivak led the highmaster down a narrow flight of stairs, along two hallways, across an outside balcony that overlooked the jungle, then back inside to a sitting room. On the other side of a door was the grand hall. "He's through there," the sivak said and stood aside.

Rivven Cairn pushed through the door and watched Cazuvel pacing back and forth alongside a large cage containing some kind of scaly, winged tiger. When he saw her, the albino pulled himself up to his full height and walked briskly over. "Your Excellency."

Another human, missing an arm, stood off to one end of the room. Rivven recognized the man as somebody Aggurat had killed several days before, although that man had possessed two arms. Rivven knew how sivaks worked, and she knew Aggurat. If the reports were correct, the missing arm was Vanderjack's doing; she'd heard that Aggurat had lost his arm to Vanderjack's blade.

"One of Aggurat's draconians just told me that the prisoners have escaped, Cazuvel!" Rivven said. "I don't believe that was on my list of instructions."

"Ah, no, it was not, Your Excellency," Cazuvel said, bowing his head. "Forgive me—I fear the sivaks are given to panic. But there is no real reason to be concerned at this point."

"So you know where they are, then."

"Quite so, Your Excellency. Might I offer you a drink?"

Rivven just stared at him, trying to figure out what he was up to. Cazuvel seemed to take that with grace and indicated the chair he'd been sitting in earlier. "Perhaps a seat?"

The highmaster sat down and propped up her chin on one balled fist, waving at the mage with the other hand. "Carry on. I'm sure we have scant moments before we hear the front gates close behind the escapees."

"Ah, but therein lies the underlying cause of my calm demeanor," the mage said, showing perfect white teeth. "The sellsword will not leave the castle, for there are three compelling reasons for him to remain."

"You have appropriated his magic sword?" Rivven said, perking up.

"Indeed. I feared that the weapon might be lost once the sivaks captured the three of them. But the kapak scouts retrieved it in the jungle. I have it safely stowed away."

"Good. I'll be taking that with me," said Rivven, feeling heartened. "All right, what are the other two compelling reasons?"

"The second is that," said Cazuvel, pointing at the slumbering dragonne in the cage.

"Yes, I see that. What is it exactly? Some kind of magical abomination you've created?"

"No, Your Excellency. That is a creature from the Dragon Isles, one of the dragonnes blessed by the gods to protect and ward those loyal to them."

Rivven's eyes narrowed.

"They were riding it when the Red Watch intercepted them."

Rivven felt her heart racing. She hadn't considered any divine interference in any of her plans, not because she wasn't herself religious, but because the sellsword was by all accounts ruled by only greed and self-interest. Rivven did not think the gods who honored those traits would have stepped in the way of her plans. Was it the gnome? Or the girl? The gnome was just another mercenary, surely no different from Vanderjack, and the girl . . . Rivven already knew about the girl.

"The third reason?"

Cazuvel pointed above his head. "The painting in the gallery," he said. "Vanderjack may be a mercenary, but he lives by his contract. My magical wards tell me that they've just located Baron Glayward's 'beautiful daughter.' Your arrival could not have been more perfectly timed."

Aggurat hadn't said a word since Rivven had arrived. In fact, he had not budged in the slightest. "What's wrong with him?" she asked, indicating the disguised draconian.

"The commander regrettably triggered one of my magical defenses," said Cazuvel. "The effect will wear off in about an hour. I could have dispelled it myself, but I felt that perhaps a lesson was in order."

Rivven frowned. "These draconians of the Red Watch," she said, "they've had more experience and training in working around magic than probably any other draconians on Krynn, other than the auraks working directly for the Dark Queen. How could he have stumbled into a dangerous ward?"

Cazuvel started to put together an explanation, but Rivven shook her head. "No, it doesn't matter. We need to deal with the sellsword and his friends. With any luck, the Ergothian will be in a position to listen to my attractive offer. Then you can do whatever you want to the gnome."

"And the girl?" asked the mage, rubbing his hands together.

"Let her go, I think. She's still under the protection of the arrangement I made with the baron. She's done her job, and if she knows what's good for her, she'll go back home and remind the baron—again—of the deal we made."

Rivven observed Cazuvel's disappointment with that. "Don't look so glum, wizard," she said. "You can keep the exotic beast. I'm sure there are all kinds of unusual magical experiments you can conduct on it, to your edification. Now let's go pay our guests a visit."

The highmaster placed her dragon helm upon her head, swept aside her flowing cape, and headed for the doors to the entrance hall. It was about time she finally met the Ergothian.

CHAPTER SIXTEEN

Vanderjack stared at the Baron's beautiful daughter.

"You knew the whole time, didn't you," he said accusingly.

Gredchen was leaning up against one wall of the gallery, running a hand through her hair. "Yes, of course I did. But I couldn't tell you everything. Lord Gilbert's orders."

"To the Abyss with the baron," he swore. "I had a signed contract and everything. Did Theo know?"

Theodenes was still lying on the floor, staring blankly up at the painting, his limbs occasionally twitching as the ghoul's paralysis worked its way out of his system.

"No, he didn't."

"So that's two of us you've been lying to. I thought this was going to be an actual rescue mission. I kind of looked forward to it—a romantic notion, I suppose. Instead it's an art recovery job. Who in the blazes pays somebody to come all the way into occupied territory for a bloody painting?"

Gredchen coughed. "Well, it's not just—"

"Lord Gilbert Glayward, expatriate Solamnic and gloomy art collector, that's who. Ackal's Teeth!"

Vanderjack paced back and forth, tugging at the collar of his arming doublet. It was chafing at his neck. His head pounded from the lump on the back of his skull, and his stomach was lurching again. He had lost his sword, he was miles behind enemy lines, and his contract was effectively a sham.

"Look," said Gredchen, a little of the steel returning to her voice. "Let's just take the painting, get out of here, and—"

"Listen, lady." Vanderjack spun about, raising his voice. "I'm not leaving the castle until I get my sword back. I am fond of that sword. It's how I pay the bills and keep myself in drink, something I am going to need a great quantity of if we ever manage to get out of this mess."

"I am sure the baron will completely cover any and all expenses, including buying any new sword you desire. This painting means more to him than you can possibly know."

A surge of anger replaced the wave of weakness and nausea that had come over Vanderjack. "No!" he yelled and slammed his fist against the wall only inches from the painting's frame. Wooden panels split, the painting rattled in its place, and Gredchen let out a shocked shriek.

"Be careful!" she said, rushing forward to steady the painting.

"That sword is irreplaceable! It was my mother's sword, and I didn't even swindle her out of it. *I need that sword, that particular sword, my sword. Mine!*"

"Separation anxiety?" said a woman's voice from the direction of the stairs.

Vanderjack and Gredchen stopped shouting at each other and turned. The red dragonarmy highmaster, fully armored, caped, and helmed, stood at the top of the stairs. Behind her were the gaunt albino wizard Cazuvel and the hulking form of one of the Red Watch sivaks.

"Ackal's Teeth!" swore Vanderjack.

"Ackal's Teeth? I heard he'd replaced them all with wood near the end of his long depraved life," Rivven Cairn said. "It's a pleasure to finally catch up with you, Ergothian."

Vanderjack instinctively reached for his sword, but gritted his teeth and formed a fist instead. "The pleasure's all yours, Cairn," he said. "Believe me."

"As I am sure you have already discovered, the good Baron has sent you on a fool's errand. I'm not sure if he's going senile in his old age or if he truly believed this would work, but you won't be returning with that painting."

"Highmaster, please, we're only here to retrieve what is rightfully his," said Gredchen, stepping forward with her hands raised and open. "Under authorized contract."

Rivven cocked her head to one side. "Do you know, Cazuvel," she said, "Gredchen here actually lied to me earlier? She told me she knew nothing about the Ergothian and was simply on the road within my lands to get supplies."

"How unfortunate," muttered the wizard, his violet eyes wandering along Gredchen from crown to heel.

Gredchen shuddered then started to say something, but Rivven cut her off.

"Enough. You've made your bed, girl, so now you're going to have to drag it home to the baron's manor and lie in it. Say good-bye to the Ergothian."

"I'm half Saifhumi, actually," Vanderjack said through clenched teeth. "Some say it's where I get my good looks."

"Do they now? But Saifhumi explains a lot," Rivven said. "The Saifhumi are all pirates, thieves, and liars."

"Guilty as charged," Vanderjack said more cheerfully than he felt, glancing around to see if there was any way out of their predicament other than through the highmaster, the wizard, and the draconian thug. It didn't look likely.

"Sellsword, I am here to collect on debts you have incurred since you signed on with the baron. You have three choices: you can repay me and the highlord of the Red Wing with steel coins, with your services, or in blood."

"Can I have a moment to think about it?"

"You can have as long as you like. Of course, you will have to do your slow deliberating back in my dungeons under Wulfgar. I'm sure you've heard that they are quite secure, unlike those beneath this castle."

"Your hospitality is legendary," Vanderjack said. "But perhaps I can pay you back in services, as you suggest. Yes, it almost appeals to me. However, I can't rightly sign up with your army without proper armor— my armor, which has been taken away from me, and my favorite sword."

"Your Excellency," said Cazuvel. "The armor in question once belonged to your captain Annaud."

Vanderjack shrugged. "He wasn't using it anymore."

"That's enough!" Rivven snapped. "I shall be keeping both your stolen armor and the sword Lifecleaver as partial repayment. You would get suitable replacements in my—the *highlord's*—army." She turned and looked at the sivak, who was lurking silently at the top of the stairs. "Bring him along. Leave the gnome to the plea-sure of the wizard."

"Now wait a minute," said Vanderjack as the sivak advanced upon him. "That sword is a priceless family heirloom."

"Gredchen, you are free to go," said Rivven coolly. "I suggest you make haste. I can't guarantee your safety for long. Apparently," she looked pointedly at Cazuvel, "some of my officers and draconians have been acting quite independently lately, and I would truly hate to have you suffer under any of their unwar-ranted misbehavior."

Gredchen looked apologetically at Vanderjack, who didn't return the favor. The sellsword's arms were yanked behind his back by the sivak, and he was forc-ibly marched out of the room and down the spiral stairs.

"Watch the head!" the sellsword called out, launch-ing into a long string of expletives.

******

Rivven Cairn moved to stand in front of the baron's beautiful daughter and pointed at the stairs.

"Go," she barked to Gredchen, "before I change my mind."

"What about Theodenes?" asked the baron's aide, looking at the incapacitated gnome.

"Does it matter?" asked Rivven.

"He is promised to me," said Cazuvel, stepping forward and hovering over the gnome, fingers laced together.

"I feel responsible for him," she said in a soft voice. "Moreover, I admit I feel a fondness for him."

Rivven hesitated, her brows knitted. "Very well." Rivven turned to Cazuvel. "Sorry, wizard. I've had a rare change of heart. You can keep that dragonne creature, but the gnome goes home with Gredchen."

"But, Your Excellency!" said Cazuvel, noting Gredchen's look of surprise at the mention of the dragonne.

"Any more complaints, wizard, and you won't even get that," she said dismissively. She motioned toward the gnome. "So pick him up and get out of here."

Gredchen nodded and stooped to lift the gnome up in her arms. "The baron isn't going to be very pleased," she whispered.

Rivven looked at her with amusement. Gredchen turned, paused to glare at the wizard, and hurried down the stairs with Theodenes thrown over one shoulder.

When Gredchen was gone, Rivven turned on the mage. "Fetch me that sword. I'm taking it with me."

"Your Excellency, is that wise? It is highly magical," said Cazuvel. "My preliminary examination of the weapon was cut short by the necessity of dealing with the dragonne, however, so I have not had time to divine its properties."

"Leave that to me," she said. "I may not have your experience with extradimensional forces, but I know magic swords when I see them. Meet me on the tower's roof in a few minutes."

Cazuvel bent low and nodded, whispering a few words in the language of mages. They were the command words for a teleportation spell, and Rivven watched as the winds of magic spirited him away, leaving behind only a brief afterimage.

Alone, Rivven Cairn turned to the portrait of the baron's beautiful daughter. She ran a gauntleted finger down the painted curve of the girl's jawline and tilted her head to one side.

"Such a terrible loss to the world," she whispered.

"Captured here in your youth and wide-eyed innocence by the skill of the artist. You're just as I remember you."

She turned away then. "No time for sentiment now, Rivven. What's done is done." She made a mental note to herself to have the painting locked away somewhere. It was an embarrassment, even there in the middle of the Sahket Jungle. She didn't like how close the baron had come to getting his hands on it, even though there was no way that could have actually happened.

Rivven extinguished the magical lamps with a spell of dismissal. She left the gallery in darkness and went down the spiral stairs. As she alighted on the upper landing, she paused for a moment. She looked over the railing to watch Gredchen carry the gnome out of the huge front doors of the castle and into the late-evening air. She smiled a little at the "Vanderjack" lying on the stairs—that had given her a momentary jolt earlier—then went on through the doors to the great hall.

The sivak had already passed through there with the Ergothian prisoner. The door near the back of the hall that led to the sitting room was still partly open. She passed the cage with its slumbering beast and, curious, stopped beside it.

"*Mencelik batin sihir,*" Rivven said, speaking the words of a spell, opening her senses to the hidden threads of magic around her. "*Mencelik tak'kalihatan sihir.*"

Sure enough, vivid purple and black bonds of power wreathed the dragonne, keeping it from waking. She looked around the room, following the lines of power unseen to those without arcane talents, and saw that they were tightly bound to the very foundations of the castle. Threads of magically infused energy wove into the walls, along the granite floor, and even around the wooden supports above.

Commander Aggurat stood motionless as ever, and Rivven could see the spell that had been placed upon him. She narrowed her eyes. It wasn't a magical trap or an accidental trigger. Cazuvel had deliberately frozen the sivak commander in place, binding him just as securely as he had the dragonne in the cage.

What in the name of the Dark Queen was the wizard playing at? She walked over to Aggurat and rested a hand on the shapeshifted draconian's shoulder. With her vision she could see both the smaller, human form he was wearing and a ghostly outline where his true form would be. The true form wasn't bound by Cazuvel's magic. So . . .

"Sihir perubhan keajukan," she intoned, passing her hand before the sivak's face, chest, and over his head. *"An-narhr sihir an-nahr."*

Nothing happened.

"Sihir perubhan keajukan," she repeated more insistently. *"An-narhr sihir an-nahr."*

The sivak's human form began to blur and swell. The illusory form of the human faltered and changed to silver scales, dragon wings, and a reptilian countenance; without the human form to attach to, the dark ropes of magic snapped free and retreated into the walls and floor.

Commander Aggurat convulsed and jerked as if he were overcome with a seizure. His eyes darted from left to right, finally settling on the highmaster, who waited patiently for him to collect his thoughts and steady himself.

"Your Excellency!" breathed Aggurat. "How . . . ?"

"You're welcome," she said. "I freed you from

Cazuvel's spell, but I had to get rid of your disguise to do it. What has happened to you and why?"

"It is not the Black Robe Cazuvel," Aggurat said, rubbing at the stump of his left arm with the clawed hand of his right. "It looks like him, and perhaps it even thinks on some level that it is Cazuvel, but it is not."

Rivven swore. "Another draconian?"

"No, Your Excellency. No sivak or aurak could maintain so skilled a transformation. This creature is almost an exact mental and physical replicate of Cazuvel. Were it not for the special training I received under the emperor and the dark pilgrims, I would not have discovered the truth."

Rivven looked toward the door out then up. "Whatever it is, it now possesses the Ergothian's magic sword. The one that removed your arm."

Aggurat growled but nodded. "That is nothing to me. But it has plans of its own, Your Excellency. I regret that I can tell you no more of what they are, but I think everything that has happened here is part of those plans."

Rivven frowned. "Aggurat, you're coming with me. I told Cazuvel to meet me on the roof with the sword. If it hasn't run off by now, I may need your help."

Aggurat nodded, following Rivven Cairn as she raced through the doors. The great hall stood quiet for a moment after the highmaster and the sivak commander left, apart from the deep and rhythmic breathing of the dragonne. Then, slowly, the massive brass-scaled forelegs of Star began to twitch and stir.

CHAPTER SEVENTEEN

Vanderjack was surrounded by stars.

On the roof of the main tower of Castle Glayward, the sellsword stood with the sivak thug waiting for the red dragnarmy highmaster to arrive. It was early evening already, the sun having sunk beneath the western horizon. Solinari was a huge silver orb just cresting the horizon to the east. Red Lunitari was absent, though he knew it would likely rise later in the night. The sky was clear, and the stars were bright and plentiful.

"Nice evening for it," he said to the sivak.

The sivak said nothing.

Vanderjack flexed his forearms a little, but the iron manacles the sivak had clapped over his wrists did not budge. He looked around a little more, seeing the Emerald Peaks limned with silver light by the rising moon, and several miles to the south he could just barely make out the lights of the city of North Keep, capital of Nordmaar and home to the young prisoner king, Shredler Kerian.

There wasn't much point in making a break for it, and while he had dispatched the sivak down on the entrance hall balcony, the one next to him was far too conscious of the sellsword's presence. So Vanderjack waited.

His anger and frustration at the revelation of the truth about the baron's beautiful daughter had subsided, replaced mostly by a different anger and frustration. He had actually been looking forward to being in the company of an attractive, appreciative woman for once. Gredchen had occasionally proven herself to be good company, all things considered, but she was the complete opposite of the beauty in the painting.

Thinking back to the baron's manor, he recalled the empty space in the baron's living room, where something that deserved pride of place should be mounted. Obviously, the painting belonged there.

Had she died at a youthful age? Was that it? Was that really his daughter, only a memory, or an image in a frame?

Standing there with the sivak beside him, another thought entered his aching head.

"Were you ever on Southern Ergoth?" he asked, looking over his shoulder at the draconian.

The sivak looked back at him, and it spoke. "Yes," it said.

"Which one were you?"

"What do you mean?"

Vanderjack cleared his throat and repeated. "Which one were you? Were you the kender? Or the dwarf? One of the two boys from Coastlund?"

The sivak looked away. Then, "I was the dwarf."

"I knew it. I *knew* it, you scaly bastard. You were the ones who killed the rest of my band and replaced them. You murdered my men and you murdered the cat and you would have done me in as well if I hadn't been wandering off drunk."

"Yes. That was us. It was a job, sellsword. We are draconians of the Red Watch. We do what we are told to do, what we are *paid* to do." The sivak went on. "My brother in the Red Watch—the one you killed on the stairs inside—how do you feel about that one dying? Do you think I should become angry at you for ending his life?"

Vanderjack ground his teeth together. He couldn't believe he was debating ethics with a sivak. "Where in the blazes is that highmaster?" Vanderjack said at last, changing the subject.

As if in answer to his question, Rivven Cairn came up the stairs from below, followed by the one-armed sivak commander Aggurat. Vanderjack winced when he saw the draconian, knowing he was responsible for the creature's missing limb—one more enemy probably wishing to kill him.

"There's been a change of plans," Rivven announced airily. She had her helm tucked under one arm, and her red cape flapped in the breeze. Her wavy blonde hair was tied back at the nape of her neck, making her pointed ears quite noticeable. Vanderjack wondered just how old she was. Those with elf blood were known for extremely long lives, even when it was muddied with the blood of humans as hers was.

Vanderjack waited.

"It has come to my attention through information passed on to me from Commander Aggurat here that Cazuvel and I are working at cross-purposes."

"Yes, he doesn't seem like a very trustworthy person. What gave him away? Was it the black outfit he tends to wear?"

"I don't have time to listen to your mercenary banter."

"I'm sorry. Please, continue with your monologue."

Rivven curled the fingers on one hand together, and a flame began to dance and skip in her upward-facing palm.

Vanderjack raised his hands. "All right, all right. Save the fiery doom for somebody else. I'm not all that fond of black robe mages myself. So what's the change in plans?"

The highmaster extinguished the flame and set the hand on her hip. "I was thinking, why am I keeping this man alive? Why don't I just kill him on the spot? It can't be your winning personality, and there are many more mercenaries out there who I could hire for less bother."

Rivven started to pace back and forth as she continued to talk. "So I have come to this conclusion: I have no good use for you. You can't pay me back what you owe me for all the trouble you've put me through because all your money is tied up in this job you're on, so I've decided. . . . "

The two sivaks moved up and stood on either side of Vanderjack, who flexed his forearms again in the vain hope that he might somehow miraculously break free of the manacles. "You know, I can easily lower my terms."

"Yes, or we can barter your terms. Which brings me back to Cazuvel. I'm very annoyed with him. I've decided I'd rather have Cazuvel out of the way than have you and your magic sword under my stewardship. Cazuvel has your magic sword, and it seems to me that you could do us both a favor by retrieving it—and killing the Black Robe."

Vanderjack cocked his head to one side. "So you *are* hiring me."

"No, just this one job. A trade for your life."

"Back up just a moment. First you're taking me to Wulfgar . . . then you're not . . . then you're thinking of having these two thugs toss me off the roof, and now you're not."

"Yes."

The thought of getting Lifecleaver back filled Vanderjack with a renewed sense of hope. Taking on a Black Robe of Cazuvel's stature without his sword was risky, but anything was better than joining up with Rivven Cairn.

"Then I'm in."

Rivven waved her hand, and Commander Aggurat unclasped the manacles on Vanderjack's wrists. Vanderjack rubbed the raw spots where the iron had chafed and dusted himself off. He gave the two draconians an annoyed look and stepped forward.

"Your payment is the sword," warned Rivven. "And then we'll be even. But I need evidence that Cazuvel is dead, so once you're finished with the job, hang this around his neck and set it alight. It will send the body straight to me."

She handed the sellsword a small, tightly wrapped parcel of what smelled like spices, tied with black flax and suspended from a leather cord. It was reminiscent of the deodorizing herbs the Saifhumi used to drop into footlockers on board ship to keep the smell of rot away.

"Burn this and the body will go straight to you. All right, I promise. Right. Do you trust me to keep my promise?"

Rivven smiled. "Look at yourself. You're a wreck. Personally, I think you'll fail, but then that's another problem out of my hair. I think you want your sword and you want your freedom. The stakes are balanced in my favor."

"I'm glad to hear it. So where is this Cazuvel now?"

Rivven shrugged. "He won't be around much longer, if he's even still in the castle. Please, give him my regards."

With that, Rivven put her thumb and forefinger to her temple and closed her eyes. A heartbeat later, an enormous dragon rose from behind the battlements, great red wings beating at the air. Vanderjack had not seen a red as large as that for years. The dragonfear flowed from the red dragon like ice water, but Vanderjack gritted his teeth.

"Cear. This is Vanderjack the sellsword. He's working for us—for the moment. Remember his face, and get a lock on his scent. If he crosses us, I'm going to let you go looking for him."

Vanderjack waved. "Always a pleasure."

Cear exhaled, a hot and dry breath that rid the tower roof of the cool, moist air. Then the dragon drew the breath in again through his nostrils, and his wide, reptilian jaws almost seemed to smile. "I will hope for the treat."

Rivven approached the dragon, and vaulted easily into the polished bronze and black leather dragon saddle strapped to his back. The sivaks flew up and found a perch behind the saddle itself, looking down on Vanderjack indifferently.

"Get the sword, Ergothian," Rivven said as the dragon lifted up from the slate roof. "And kill the wizard. Then go home—wherever home is—and stay out of trouble."

"Get sword, kill wizard. Right."

She placed the helm on her head, gave a final

command, and the dragon threw himself into the air with a mighty thunderclap of his wings. The force of the departure almost knocked Vanderjack off the battlements, but he steadied himself and let out a long breath.

"Ackal's Teeth," he muttered. "What have I got myself into now?"

******

Theodenes stared up at the stars and let the blood flow back into his extremities.

He was lying on the side of the Baron's Road. The road wound its way up the jungle-covered foothills of the Emerald Peaks toward Castle Glayward. It was edged by wet grass and mud, which meant that Theo's back was soaked with muddy water.

Theo's muscles and tendons had released after hours of painful tension and an inability to move. Even the tiny muscles around his eyes had been rigid, and he saw nothing but an out-of-focus blur for the bulk of the time he was paralyzed.

His hearing had been unaffected, however, so he had heard the exchanges between Vanderjack and Gredchen, between the two of them and the highmaster, and the outbursts of the wizard. He had heard everything that happened.

He was furious. And with his mouth, larynx, and lungs free of paralysis, Theodenes was able to loudly vent his displeasure.

Gredchen came running over from the trees. She heard the gnome screaming expletives in rapid-fire succession the likes of which had not been heard outside of a gnome research and design committee exploring the benefits of curse words as sonic weapons. The explosion of expletives had come on so suddenly and with such violence that the baron's aide dropped the herbs and fruits she'd been collecting to see what kind of monster had come lurching out of the rainforest to devour the hapless gnome.

"Theo!" she called, almost tripping over a fallen tree and stopping beside him in a crouch. "What is it? Are you hurt? Did you see something?"

"Hurt? See something? You blistering imbecile! You unfathomably moronic she-creature! Of course I'm hurt! I was paralyzed for three point eight hours and forced to endure irrational and inconceivably humiliating acts on the part of Vanderjack and even you! Hurt? See something? Thundering pigswill!"

Gredchen cleared her throat. "Well, yes. I apologize for the bit with the wagon and the sheet over your head, but—"

"And all of that carrying on with the highmaster and the wizard and that brainless thug of a mercenary, who I should have had killed years ago!"

Gredchen went off a short distance, then returned with a piece of cloth she'd bundled up. Unfolding it, she revealed a pair of ripe nectar plums and a cluster of unpeeled tree nuts. "Hungry?" she asked meekly.

Theodenes pulled himself into a sitting position. "Hungry? Are you categorically psychotic?"

"Well, I thought you might be hungry after all of the paralysis."

Theodenes took a deep breath and shut his eyes. He opened them again, looked at Gredchen, then looked at the food.

"I am *starving*."

"Good. Then I'll prepare this and we can start to make plans for going back into the castle."

Theodenes sputtered. "Back into the castle? Witless

harridan! We have escaped with our lives from the dragonarmy highmaster of Nordmaar and her draconian elite. What could possibly make you want to go back inside?"

"Good question," said Gredchen, peeling the green flesh from the nuts with a small knife. "There's the painting, which I really do want to bring back to the baron."

"Insanity," muttered the gnome.

"Then there's Star."

Theodenes paused. "Star?"

"Oh yes. You probably didn't get all of that, but Star's alive somewhere in the castle. I think Rivven told the wizard he could have him."

Theodenes scrambled to his feet and promptly fell back down again on his rear end. "A wizard? The only thing a wizard would want to do with Star is conduct some sort of foul thaumaturgical rite upon him and extract his essence or harvest his remains for supernatural reagents!"

"Right. I knew you wouldn't be very happy with that idea."

"What about the highmaster?"

Gredchen handed some nuts to Theodenes, who sniffed at them before popping them into his mouth and chewing them noisily. "She's taking Vanderjack back to Wulfgar. They made some kind of strange bargain. Vanderjack wasn't pleased to find out that he had come all this way to bring the painting back and not some beautiful woman."

"I ab nob surpbride," said Theodenes, his mouth full of chewed nuts. "I woub be agry doo ib I fow dout."

Gredchen frowned at him, finishing the nuts and turning to the fruit. "So you're angry too?"

"I am angry to the core!" he said, greedily eating the

sliced fruit and getting juice all over his beard.

"About the painting?"

"That is between you and Vanderjack," said Theo, remembering to swallow first. "But the sellsword has a financial obligation to me, he can't just disappear; he owes me big for all he's done, right down to killing my cook!"

Gredchen brightened. "So you'll return with me to the castle?"

"Do you think my expandable conflict primacy attainment utility is there too?"

Gredchen squinted. "Your what? Oh, your polearm? I'm sure it is; it's such a valuable weapon."

"Excellent! Then in an effort to rid myself of unnecessarily distracting anger and resentment, I shall accompany you—with addenda to be added to our contractual agreement at a later date—and retrieve both the painting and Star from the castle. Vanderjack too, if he's still around."

Gredchen smiled. "Thanks, Theo. That means a lot to me."

"Nonsense," Theo said. "As a mercenary, a master of weapons and tactics, an expert at overcoming obstacles, and as a gnome, I forsake paltry gratitudes. I shall be doing this for the glory of discovery and the attainment of purpose."

Theodenes stood up once more. He smiled at his success, put one foot before the other, and fell flat on his face in the soft mud.

Ten minutes later, with their stomachs full and mud wiped away, Gredchen and Theodenes packed up what remained of their temporary camp and headed back along the road to Castle Glayward. Along the way, Theodenes began to formulate a plan.

"How long have you known this wizard?" Theo asked.

"About ten years," she replied. "It's complicated. He's been working for Rivven Cairn at least as long as the occupation of Nordmaar."

"Is she not herself a sorcerer of some description?"

Gredchen nodded. "Yes. Studied under Emperor Ariakas. But mages are a strange lot. Very few of them master all of the different fields of magical study. Rivven never really studied the arts of conjuration and binding pacts of dark magic. She's more ambitious and a little obsessed with fire and war."

"Sensible, given her position," said Theodenes.

"So she hired Cazuvel years ago to work for her. She had some contacts within the Towers, I suppose. Mages who were more afraid of her and of Ariakas than they were of the Conclave."

The two of them rounded a bend. The castle loomed over them from atop its mesa, awkward and towering in the early-evening gloom.

"I have dealt with wizards and their ilk before," Theo mused. "If, as you say, this Cazuvel has been working with the highmaster for a decade, he must surely have the advantage of knowing this castle better than we do."

"I know it just as well as he does," Gredchen said. "I grew up here."

Theo looked at her. "You were here as a child?"

Gredchen stammered. "Well. Yes. Sort of. I mean, you know how it is in castles. There's a lot of people living and working inside of them. Like a small town."

"How long, exactly, have you been working for the baron in your current capacity?"

Gredchen ran her hand through her hair. "Oh, roughly ten years."

"Interesting," said the gnome and said nothing more as they walked.

When they had arrived at the last sloping approach to the main gates, Theodenes stopped and pointed. Several figures were moving around in front of the castle walls, near the top of the approach; despite the darkness, the gnome could make out their features. They were draconians.

"Kapaks," he whispered. "See the wings, tightly folded behind them, and their stature—hunched yet nimble. Not dull brutes like the baaz draconians, nor walking arsenals like the sivaks."

"I know what kapaks are," she hissed back. "Those must be the scouts that have been ranging through the jungle hereabouts. Rivven must not have taken them with her."

"I count at least six," said Theo. "If we walk up the slope to the front gates, we shall be immediately set upon by the venomous blades of a half dozen kapaks."

"Do you have any better ideas?" Gredchen asked.

"Quite so!" said Theo. He pointed at a number of heavily-vine-laden trees hanging over the road. "We'll need your knife to cut those down. And those spiked floral arrangements over there."

A short time later, thanks to the ingenuity of the gnome, Theo and Gredchen had two serviceable grappling hooks fashioned out of thorny spiked vegetation and sufficient lengths of vine to pass for rope. Gredchen located a likely place from which to toss the grapples upward, and together they scaled the sheer, hundred-foot side of the massif upon which the castle stood.

Theo was the first over the side of the cliff, and he looked around. Gredchen came next, but by that point, the gnome had scurried over to a heavy cornice along the base of the castle wall and poked his head around the corner.

When Gredchen joined him, he said, "Four of them appear to have walked in the other direction around the castle. There are only two standing at the gate now. If we are stealthy, we can attempt to overpower them."

"With just a paring knife?" asked Gredchen incredulously. "What are you going to use?"

Theo tapped the side of his head. "Gnome tactics," he responded.

Gredchen skeptically agreed to follow his lead, and with their backs pressed firmly against the massive, ivy-covered walls of the castle, the two would-be infiltrators sneaked along in the direction of the front gates.

They had almost reached their targets when Theo heard a loud, choking cough from behind him followed by a sneeze. Horrified, he looked up and saw that Gredchen's face was blotchy and red, and her eyes were watering.

"My allergies to ivy," she whispered apologetically, but it was too late. The two kapaks, their copper scales gleaming in the silver moonlight, had heard the noises. Their heads jerked back and forth, sniffing, listening, and they turned to look straight at Gredchen and Theo.

"To arms! To arms!" cried Theo.

The little gnome dashed across the flagstones in front of the gates, straight at the nearest kapak draconian. The two draconians were quite astonished to be charged by such a pint-sized creature, and by the time they could react, the gnome had flung himself into the air and tackled the first creature around its midsection.

Gredchen drew her knife and followed the gnome. The second kapak had leaped backward and looked up to see her charging. It drew what appeared to be a hatchet, licked the business end with its long tongue, and ran to meet her. The axe head was coated in greenish spittle, which Gredchen knew was a deadly poison. She needed to get her knife in quickly before the kapak landed any blows.

Theo and the first kapak were rolling over and over, stopping just shy of the edge overlooking the jungle floor below. Theo had no interest in falling a hundred feet, so he got up quickly and began kicking the kapak while it was still lying flat on its back. Somehow, he had also come away with the kapak's hatchet, and when the creature leaped to its feet, he swung it with all his might at the enemy.

Gredchen and her opponent circled each other. The kapak feinted to bluff her into thinking it was going to swing the axe. Abandoning all thought of self-preservation, she lunged at the kapak with the knife and her arm fully extended. She succeeded in poking a vicious hole in its shoulder, causing it to yelp and retreat a pace or two.

Theodenes' axe had just connected with the kapak's head. The gnome heard a sickening crunch and realized the hatchet hadn't hit along its edge but on the flat. Regardless, the kapak clutched at its temples, hissing and screeching. Theo swung again, chopping into the kapak's left wing and forcing it back. Unfortunately for the kapak, there was nothing behind it but open space.

Theo's kapak fell backward, and with one wing badly mutilated, it could not arrest its fall. Theo gazed over the edge to see the kapak sprawled below, its death throes kicking in. The body of the draconian was engulfed in noxious smoke and noise as it broke down into an acidic sludge.

Gredchen glanced over at Theodenes and smiled—making the mistake of taking her eyes off her opponent at a crucial moment. Her kapak ducked, sidestepped, and brought its axe up along her leg and into her thigh.

The baron's aide screamed and fell backward. The kapak leaped atop her and brought down the axe, once . . . twice . . . three times. Theodenes ran to help.

"Gredchen!" screamed the gnome.

The kapak spun about, hissing in Theo's face. He could smell the acrid stench from the draconian's toxic spittle. Ducking to avoid any poison aimed at his face, he weaved and sprang at the kapak, axe held high above his head.

The kapak threw itself out of the way. Theo had to avoid tripping over Gredchen's fallen body but kept his footing and angled himself around to meet the kapak's axe straight on with a loud *clang.* Theo stooped, plucked the knife from Gredchen's hand, and lunged forward with it. The kapak was taken completely by surprise, and before it had time to bring its axe up to deflect the maneuver, the knife was up to its hilt in one of its eyes.

The kapak staggered away, screaming, trying to remove the knife from its face. It managed only three steps before it collapsed, dead, its body beginning to bubble and dissolve.

Theo grabbed Gredchen's ankles and pulled her clear of the slowly growing pool of the kapak's acidic remains. He tossed aside the axe, knelt next to Gredchen's head, and looked over her wounds.

He gasped.

Although her tunic, sleeves, even her leggings were torn and ripped by the axe, her body was whole and unharmed. She opened her eyes and looked right at him.

"Am I alive?" she said weakly.

CHAPTER EIGHTEEN

Vanderjack stared up at the kitchen ceiling and let the nausea slowly fade away.

He had descended from the tower roof, taken the path through the upper levels and along the balcony in the direction of the great hall. Before reaching the sitting room, however, he'd decided instead to duck into what he reasoned to be kitchens and dry heave again. He was dripping with perspiration, his hands and feet felt as heavy as lead, and his stomach felt like a portal to the Abyss. So he simply lay there and waited for it to pass.

"This is ridiculous," he told himself. "I've been in the mercenary business for decades. I've fought in battles, killed ogres, and faced down dragons. My job is killing things for a living. I am not just a . . . " He rolled onto his side and retched again. "A pair of legs for a magic sword," he muttered, wiping at his face.

He didn't believe his own words. With the ghosts around to provide commentary and assistance, he had gained a reputation as one of the most proficient sword masters alive. Without them, maybe he was just an old man lining up for an exit interview with Chemosh, the god of the dead.

"Get up, old man," he grunted, and pushed himself first to his hands and knees, then to his feet. He needed to find Cazuvel and get the sword back. Then it would all be as it was.

Vanderjack returned to the sitting room and slowly, with his foot, pushed open the door into the great hall. He peered in through a thin crack and saw only one end of the great hall. Nobody there, apparently, for the moment. He took a deep breath, and slid into the hall as quietly as possible.

Then he smelled something strong and pungent, like scalded leather; it was pervasive, surrounding almost everything with its smoky odor. He had smelled it once before, after a mage duel in Neraka. It was the smell of burned-out magic.

There was a huge cage in the center of the room—a huge, empty, steel-reinforced cage. On his way through there earlier, he could have sworn Star was lying on the floor of that cage, unconscious. The dragonne was gone.

No blood, Vanderjack thought. They hadn't slaughtered the beast, nor had there been a fight. He walked farther into the great hall, checking behind stacked tables, crouching and looking for the booted feet of guards or draconians—nothing.

Then, crossing to the opposite side of the room, he realized that the door to the cage had been bashed open from the inside. So Star had broken free. Had they been keeping him under magical sedation, a spell that wore off? All he remembered was him slumbering earlier. If the spell had worn off, that would explain the after-magic smell.

Surely the only way out of there—at least for a

dragonne such as Star—was out the front doors. Vanderjack stepped out onto the landing on the upper balcony of the entrance hall. There was no sign of anybody there either—no wizards, no draconians, no huge dragon-tigers.

Vanderjack was almost halfway down the wide marble stairs that descended to the entrance hall when the front gates swung inward. He took a step back and braced himself for the worst. A rare feeling of relief washed over him when he saw that it was Gredchen and Theodenes.

Theo was ambulatory, so the paralysis must have worn off. Gredchen looked a lot worse than she had last he saw her; her tunic and leggings were cut and torn. Theodenes seemed to be supporting Gredchen as they limped in.

"Vanderjack!" Gredchen called out. She broke free from Theodenes and hurried up the stairs. The gnome scowled and followed at half the speed.

"Well, hello," Vanderjack said, smiling weakly. "Nice of you to come back. Probably to get the painting, not rescue me, huh?"

"Vanderjack, I'm sorry. About the painting. About the whole contract. I should have told the baron not to do it, but he's been wanting that painting for so long—"

The sellsword raised his hands. "Hold on," he said. "Can we talk about this out of earshot of any surprise monsters or evil villains? And knowing Theodenes, I'll bet he wants to put in a few words, once he catches his breath."

The gnome, coming up behind her, nodded, panting heavily. The three of them walked around the balcony and into a side room filled with overstuffed chairs and a long, low table. It was the kind of room one sat in if one wanted to be served tarbean tea and sugared buttercakes. Vanderjack dropped into a seat, and the others followed suit. For a moment they all stared at each other. Then all three started to talk at once.

Theodenes launched into a diatribe about the way he had been treated. Gredchen complained that the highmaster had it in for her and never really liked her very much and not to blame the baron. Vanderjack tried to answer both of them, barely getting a word in edgewise, until finally he sat back and closed his eyes and just listened.

The girl and the gnome stopped, staring at him.

"I have a confession to make," he said.

They just looked at him.

He opened his eyes again and looked at each of them in turn. "I'm working for Rivven Cairn now."

Theodenes leaped out of his seat in a fighting stance, while Gredchen almost fell out of her chair. Vanderjack raised his hands again and blurted out, "Wait wait wait!"

"What do you mean you're working for her?" demanded Theo.

"Up on the roof, earlier this evening," he said. "She said she and Cazuvel were no longer allies. She decided it was better for me to be alive than him and said I should find Cazuvel and kill him. If I did that, she'd let me live, and I could keep my sword, which the wizard's got."

"For a moment there, you jackanapes, we thought you meant you'd been working for her the whole time!" said Theo.

Vanderjack laughed. "No! Are you crazy? This is just a short-term deal. Long-term—we're still on bad terms."

"So that's the confession?" Gredchen said, sitting back in her chair again.

"No. Actually, the confession is related to that. It's about Lifecleaver."

Theo cocked his head. "That sword? What is it? A fake? The wizard has a fake! Huzzah! Threw the wool right over his eyes."

"No," said Vanderjack, smiling grimly. "The fake is me."

There was a moment of silence.

"The sword's haunted. There are seven . . . eight ghosts now that Etharion's joined them. The Sword Chorus. Ghosts of people who were killed with that sword before their time to die was upon them."

Gredchen narrowed her eyes. "Go on."

"When I'm in a fight, it's the Chorus that give me eyes in the back of my head. All of that clever maneuvering and leaping about is only possible because they call out the locations of my enemies, suggest tactics, and tell me to duck or to dodge or to weave. It's always been the ghosts."

Theo said, "So you're saying you don't have any actual skill at arms?"

"That isn't what I said! I'm a passable soldier. But without the ghosts, without Lifecleaver, I'd be a passable soldier with a sword in my back or a fallen boulder on my head."

Theo scratched at his beard and exhaled. "So you need the sword back in order for the ghosts to once again tell you how to fight like the legendary mercenary captain you are reputed to be. I see. This is so very typical of you."

"How is this typical of him?" Gredchen said, exasperated. "This can't have been very easy for him to confess. I find it very . . . uh, touching."

Theo shrugged. "He's always so secretive."

Vanderjack closed his eyes again. "Think what you like. I've come to the conclusion that Rivven believes I won't be able to defeat this wizard without my enchanted sword. She's back in Wulfgar, laughing her pointed ears off, thinking I might just sit it out and sink into depression."

"But now we're here," Gredchen said, "and we can help you."

"She's also full of secrets," said Theodenes.

Vanderjack looked at Gredchen. "Oh, some little secret other than the fact that this whole expedition was a fabrication?"

"That's just it. It wasn't. The baron wants his beautiful daughter back."

"His painting of the beautiful daughter."

Gredchen shook her head. "No, sellsword. That really *is* his daughter. A spell has bound her to that painting."

Vanderjack stood up at that, gaping. "So now you're saying that's a *real person* stuck in a picture frame?"

Gredchen nodded. "It's a little more complicated than that, but basically, yes."

"And Cazuvel wants it here why?"

"He's the mage responsible for the enchantment in the first place," said Gredchen. "So long as it was kept here, out of harm's way, the highmaster could continue to hold it over Baron Glayward and he'd be unable to lift a finger against her. But it was a rare enchantment. And the wizard has been studying the magic, trying to duplicate his feat ever since. Without success, or so I'm told."

"To the Abyss with wizards!" said Theodenes. "And speaking of magical curiosities, I should also note that Gredchen here—"

"I can't be hurt," the baron's aide admitted.

Vanderjack sat down again, rubbed his palm over the stubble of his scalp, and swore. "What? You're immortal, then? Congratulations. Is that the end of the secrets?"

"It's really only here at the castle or in the grounds. At least I suppose that's how it works."

Vanderjack smiled weakly. "How incredibly convenient for you. Theo? Any heartwarming truths you'd like to air? We're all having a moment."

"No."

Vanderjack clapped his hands together and rose one final time. "Excellent! Well, for your information, Theodenes, I think Star's alive and well and escaped a short while ago from the cage in the hall. And for you, Gredchen, the highmaster said nothing to me about not taking the baron's beautiful daughter along with me when I went to Wulfgar, so I believe we can go upstairs right now and fetch the painting and be done with that part of the job."

Gredchen's eyes widened. "You're serious?"

Theodenes perked up. "Star's escaped?"

"Yes to both. In fact, I think it may make getting to Wulfgar a lot easier if we had Star's help. You don't mind a short stop in Wulfgar before we head back to the baron, do you, Gredchen?"

Gredchen nodded. Theo's eyes narrowed.

"Then it's settled." Vanderjack dusted himself off. "I may not be the world's greatest swordsman, but I know a good plan when I come up with one. Let's go."

Vanderjack led them back to the entrance hall's balcony and up the spiral staircase to the gallery. Gredchen did the honors, stepping forward and pulling on the silken rope. The gallery's lamps fizzled and popped into radiant life, revealing the painting once again in its place.

Gredchen gasped. Theodenes sighed. Vanderjack clicked his tongue and walked over to the portrait with a frown.

The painting looked as if somebody had taken to it with an axe.

"Why would the wizard have done this?" Vanderjack asked.

"Oh, no!" Gredchen cried, darting forward to trace her hands over the places where the axe head had struck. "Wait."

"Yes, I see now. Those aren't actual cuts," Theodenes observed, folding his arms across his chest. "Those have been *painted* on. Under the varnish. Clever. But why?"

Vanderjack turned to Gredchen. "Got an explanation for this one?"

* * * * * *

Cazuvel swept through the dusty halls of the Lyceum.

Once he had left the highmaster's presence, he had spoken the words of power that brought him back to his sanctum, the place he had hidden Vanderjack's sword. His eldritch connection to the wards set up around Castle Glayward had triggered shortly afterward, alerting him to the highmaster's interference. With Aggurat freed, the highmaster would know that Cazuvel had been acting behind her back. The half-elf was a powerful enough mage that she had somehow untethered the draconian from Cazuvel's mystic bonds, despite all of the energy he had flooded into them.

Cazuvel did not care. It was just a slightly premature digression from a path he had carefully laid out, the path that had begun months earlier. He had his mirror and its magic. He had the star metal–forged sword of Vand Erj-Ackal, and he suspected there was a great deal of powerful enchantment tied up into that weapon.

The black-robed mage arrived at the grand cloister, the chamber in which the mirror hung suspended within its multiple arcane wards. He walked in and looked to the center of the room. The mirror was exactly as he had left it, so he proceeded over to a narrow table against the far wall, outside of the complex summoning circles and runic labyrinths. Lying upon the table was Lifecleaver.

Cazuvel had not yet drawn the sword. One of the kapak scouts had tried doing just that after he had recovered it from the jungle, and within moments the draconian shrieked and collapsed, catatonic. The mage wasn't prepared to have that happen to him, so he'd been careful to relocate the weapon from the baron's castle to the grand cloister without physically touching it. It was wrapped up in thin layers of magically resistant cloth, preventing whatever effect that had felled the draconian from plaguing him.

Looking over again at the mirror, Cazuvel spoke the incantations that would bring the imprisoned Cazuvel to the mirror's surface so the fiend who had taken his place could draw additional power.

"Cermindaya, cermindaya, saya memanggil anda dan mengikat anda!"

The surface of the mirror became briefly incandescent, and the brilliant metal swam with an image. It coalesced, and the true Cazuvel, his cheeks sunken and eyes rheumy, appeared within the mirror.

"I have nothing left. Nothing left to give you. You already took it all," said the weary voice.

Cazuvel snatched up the sword by the hilt, and stalked back to face the mirror, pointing one slender finger at the image of his captive. "Lies!" he shrieked. "I know how the enchantment works. You are a catalyst, an intermediary between me and the limitless powers of the Abyss. I need more power, and you will grant it to me!"

The Cazuvel-image moaned as his captor seemed to claw at the air with his hand, as if clutching something thick and viscous. Arcs of lightning once again leaped from the hammered-steel mirror and into Cazuvel, filling him with the howling forces he demanded. The image screamed, Cazuvel laughed. The noise was so loud and the play of purple and orange electricity so bright that at first the fiend did not notice the eight spectral figures manifesting behind him.

"Cease this!" bellowed the Conjuror above the din.

"Leave him alone!" cried the Apothecary.

"Your dark work is over!" said the Aristocrat.

Cazuvel stopped, and the myriad threads of energy feeding into him abruptly vanished. The man in the mirror looked emaciated, his stark white skin stretched across his skull, eye sockets sunken, lips drawn back in a hideous grimace.

"What is this? How did you get into my sanctum?" demanded Cazuvel to the array of spirits floating before him.

"We are the Sword Chorus," said the Philosopher.

"You are not of this world," said the Balladeer.

"You don't even smell human," the Hunter sniffed.

"Sword Chorus?" repeated Cazuvel. "So you are the sword's enchantments?"

"We are the souls of those slain by the sword before their time," explained the Cavalier.

"Fascinating. And you haunt the bearer of the weapon?"

The wizard splayed his fingers over the blade,

invoking the magical forces he'd just drawn from the mirror and using them to peer into the sword's construction, revealing layer upon layer of eldritch craftsmanship.

"A nine-lives stealer!" Cazuvel said, triumphant. "One of the legendary soul swords, said to have been crafted by the Smith God himself in the Age of Dreams. I should have recognized it, the blue-black star metal blade, and the sigils in ancient Ergothian. How fortuitous! There is magic bound into this blade, magic that the wizard whose form I have taken sought all of his life to master."

"This sword is not yours," assured the Aristocrat.

"We've been watching you, you know," said a ghost who had not spoken yet. "Don't think we don't know what you're up to."

Cazuvel narrowed his eyes at that eighth ghost, who appeared to be dressed in a cook's apron. "You are but a bound spirit," he hissed. "And I am—"

"A creature of the Abyss," finished the Conjuror.

"You're a fetch!" said the Cook. "Of course! A mirror fiend!"

"Fetches are incapable of taking mortal form," said the Balladeer.

"Nightmares that strike from the Abyss through reflective surfaces," said the Philosopher.

"It was the real Cazuvel, wasn't it?" said the Cook. "Black Robes are always making dark pacts with evil. Did he realize what he was doing?"

"He tried it once before," said Cazuvel. "The painting in the baron's castle. An imperfect medium, the wrong subject. He needed a true reflection, a reflection of himself. He—"

"He needed a mirror," said the Cook. "He'd created

that painting of the baron's daughter, but that was just practice."

The other ghosts were quite different from the Cook, Cazuvel realized. Cazuvel spoke a word of divinatory magic at the Cook, but it failed, dissipating before it could reveal anything. "You. Ghost. You are the most recent addition to this Sword Chorus, aren't you?"

"Silence, fetch!" said the Cavalier.

"You shall not gain the sword's power," said the Aristocrat.

"Vanderjack will find and defeat you," said the Hunter.

"I doubt that," said Cazuvel. "Even now, I would hazard a guess, the highmaster has thrown him into a cell beneath Wulfgar so that he might rot away for his interference."

"That's where you're wrong!" said the Cook.

The other ghosts moved close to the Cook, muttering at him. Cazuvel stared, curious, as they tried to stop the cook from blathering and boasting. Still, he reflected, they were behaving quite oddly for bound spirits.

"I've figured it out. You fetches are fiends from the Abyss," the Cook continued, despite the protestations of his fellows, "servants of the powers of darkness and chaos. You've been using this mirror to keep your connection to the Abyss active? Give you power!"

"Yes," said the fetch, pleased that somebody had noticed his extraordinary work. "It is not perfect power, but it has its definite uses. No other wizard on Krynn has access to it in the way I do. I can use the Black Robe's imprisoned soul as a template, channel raw power from the Abyss and through him. In doing so, I eschew the magic of the moons, the magic of the gods."

"Ingenious but aberrant," the Conjuror said begrudgingly.

"An active conduit like that could backfire," warned the Cook, "funnel magic back into the Abyss, or worse, open a permanent gate. The consequences could be catastrophic!"

"He speaks the truth," said the Conjuror. "What you are doing will have far-reaching effects. You cannot do this."

"He's right," echoed the Cook. "That conduit you're using now, the mirror, is almost expended. The wizard's just a mortal being, and you've been abusing him so much that he'll be consumed the next time you draw power through him."

Cazuvel looked toward the mirror, saw the almost mummified visage of the real Cazuvel, and muttered, "Perhaps. But I have his memories, his knowledge. This mirror was to be his crowning achievement."

The other ghosts had begun drifting slowly away, spreading their circle outward. Cazuvel didn't notice, focused as he was on the words of the Cook. "And now I have the sword," Cazuvel continued. "Its soul-draining properties may be just what I need to refine the process, perfect the conduit."

Etharion's spirit looked quickly in the direction of the retreating ghosts and back at Cazuvel. "Well, in order to do that, you'll need a lot of souls. Lots of . . . people. All in one place. Oh, and . . . another conduit, like this one, something to replace the mirror, only one that the real Cazuvel didn't mess up."

Cazuvel's eyes widened. "Yes! You have the right of it! A place of great death."

The Cook egged him on. "And another conduit."

"The painting! Of course. You are right. I had not

planned on using it, believing it to be nothing more than a bargaining chip and an amusing trophy. But it was his first success. It could be improved upon, perfected."

"I've said too much," said the Cook, raising his spectral hands. The other ghosts had gone. The Cook began to fade also. The wizard waved good riddance to them.

Cazuvel passed his hand before the mirror, once again obscuring his decrepit prisoner behind thick clouds in the polished surface. He returned to the table, gathering up the sword's scabbard and belt.

"Now, Highmaster," said the fetch. "In due course, you shall see just how powerful my magic is. When you stand before the great storm of the Abyss, a storm that I conjure forth, you shall know. We shall see who pleases the Dark Queen then, won't we?"

His laughter echoed throughout the halls of the Lyceum, even after his magic spirited him away.

CHAPTER NINETEEN

Vanderjack tore the baron's beautiful daughter from the wall of the gallery.

It had been firmly attached to the paneling, and they were in a hurry. Gredchen covered her eyes, and Theodenes stood over by the top of the spiral stairs, making sure nothing came running in after hearing the noise.

It made a very loud noise indeed.

"Ackal's Teeth!" cursed the sellsword. "It's a good thing the frame's made of ironwood, or that would be the end of it." Vanderjack held the painting out. "Gredchen. The painted-on axe cuts match up to where you say the kapak chopped at you, right? I think it's obvious that you and this painting are connected in some, dare I say it, secret fashion."

"If so, then I'm in the dark about it, Vanderjack," Gredchen said. "I swear. It must be the work of Cazuvel."

Theodenes snorted. "Wizards."

Vanderjack eyed her skeptically and indicated the painting. "So other than the new additions . . . ?"

Gredchen inspected the painting, frowning at points, but then nodded. "It's the same," she said. "Fine."

"Can we go now?" Theo grumbled, looking around worriedly.

"After you." Vanderjack indicated the spiral stairs and followed Theo down. Gredchen brought up the rear, and when they reached the landing below, she stepped over to the grand hall doors and peeked inside.

"No sign of Star," she called. "Where should we look?"

"The roof," Vanderjack said. "The dragonne will be flying about outside, more than likely. Besides, if those kapaks are still around, they're going to be down that way." He pointed over the balcony toward the entrance foyer and the big gates.

The trio hurried through the great hall, on through the sitting room, making their way out with occasional stops for Vanderjack to adjust the painting or for Theodenes to scout ahead. When they scaled the stairs to the tower roof and felt the moisture-laden night air of the Sahket Jungle, Gredchen took a deep breath and exhaled slowly.

"No draconians!" she said. "But no Star either."

Theodenes walked to the edge of the battlements and began scanning the silver-edged landscape around the tower with his keen eyesight. Vanderjack left him to it and set the painting down against a crenellation. He looked at his hands, spread before him, and watched them shake noticeably.

"It's getting worse, isn't it?"

He looked up and saw Gredchen standing there watching him. "Yes. This happened to another swordsman I served with, back in the war," the sellsword said. "He was a fine soldier, came from a family near Thelgaard. He had a big two-handed sword." Vanderjack raised his arms and held his hands apart to show just how big. "His grandfather's, he said. Family heirloom."

"Magic?"

Vanderjack shook his head. "Oh, no. These days, every two-bit adventurer and freebooter from Kharolis to Khur says he has a magic sword. Back then, in the middle of the war, most of us had never seen one."

"Except you."

"I never told people Lifecleaver was magical. Whitestone or dragonarmy. Not even the officers knew."

"So this other warrior?"

"Right. His name was Orbaal. We were on a mission near Kayolin, the dwarf stronghold. This was before they had signed up. I don't remember the details, but Orbaal and two others from our unit were jumped by bugbears. Big, furry, ugly goblins. You know?"

Gredchen nodded. "I've heard of them."

"Orbaal fought them off, but in the process he put his foot through a thin patch of rock over a sinkhole. He fell in, took three of the bugbears with him. He ended up on a ledge, but the sword kept on going."

"You couldn't get it back?"

Vanderjack smiled weakly. "The dwarves have it now, I bet. It went down a long way."

"So what happened?"

"Orbaal went crazy. We pulled him out of there and regrouped; the bugbears were taken care of, and we returned to the camp. Only Orbaal couldn't sleep. He would rant at the officers, demanding we make a deal with the dwarves to get his cherished sword back. It was messy."

Gredchen looked down at her feet. "You think that's happening to you."

"I know for a fact Orbaal didn't have voices telling

him how to fight, where to look. Me, I've had those seven ghosts with me for years now. I can't shake this headache, my stomach's rebelling, and my nerves are shot. Something's going rotten, I know that for sure."

"You're tough, Vanderjack. You can get through this. And when you get the sword back again, you'll be fine. When you're in the middle of your next fight, just ask yourself what they'd be saying if they were still there."

The baron's aide was grinning, that one attractive feature she had in an otherwise ugly face. "Just ask, what would this ghost say? What would that ghost do?"

"That's the stupidest idea I've ever heard," Vanderjack said, awkwardly glancing away from her.

Gredchen leaned back, her hair blowing in the rooftop breeze. For several seconds neither of them spoke. Then Vanderjack glanced over at her, intending to mumble his gratitude. Only she wasn't there. One moment she had been there, sitting on the battlements, and the next she was gone.

"Gredchen!"

The sellsword rushed to the edge, gripped the crenellations with his calloused hands and looked over. Nothing. "Gredchen!"

Theodenes raced over, patting around his belt and back for weapons that weren't there. "What is it? Where is she?"

A small explosion of fire, ash, and concussive force knocked both the gnome and the sellsword flat. Chunks of brick and masonry blew outward. The explosion detonated somewhere in the middle of the tower roof. Vanderjack rolled onto his back and curled up into a sitting position, shielding his eyes from the smoke.

"Ackal's Teeth! Theo, are you all right? Theo? Blast it all!"

He couldn't see anything; there was too much of that thick, acrid smoke. Something had blown up. He looked to his left and checked on the painting. It was still there and unharmed. He got to his feet. "Theo?"

"Right here," said a voice from the smoke. Theodenes, his face black with soot, emerged. "Vanderjack, I think that was a display of invoked pyrothaumaturgics."

"A what?"

"A fireball. We're under attack!"

Vanderjack grabbed Theodenes and ducked behind a low brick wall as a whistling sound heralded another explosion.

"Where's it coming from?" asked Vanderjack.

The gnome poked his head around the corner of the wall then quickly drew it back. "It's him. It's Cazuvel."

"Oh, fantastic. I thought I'd have a little time before he showed up."

"Sellsword!" called the Black Robe's voice above the sizzling sound of many small fires burning the rooftop tar. "I have the girl! Give me the painting! We'll call it a fair trade."

Vanderjack blinked and looked behind him. He clasped Theodenes on the shoulder and whispered, "He's got Gredchen. Duck over there and get the painting before he sees it, Theo. I'll . . . distract him."

Theodenes looked from the sellsword to the painting, which was indeed out of sight, and nodded.

Vanderjack jumped out from behind the wall. "Over here!" he shouted. "Looking for me?" In his mind, he recalled Gredchen's advice and tried to imagine what the Balladeer might prompt him with. The ghost was always suggesting one insult, taunt, or jibe after another. What were some of the best ones he'd used before?

He saw Cazuvel stalking across the tower roof, his black robes flapping in the wind. His cowl was pulled over his head so all the sellsword could see were those violet eyes and the peculiar grin. With a twinge, he also caught sight of what might have been the hilt of Life-cleaver, strapped to the mage's belt, beneath the robes.

"So the highmaster left you behind, did she?" said Cazuvel, shaping a gesture with one hand while the other gripped the sword hilt. Vanderjack saw him look briefly to the side and say something under his breath then shake his head.

He was talking to the ghosts!

"She figured you and I should have a little parley!" Vanderjack said, holding up his hands. A memory of the Balladeer's voice came to him, and he ran with it: "But I thought, why tease you with big words you don't understand?"

The kender race produced the most accomplished insulters and taunters in all of Ansalon. Vander-jack was no kender. But his sarcasm seemed to have struck some nerve. The wizard completed whatever spell he was casting, and a streak of black lightning arced from his fingertips to a spot just to the left of the sellsword. Where it struck, chunks of rock exploded upward, catching Vanderjack across his side and along his upper arm.

"She sent you after me, did she? Madness! You haven't a chance against my magic, sellsword. Give me the painting, or I will wipe you off the face of Krynn!"

Vanderjack took a quick look around. "Or I'll give you the painting and then you'll wipe me off the face of Krynn! See what I mean? All you've got is fakery and grandstanding and simple words of one or two syllables. It's really kind of embarrassing." In his mind the memory-voice of the Hunter was telling him to watch his flanks. Sure enough, the sellsword spotted two kapak draconians clinging to the battlements on either side of him, crouching, unmoving.

The sellsword hoped Theo had moved the painting or was at least making his way to the stairs. He couldn't see him anywhere; the collateral damage from the mage's destructive magic had stirred up so much dust and smoke.

"The painting, sellsword!" said Cazuvel, emerging from the nearest bank of smoke. Vanderjack had no weapon and still couldn't see Gredchen. Had one of the kapaks grabbed her?

"Painting?" Vanderjack said. "Now where did I put that thing . . . ?"

Cazuvel snarled and started to frame another spell. Vanderjack wondered what the Conjuror would say about that. Maybe . . .

Vanderjack dropped to his left, somersaulting out of the way just as a chilling blast of frost sprayed the spot he just left. When he came up, he knew he needed to take the initiative and just grab the wizard. With luck, he'd take the sword from him and it would all be over.

Vanderjack dived at Cazuvel, aiming for his midsection. The wizard brought his knee up, hoping to catch the sellsword under the chin, but was a fraction of a second too late. Vanderjack knocked the wizard backward into another low wall, one hand up to grab the wizard around the throat with the other reaching for his sword.

His fingers wrapped around the hilt, and in that instant Vanderjack spied the ghosts arrayed around

them both—the Cavalier, the Hunter, the Apothecary, the Aristocrat, the Conjurer, the Philosopher,
and the Balladeer. And there, in front of them all, stood
the Cook.

"Etharion?" said Vanderjack.

"Get back!" they all shouted in unison.

Cazuvel brought the heel of his palm up against
Vanderjack's nose. The sellsword felt his nose break,
the blinding pain lancing all the way to the back of his
head. He let go of the sword, and the ghosts vanished
from his sight. Then something even worse happened.

Cazuvel triggered a spell, obviously connected to the
act of making physical contact with his opponent. A
sudden wave of nausea and muscle cramps struck the
sellsword only a heartbeat after his nose was broken.
He slumped to the side. The wizard leaped to his feet,
and Vanderjack felt a hard kick in the ribs from a hob-
nail boot.

"Aaaargh!" he screamed, clutching his injury.

Cazuvel looked off to the side. A smile crept across
his face, and he looked back down again at Vanderjack.
"I have what I came for!" he said, triumphant, and
dashed away.

Vanderjack struggled to get up. Blood was streaming from his nose, and his chest felt as if a lance had
pierced it. He looked around, desperate, unable to see
Theodenes, the painting, Gredchen, or anything except
flashes of color in his left eye and smoke everywhere.

Then, as if it could get any worse, there was a high-
pitched screech as the kapaks leaped out of the darkness
toward him. Vanderjack braced for their impact.

A deafening roar split the night, knocking the
two kapaks out of the air with the force. The smoke
was blown clear. Vanderjack rolled onto his belly and

pushed himself up onto his elbows to see the welcome sight of Star rising up above the battlements, Theodenes straddling his back.

"The wizard!" Vanderjack coughed, pointing in the general direction of where Cazuvel had gone.

"Too late for that now," said Theodenes. "He has the painting and Gredchen and he's teleported both away from here."

Vanderjack felt the world around him spin, and he had to steady himself against one of the crenellations. "Then we've lost. We've lost everything. Ackal's Teeth, what do we do now?"

"A rescue mission, of course! We leave immediately for Wulfgar," said Theodenes.

"How could you possibly know that's where Cazuvel is going?"

"Because," said Star, his resonant feline voice dispelling the fog in Vanderjack's head. "Your ghosts are telling me."

Vanderjack managed a smile. Now *that* was more like it.

******

Rivven Cairn instructed Cear to land in the courtyard behind the khan's palace in Wulfgar.

"All of this traveling back and forth is distracting me from what I need to be doing, Cear," she said, patting him on the snout as she dismounted. "Stick around, though. The chariot racing starts tomorrow. I know how much you like that."

"I like it more at night," said the dragon, his jaws dropping with thick, sulfurous spittle. "When everything's on fire."

Rivven smiled. "That's only when you get carried away, Cear," she said and walked away from him. Cear was as much in love with fire as she was, but then, he had an excuse. She was the perfect partner for one of the mighty, inflammatory reds.

Rivven had no doubt that Vanderjack would probably find Cazuvel at some stage. She didn't believe he'd have any luck taking him on, however. Since Rivven knew he wasn't truly Cazuvel, she had dedicated some of her time on the flight back from Castle Glayward to figuring out what he was.

She had come to the conclusion it had something to do with Cazuvel's field of expertise—summoning, binding, and trafficking with dark forces. The real Cazuvel had been almost as ambitious as Rivven herself, although his reach frequently exceeded his grasp. Early in their career together, Rivven had come to the mage with a task that would have gotten him thrown out of the order of High Sorcery; she had asked him to develop a means to keep the emperor of dragons alive.

It was five years after she had been recruited to serve under Dragon Highlord Phair Caron. The brutal highlord, handpicked by Ariakas, desired only female highmasters to fly alongside her. Rumors of her romantic preferences were rife, but Rivven paid no attention to them. The half-elf was there because of Ariakas, not Phair Caron.

In the three hundred forty-seventh year after the Cataclysm, prior to the dragonarmies' invasion of Ansalon, the cabal of lesser wizards and priests surrounding Ariakas had determined that a safeguard against assassination was needed. Rivven, as a student of Ariakas and a mage in her own right, was among those chosen to produce a solution. Although it wasn't her field, Rivven knew somebody who might be able to help her.

Recruiting Cazuvel, Rivven had charged him with the task of developing a contingency plan should a rival or an enemy kill Ariakas. She knew the Queen of Darkness would not simply resurrect Ariakas, even though he was foremost among her highlords. That would imply weakness, and she could not abide weakness. The goddess liked her highlords to take care of themselves. Thus, Rivven intended to give Ariakas a means to return from the dead independent of Takhisis, and to do that, Cazuvel would need to delve into the darkest of magic.

Cazuvel initially had presented Rivven with the idea of keeping the emperor's soul safe in a phylactery, but Rivven said no. That was the basis of lichdom, a path that Ariakas would never accept. Even if it meant living forever, Ariakas would not agree to become one of the undead. No, Cazuvel would need to accomplish something similar without necromancy, and therefore, he came up with the idea of the painting.

It was, in a way, sympathetic magic. Essentially, a painting of Ariakas could be created, as exact a likeness as possible. A powerful link would exist between the painting and the subject of the portrait, one that defied death. In the event of his untimely end, the painting would serve as the means of bringing him back, the template for his resurrection.

The accuracy of the image was crucial, but the composition of the oils, the tinctures, even the canvas and frame were also critical. Ariakas would need to surrender some of his blood, and at least pose for the portrait. Painting him from memory would never work. Rivven thought she could arrange all of that, but she wanted Cazuvel to test the process first.

Rivven needed a test subject, somebody to be painted,

somebody for whom the possibility of death was imminent. She could simply have chosen some peasant or minor soldier from the Red Wing, but she had a much better idea.

In the weeks before the initial invasion of Nordmaar, the first region to experience the true power of the newly organized dragonarmies, Phair Caron had held numerous strategic meetings with her highmasters, with her fellow highlords, and with Ariakas himself. Nordmaar was ideal because it was close enough to Neraka and Kern, where the armies were based, and it represented the nearest free, independent kingdom. Success in Nordmaar meant success elsewhere in Krynn. In a way, Nordmaar was the prototype for the rest of the war.

The half-elf approached Phair Caron with a plan. Rivven knew an important nobleman in the region, a man with the ear of the king. He was a Solamnic exile, and he kept many secrets. If she could get to him, he could provide valuable information that would benefit the invasion. The highlord agreed to her plan, and the red dragonarmy sat poised to overwhelm Nordmaar's borders, contingent on Rivven's intrigues.

Rivven knew at the time that the nobleman, Baron Gilbert Glayward, had a daughter who was stricken with a fatal malady. She told him she had a means of saving the girl's life, but it would require his cooperation. The daughter was a natural beauty, his only child; convincing him to betray the king proved easier than she had thought.

Unfortunately, the experiment failed. The daughter died prematurely, and the painting . . .

Pushing away those thoughts of the past, Rivven rushed through the tall, arched doors into the administration wing within the khan's palace. Servants ran back and forth, mostly getting out of the highmaster's way. She passed a series of open doors, each leading into a room full of scribes, factors, and bureaucrats keeping track of her finances, her taxes, and more. Her destination was the large and opulent chamber at the rear of the wing.

"Aubec," she said, nodding at her aide-de-camp. He stood, waiting, beside the enormous table covered in maps and plans. "What news?"

"All is in readiness for the chariot races tomorrow, Excellency," the aide said, bowing. "Local warlords, all of whom have paid their taxes in the last week, have their retinues and are on the way. The people of Wulfgar are ablaze with gossip over their favorites in the arena. Your masters of horse and your marshals of arms have selected the best of the best, and—"

Rivven waved her hand. "It all sounds good," she said. "Cear and I are looking forward to it."

Aubec bowed again and cleared his throat.

Rivven looked up from the table, absentmindedly shuffling papers about. "Yes?"

"Forgive my impertinent observation, but you seem more than a little preoccupied, my lady."

"Oh, yes. Well. It's Cazuvel."

"The Black Robe?"

"Yes. Or whoever he is, yes."

Aubec hesitated as a scribe ran in, handed something to him, and ran out. He made a notation on his tablet and looked up again at the highmaster.

"You suspect he might be some kind of imposter, my lady?"

"I *know* he is an imposter. And it makes me wonder what else has been going on behind my back while I've been so preoccupied with the bloody sellsword and with the baron's efforts to strain our relationship."

"I can assure you, Excellency, Nordmaar is securely in your hands, even now."

"That's what it looks like. But I have mercenaries flying in behind enemy lines on the backs of mythical beasts, fake wizards conjuring up who knows what, and gnomes acting very ungnomelike. Even the baron's ugly servant is causing problems when she knows better."

Aubec shrugged. "I regret I can do no more to help."

Rivven exhaled. "At least you're doing what I ask you to do. Thank you, Aubec. You're dismissed."

The aide-de-camp slipped out of the room, closing the door behind himself. Rivven snapped her fingers and the many lamps and braziers that lit the room burned down to a low smolder, leaving only a single bright candle burning nearby.

Rivven lifted a large dish full of water onto the table and began reciting the necessary incantations to still the water's surface and send forth a summons of communication. She wasn't sure she would get an answer and was, therefore, surprised when the wizard Cazuvel's face—the imposter's face—appeared in the water.

"Sending a sellsword to do your dirty work, Highmaster?" The mage sneered, lips curled back.

"Did I? Probably just an afterthought." She studied the face in the water critically, smiling thinly.

"Unlikely," Cazuvel said. "Vanderjack has been the only thing on your mind for over a week. Did you think you could eliminate two threats at the same time this way? Are you that naïve?"

"You're one to make accusations of naïveté, wizard," she said. "I know now you're not the real Cazuvel. I'm going to find you, and when I do, I'll cut off your hands and feed them to my sivaks."

"Oh, but you are blind, Highmaster! You are too wrapped up in your own ambition. If you weren't so preoccupied, you might have seen the clues years ago, Rivven Cairn."

How odd, Rivven thought. He's actually gloating. Not only gloating, leaking useful information. Imposter though he was, he had Cazuvel's insecurity mimicked almost perfectly.

"You're just one man, wizard. I have the resources of an entire wing of the red dragonarmy at my disposal. I only need to speak the word, and a flight of dragons and draconians will fall upon you and tear you apart."

The wizard laughed; his laughter shook the surface of the water, causing ripples that distorted the wizard's image. "I think it will not be that easy. Perhaps your own mistakes will fall upon you and tear you apart."

"Is that a threat, wizard? I'm the one who contacted you."

"Yes, Highmaster. And you will note that I still answered."

Astonished at his bravado, Rivven ran several responses through her head, readying at least one of them, but before she could say a word to that effect, the water erupted in her face. A thin, bleach-white fist thrust up through the scrying dish and into her jaw, sending her spinning backward into a row of chairs, trailed by a spray of blood.

The voice of Cazuvel called out from the water. "I am the greater sorcerer! I am the true heir to the power of the Abyss! You are nothing! Prepare yourself for your doom, Highmaster!"

Her mouth formed a tight line as Rivven stood and

lashed out at the upstart. Fiery magic rose rapidly to the surface of her conscious mind. A blast of white-hot flame incinerated the dish, the water boiling instantly away into vapor, the papers and maps and the table itself bursting into flame. Only then did she collapse back into the broken chairs and, somewhat ruefully, nurse her split lip.

When Aubec and the other servants raced in, Rivven had already placed the helm back on her head and was on her feet. The table was still on fire. The servants dragged flammable objects and materials away from the scene of destruction. Rivven simply stood to one side and watched, collecting herself and her thoughts.

"My lady?" asked Aubec without raising his voice. She admired that calm quality about him.

"Yes, Aubec."

"Shall I fetch a new table?"

"Yes, Aubec."

Rivven sighed. Either the wizard masquerading as the real Cazuvel was more powerful than she realized or he was more than just a wizard. If not a wizard, then what was he?

CHAPTER TWENTY

Vanderjack was on a rescue mission.

Technically, it was the same mission, but prior to that, he had apparently been contracted not to rescue a person but a painting. He was still trying to retrieve the painting, but in addition he had Gredchen to rescue.

Despite a broken nose, one or two broken ribs, some serious burns, a lingering concussion, and an admitted dependency on a magic sword that he still hadn't won back, Vanderjack felt excited by the challenge. While the flight to Wulfgar meant at least three stops along the way to hide from dragonarmy scouts, he estimated that he, the gnome, and the dragonne they were riding would arrive in the legendary City of the Plains by sunrise. Then . . . action.

The other thing that had Vanderjack excited was that his ghosts had returned, albeit beyond his capacity to perceive them. The dragonne could see them, however, so through a process of Star acting as translator, the ghosts and Vanderjack could maintain a sort of conversation. It was in that manner that the sellsword learned of the truth behind Cazuvel, the black robe mage.

"So what's a fetch?" Vanderjack asked after listening to a long explanation of events that left him scratching his head. Star repeated the question and related the answer.

"A creature of the Abyss," the Conjuror responded. "It comes at its victim through mirrors."

"This one's more powerful than the stories would lead us to believe they can be," said the Cook.

"It has found a means to manifest itself in the material world in the form of its victim, and indeed it has trapped that victim within a mirror," said the Philosopher.

"That victim is the true Cazuvel, and while the mirror appears to be keeping him in a form of stasis, the fetch has been drawing power through the mirror," said the Apothecary.

"In a sense, the fetch is using Cazuvel as a template through which to clothe itself in a mortal guise, and to cast spells," said the Balladeer.

"Magic that comes straight from the Abyss," said the Cook. "The mirror's a portal. And this is all connected to the painting of the nobleman's daughter."

Aha! Vanderjack turned to Theodenes. They were flying over the last stretch of jungle before emerging onto the plains, less than an hour from Wulfgar. "Did you realize your cook was such an expert on fiends from the Abyss?"

"His candor and knowledge are a great deal more inclined toward the arcane and supernatural than they are toward camp cuisine," conceded Theodenes. "When I hired him in Pentar, I perhaps did not probe his past as much as I might have. When he told me that he had been with the Solamnic forces, I asked him if he could cook, and he said that's what he did best. At the time, I needed a cook."

Star rumbled his agreement. "The one known as Etharion is more than he appears to be," said the dragonne. "The ghosts are making every effort to distract us from knowing this."

"Etharion," asked Vanderjack directly. "How does a cook who served time in the Solamnic army—the army voted most likely never to work with a wizard, ever, even if asked nicely—know so much about this kind of thing?"

Star related the ghost's response with a chuckle. "He says he has been 'around a lot' and 'knows a little bit about everything.' "

"Fantastic, Theo. You hired a journeyman, not a cook. Not a bad thing for us, as it turns out."

"Not so good for him," pointed out Theo. "Considering he was run through with a sword and killed by you."

"Look, how many times do I need to apologize for that?"

Star cocked his head, listening to the dead cook. The dragonne said, "He tells me it has placed quite a damper on his cooking, but he is pleased to be able to help in some way."

Vanderjack squinted. "Whatever floats his ghostly boat, I suppose. All right. So Cazuvel's a fetch, using a magic mirror to cast evil spells. And the real Cazuvel is the one who fashioned the enchanted portrait of the baron's beautiful daughter. Got it." Vanderjack rubbed his itchy scalp. "Ask the ghosts," he said to Star, "what they think we need to do to defeat this feckless fetch."

"The fetch may only last for a short time outside the Abyss without a functioning portal," said the Philosopher.

"The mirror is, for all intents and purposes, no longer sufficient for Cazuvel to maintain his power," said the Conjuror.

"I managed to trick him into taking the painting," the Cook said. "He wants to try and replicate its powers. I didn't think he would take Gredchen. I'm sorry about that."

"He goes to Wulfgar," explained the Cavalier, "because he needs a large number of souls departing their bodies within a very short time in order to solidify his dark magic."

"It turns out Wulfgar has a huge chariot race and gladiator battle every year," said the Balladeer. "Which, this year, is today."

A brief, ominous silence reigned.

"But Rivven Cairn is a pretty powerful wizard herself," said Vanderjack. "Won't she sense him in her city and then give us all a display of her magic-fueled wrath?"

"If we are fortunate," said Theodenes. "But what about Gredchen and the painting?"

"We need a plan," said Vanderjack aloud. "That's an understatement," he added to himself.

Somehow the ghosts must have heard him because they all nodded sagely.

* * * * * *

The city of Wulfgar was founded only a hundred and fifty years earlier. Before that, the land on which Wulfgar stood was a campsite for the native Huitzitlic tribesmen during the winter months. Solamnic Knights garrisoned at the nearby fortress of Qwes warred with those natives, but once peace had been established, they drew up plans for a major settlement.

In less than two years, natives and settlers working together erected the mighty walls and sturdy buildings. Initially designed to repel ogres from the south, they proved to be no match for something they had no concept of defending against: an airborne attack by the dragonarmies.

Ten years earlier, when the Red Wing swung out of Neraka and into Nordmaar, the city of Wulfgar was taken completely by surprise. The Solamnic Knights had already lost Qwes to Highlord Phair Caron, and those survivors who limped back to Wulfgar found it occupied by Highmaster Rivven Cairn and the Twelfth Red Dragonarmy, most of whom were kapak draconians and mercenaries from Neraka.

Wulfgar was a mile in diameter, constructed as an almost perfect circle. The palace was in the center, on a raised plateau at least twenty feet above the wide paved streets that surrounded it. Also upon that plateau, accessible to the residents of the city by enormous ramps closed off by gates when not in use, was the Horseman's Arena. Its proximity to the palace and its central position spoke volumes of its importance to the city's population before the war. After the occupation, its importance had become twisted into an obsession, and simple horse races and mock battles had become bloody reenactments.

Getting into the city was not going to be the difficult part. Theodenes had a cousin in the Guild of Sewers, Waterways, Reservoirs, and Wells who had liked to talk about his job when they were younger. They'd go underground, even though it meant leaving the dragonne behind. They instructed Star to stay in a cluster of lightly wooded hills a half mile north of the city while they crossed overland to the city walls.

Vanderjack's cracked ribs slowed their pace. For once, Theodenes' short legs could easily keep up with the limping sellsword. Yet they reached the walls before the half-light of dawn. Vanderjack heard the sounding of horns and the clatter of horse hooves along the main roads leading into the city, out of sight as they crouched beside the century-old stone.

"I hadn't counted on this," said Theodenes, looking down the curving length of the outside wall.

Vanderjack was catching his breath. "Hadn't counted on what?"

"No outside sewer grates, no reservoirs, nothing."

"It's a city; there's always a sewer grate."

Theodenes shook his head. "I believe all of the city's effluent, all of the sewer works and so forth, are inside the walls, directed underneath the city proper."

"Clever Solamnics," muttered Vanderjack.

"So either we try the front gates," said Theo, "or we go over the wall."

"We'll be a little conspicuous, won't we? Mercenary and gnome."

Theodenes stroked his beard. "Then we do both."

Vanderjack looked at him. "We split up?"

Theodenes nodded. "I scale the walls. It will be a simple matter for me, especially with my mountaineering skills and well-honed physical prowess. You go around to one of the gates and find a way in. I suggest the west gate because it leads straight into the merchants' quarter."

"Sure. Nobody will notice a tall black bloody-nosed guy in an arming doublet tripping over himself." He paused. "And we're meeting where? And you know all of this local geography how?"

Theodenes sniffed. "Because I make it my business to know about my areas of operation. Now let's see. We want to attend the chariot race because that's where Cazuvel is most likely to reveal himself. Correct?"

"That's right. Hopefully, he'll reveal himself, Gredchen, the painting, my sword, and anything else worth revealing."

"Then we should meet at the Alochtlixan Fields."

Vanderjack gingerly pressed around his nose with a cloth to make sure he hadn't just started bleeding again. "The where?"

"All of the equine specialists, representatives from the stabling yards, practice tracks, chariot builders, and those trained in animal husbandry frequent the Alochtlixan Fields, which are in the southeastern quarter of Wulfgar. Famous place."

"Carrying a copy of *Bertrem's Guide,* are you?"

"I most certainly am not. *Bertrem's Guide* is notoriously unreliable. Might as well have a kender map. How does midday sound to you? When the sun is overhead?"

"How long is it until the games in the arena?"

"They begin midafternoon. We shall have more than enough time, assuming you are not caught or captured."

Vanderjack grinned. "Now how often does that happen?"

Theodenes gave him an icy stare, and the sellsword laughed and sauntered off, not feeling as confident as he acted. The ground seemed to lurch beneath him; he was still feeling wobbly and weak. He was on an important rescue mission, he reminded himself. Lives and riches hung in the balance. Somehow he would have to get the job done.

******

Theodenes dropped to the ground on the other side of the city walls and looked around for a long stick.

Losing his multifunction polearm had been a blow, but he should be able to construct a new one. All he required was a little time and some materials, most of which he'd be able to scrounge together in any large and well-stocked city. He suspected Wulfgar was just a little too backwater for that, and there was not time for tinkering there anyway. It was a shame, he thought, so he would have to improvise.

In place of the polearm, Theo settled on a pitchfork. He pulled it free from a bale of hay, one of hundreds of hay bales stacked against the inside of the walls of the city. Theodenes also thought to snatch up a wide-brimmed hat from atop a sleeping local. With that and a poncho he tugged down from a nearby drying rack, he had the makings of a disguise. Of course, he was half the height of any other Nordmmaaran peasant, but he supposed if he hid his face and walked about as if he belonged, nobody would be the wiser.

The part of the city he was in was something of a residential district. It wasn't the famed Solamnic Quarter, at that time almost completely turned over to the dragonarmies, and it wasn't the Warriors' Quarter, where the legendary Plumed Jaguars of Wulfgar would be carousing if the highmaster hadn't driven them all from the city. The dilapidated single-story dwellings around him were more common in the city, which had been almost burned to the ground at the opening of the war.

He rounded a corner and saw, at the end of a wide street crusted with muddy clay, horse droppings, and straw, the wooden fences that divided the Alochtlixan Fields off from the city. Good. He was close to his destination, but glancing up at the sun, he saw that he had at least an hour in which to investigate the city further, so he made a mental note of his surroundings and headed due west.

The palace of the khan rose majestically above the streets; between it and Theo was the high-walled Horseman's Arena itself. Theodenes crossed over the paved avenue leading directly from the south gate to the foot of the arena's entrance ramp. Dragonarmy soldiers lined the street, most of them looking as though they needed only slight provocation to take a swing with their weapons. Here and there, Theo saw pairs of kapak and baaz draconians. As he recalled, they were expensive for the highmaster to keep stationed there. Where once she would have boasted whole brigades of kapaks, baaz, and even bozaks, nowadays she was scraping the bottom of the coffers.

His thoughts were interrupted by the commands of a heavily armored dragonarmy officer who shouted out to the pint-sized peasant from the opposite side of the street. The officer was accompanied by two thugs, Theo noted.

"Well, well, what have we here," said the officer. His accent was strongly Nordmaaran, not uncommon in those days among the dragonarmies. "Is this one of those dread kender, boys?"

"I am but a simple gnome farmer," said Theo, trying for honesty, hoping his voice sounded even and humble.

"A gnome?" said the officer, incredulous. "You're a long way from home, aren't you? A gnome away from home. Ha, ha, ha."

The thugs joined the officer in laughing at his jest but showed no sign of actual merriment on their blunt and heavy features. Theo's neck became hot and prickled.

"Surely your honors have heard of the gnomes of . . . " Theo's mind raced. ". . . the Great Moors?"

The Great Moors was an enormous, swampy region in the southeastern corner of Nordmaar, a trackless waste of humid marsh and bog that nobody in his right mind would ever enter lest he be eaten by predatory lizards or devoured by swarms of giant, blood-sucking stirges. Theo hoped the gazetteer he'd read as a young gnome about the Great Moors was right and that it was still largely a mystery to even the most widely traveled of Nordmaarans.

"A gnome from the Great Moors?" the officer said, scratching at a loathsome boil behind his ear. "Are your hands and feet webbed, like they say the tribesmen from there are?"

Theodenes swallowed. Best not to make any bold-faced claims. "By the Abyss, no," he laughed. "We Moorish gnomes are but simple folk, like thee and thou, sure enough."

The soldiers squinted.

Theo added, "In service to the Queen of Darkness, of course."

"Dark gnomes, then!" The officer beamed.

"Yes, of course," said Theo, who was beginning to wonder where the conversation was going and how he was going to derail it. "Dark, savage gnomes. But without webbed hands or feet."

"Just evil." The officer nodded.

"Very," said the gnome.

"All right, then. That's good enough for me. What do you say, boys? Shall we let the evil gnome go about his business?"

The two thugs shrugged and grunted something incomprehensible to their officer, and the officer nodded. "All right. On your way, little gnome! And watch where you're swinging that pitchfork."

Theo breathed a huge sigh of relief. He touched his hand to the brim of his hat and turned to walk away. He'd gone no more than three steps when a new voice, deep and sibilant with a Nerakan accent, said, "What in the name of the Dragonqueen is a dark gnome?"

He froze. Thinking it a bad idea to scurry away suspiciously, he leaned his pitchfork against an adobe wall and crouched down idly, as if to lace up his boots.

"From the Great Moors," said the officer's voice.

A snort greeted his intelligence.

Heavy footsteps pounded on the paving stones, coming toward Theo. It was a one-armed sivak draconian, wearing the markings of the Red Watch. Theo turned to run just as the sivak reached out with his one good arm and lifted him off the ground by his collar.

"Dark gnome, is it?" barked Commander Aggurat.

"I demand to be taken to your leader!" said Theodenes feebly.

"With pleasure," said the sivak, and flew off toward the khan's palace.

CHAPTER TWENTY-ONE

Vanderjack leaned against a post, arms folded, watching the column of arrivals enter the city by the west gate.

Leaning against the post and folding his arms wasn't just for appearances. He badly needed a breather, and when his arms were folded across his chest, it kept his rib cage in one place too. He was trying to appear confident, calm, and in control of his life—all part of the illusion.

Vanderjack took note of who was arriving in the city for the games. Many of them were Nordmaaran natives, both the rugged horse barbarians of the grassy plains to the west and tribal folk from the Sahket Jungle. There were a handful of banners from mercenary companies, war bands, and minor nobles who had benefited from the dragonarmy occupation.

In addition to the spectators, Vanderjack observed a few groups of large and intimidating men who he identified as gladiators. In occupied Nordmaar, as with other regions of Ansalon still under the control of the highlords, slavery and gladiatorial combat were rife.

Many gladiators were free men, used to the lifestyle and capable of making more of a living killing others for glory than killing others for a cause. Vanderjack had known a few. He realized as he watched them move along, some sitting on wagons and others talking among themselves on foot, that he could probably join up with them.

As soon as the next group passed him by, he flagged the man in front. He was tall, tanned and skinny, but had muscles like steel ropes and sharp features. He was probably the lanista for the men with him, a combination of trainer, manager, and representative. They weren't slaves because they weren't in chains. That meant they might be amenable to a recruit.

"I'm looking for work," Vanderjack told the lanista, who was staring at him, up and down. "I'm a freeman from Ergoth. Fought in the pits in Gwynned, and I know my way around a chariot, horse, meredrake, whatever you like."

The lanista nodded appreciatively. "From Ergoth, huh? My last Ergothian got himself killed in the round in Jelek. Been looking for a replacement. Chariots, huh?"

Vanderjack shrugged. "You know how it is. Can't ride a chariot in Ergoth, may as well just kill yourself."

"Thought you were all sailors and pirates!" exclaimed the lanista.

"On my mother's side." Vanderjack grinned.

The lanista scratched his chin. "All right," he said, cracking a smile. "My name's Broyer. Jump on the wagon. You look like you could use some patching up, though."

Vanderjack shook the man's hand and headed to the wagon, where four other gladiators reclined, sharing a skin of wine. He pulled himself up onto the back and groaned as the movement shifted his ribs. One of the swarthier gladiators, an Estwilder by the looks of him, leaned over, helped him on, and said, "Need bandage? Got bandage."

Vanderjack nodded. The Estwilder reached into a box at the front of the wagon and pulled out a thick wad of linen soaked in liniment. It looked dirty and well used, but the liniment smelled strong, so Vanderjack pulled his arming doublet over his head, tossed it to the floor of the wagon, and wrapped his ribs. He oiled his other cuts and bruises as the wagon passed through the gates of Wulfgar and into the Merchants' District.

"So, Ergothian," said Broyer as the wagon came to a halt in front of a scorched tavern or alehouse about a hundred yards inside the gate. "Got a name?"

Vanderjack thought about it for a moment. "Cordaric," he said. He figured the Cook wouldn't mind Vanderjack borrowing his last name.

"Nice name," Broyer said. "You get an hour to sleep, then we're in line to go to the Horseman's Arena for the opening races. We'll get you a chariot, don't you worry. But you don't get paid until after the games. If you stay alive."

Vanderjack nodded. Then he went to sleep for an hour on a lumpy, straw-stuffed mattress inside the tavern, in a dormitory alongside the other gladiators. As he rested, he dreamed of the Sword Chorus, murmuring their advice to him over and over: "Look to the left!" "Hold your breath!" "That wizard is trying to set off a bolt of lightning!"

"Wizard! Bolt of lightning!" echoed Vanderjack, opening his eyes with a start.

The gladiator who had woken him frowned. "Cordaric?"

Vanderjack swallowed, blinked a couple of times, then sat up. "Sorry about that. Dreaming. What hour is it?"

"They rang the bells for Seventh Watch a little while ago." That was an hour after midday. He'd completely missed his meeting with Theodenes. "We're heading over to the arena soon."

Vanderjack rose and dressed. He met with the other gladiators in the common room, sharing their food and listening to their banter. The liniment and the sleep had revived him somewhat, and the food tasted good. When the conversation between the gladiators turned to the highmaster, he began to pay strict attention.

"Every year it the same, yah. Rivven Cairn stop what she doing and attend the games, yah."

"Cairn used to be a gladiator herself. Oh, yes. So the rumor goes."

Vanderjack leaned in, helping himself to a chunk of bread on the table. "She fought in the round? Where?"

The first gladiator shrugged. "Some say Lemish. Before she learned magic. Anybody who has seen her fight knows what I'm talking about."

"She have a good fighting style, does she?"

Another gladiator nodded. "Oh, sure. You seen that sword on her back? It's an elven sword, so sharp it could cut you in half and you wouldn't know it until the top half fell to the ground and you saw your legs just standing there."

One of the other fighters shrugged. "Yeah. You know, she's half-elf, see. She can pull it off."

Broyer the lanista stepped in through the door of the tavern and clapped his hands. "All right, boys. Time to go. We kit up in the arena dungeons, as usual. When it's showtime, we'll take the elevators up to the track."

Outside, it had begun to rain again. That suited Vanderjack fine because it meant he had an excuse to throw a cloak over his head and shoulders as he walked through the city. He couldn't believe his luck; if what Broyer said was the case, he would be right underneath the arena. His only concern at that point was how to hook up with Theo.

"So, Cordaric," said Broyer as they approached the center of the city. "If at any point you want to grab a charioteer and pull him off the thing and commandeer one of those chariots, the crowd would love it. Extra pay too."

Vanderjack nodded. "I'll try."

"Good man. Any preferences for kit?"

"Sword. If you've got scale mail, that'll do too."

Broyer slapped Vanderjack on the back. "I think we can do that."

The avenue they walked led upward on a ramp at a sharp angle and provided access to the elaborate porticos in the front of the Horseman's Arena. Mighty pillars supported the arena's walls, which were essentially the backs of the stadium seating. The arena was modeled after ancient Istarian coliseums, oval in shape and featuring row upon row of stone benches rising up and away from the arena floor. Spectators walked along a colonnade and under the eaves of the portico, after which they would take stairs to reach their seats. Gladiators, on the other hand, were directed down ramps into the tunnels underneath the arena, where it was said the most unfortunate of Rivven Cairn's prisoners and captives were locked away.

Despite the rain and the rumble of thunder over the

plains to the west, the city was filled with crowds. There were thousands of people there, thronging toward the city center to attend the games and overburdening the Merchants' Quarter with their patronage.

As Vanderjack's gladiator band descended into the gloom of the arena dungeons, the sellsword felt the blood in his veins thundering in time with the storm outside.

Armor was strapped on. More wine was drained from clay jugs. Weapons were passed around, and the steady noise of blades and points against grindstones echoed throughout the staging area.

Broyer disappeared for a few minutes then returned. There was a big grin across his hawklike face.

"It's going to be a special day for you, Ergothian," he said, looking at all of the others. "All of us!"

"What is it?" said one, lacing up a tunic of chain mail. "News from the arena?"

"Big news," Broyer said. "It's not just other pit fighters and gladiators you're facing this year. No, the highmaster's said to have a big surprise for the ending."

Vanderjack frowned. That didn't sound good. "A big surprise? What does that mean?"

The lanista shook with excitement. "Nobody's saying what it is, but I happened to pass along the hallway where they keep all the caged animals. She's got something new down there, something nobody's ever seen before."

The sellsword rubbed his scalp and feared he knew what that something was. That wasn't good. "Big cat, brass scales, wings?"

Broyer stopped, gaping at Vanderjack. So did the other gladiators.

"How did you know?" he asked.

* * * * * *

Rivven Cairn stood in the palace of the khan, looking out over the rain-swept Horseman's Arena from the covered section of the balcony.

"Aubec," she said, lifting the chilled wine to her lips then pausing. "Would you see if our guest would like something more to drink?"

"Yes, my lady," the aide-de-camp at her side said and crossed over to where Theodenes the gnome sat in the rain, arms folded tightly.

"I most certainly would not like anything more to drink," the gnome said, soaked to the skin. "In fact, I would very much like to come inside."

"Do stop complaining, Theodenes," the highmaster said smoothly. "It's only water."

"It has not escaped my observation that you are standing underneath cover," said Theo. "Nor has it escaped my observation that you only moved me out here when it did, in fact, start to rain, and that I am unable to move due to the shackles you have around my ankles."

"I don't want you running off."

"Where would I run off to? I'm in the middle of your city, and you have armed guards and draconians at every major vantage point. Clearly, I have no hope of running off."

Rivven smiled. "All right. Aubec, would you have our guest brought in?"

The aide-de-camp signaled to a pair of burly guards who stood by the doors. They walked out, picked up the gnome and his chair, and carried both inside. Theodenes was set down upon a raised marble dais underneath a colorful wall mosaic. The mosaic depicted the legendary Knight of the Sword, Sir Janothon Wicturn, clasping hands with Nordmaaran King Chialpa of the Quintalix. It was a striking image, especially as it depicted a kind of solidarity and union that was no longer present in Nordmaar under the dragonarmy occupation.

"Is that better?" she asked the gnome, who accepted a towel from Aubec and was drying himself off.

"Hardly," the gnome snapped. "To be informed by you that not only am I to watch as you subject my pet dragonne to unimaginable tortures in these ridiculous games of yours, but also that you never had any intention of honoring your deal with the sellsword does not speak to a more comfortable future."

Rivven looked at him with amused eyes over the wine she was savoring.

"Might I also say that I continue to strenuously object to having my mind invaded by your magical arts? You have no right to delve into my thoughts in such a manner."

Rivven chuckled. "Theodenes, you have an incredible resistance to my divinatory skills, magic or otherwise. As it happens, I didn't find anything in your head that I didn't already piece together from the evidence."

Earlier, her scouts had come to her with news of the dragonne lurking in the hills to the north. She'd sent two of her remaining bozak draconians out to investigate, with orders to use sleep magic on the beast if the reports proved correct. If those spells had already worked on the dragonne before when Cazuvel had captured it, they would likely work again. She was right. The dragonne was safely secured beneath the arena.

But why would the gnome come to Wulfgar? Where was Gredchen? Rivven had tried to work her magic on the gnome to get him to talk, but gnome minds were almost impenetrable; all she had pulled from him was an image of Vanderjack. The sellsword must have tracked Cazuvel there to Wulfgar.

"Do you intend to kill Vanderjack?" asked Theodenes after a long pause, his defiant tone altered, his manner subdued. He folded the towel up neatly and set it aside.

"Not if I don't have to."

"My bet would be on him in a fair fight," Theodenes said in a low voice.

Rivven walked over to the gnome and slapped him across the face almost hard enough to knock him off the chair.

"Fair fight!" she said, chortling, as she handed her glass off to Aubec. "Quaint idea for a gnome."

She walked back to the balcony, leaving the gnome to rub at his jaw. "See if you can keep quiet for a while," she said. "I see the chariots are coming out now."

Theodenes said nothing more as the first race began.

It featured no fewer than a dozen chariots, each drawn by a pair of horses. The horses were well trained, and the charioteers knew how to draw out the crowd's enthusiasm.

As Rivven watched and the hour drew long, she could feel the gnome's gaze burning into the back of her head, so when the race was over and the winning chariot was given the thundering applause of the crowd, she came back inside the palace and had Aubec refill her glass. While the aide-de-camp did so, Rivven sat on a divan near the gnome's chair and studied him. Silently, he was also studying her.

"I have spent ten years solidifying my power structure here in Nordmaar," she said finally. "I've done so despite the rotating roster of dragon highlords, the threat of Solamnic Knights and their allies on my doorstep, the rising costs of maintaining this occupying force, and the upsurge of mercenary activity within the region. You can be sure that when a legendary mercenary such as

Vanderjack takes a job for a nobleman who, until now, has been content to sit in his manor and enjoy the fruits of his exile, and when that mercenary's former associates come looking for him and mysteriously join his cause, I take notice. I have taken notice of Vanderjack and of you, gnome, but I haven't made up my mind about you. You amuse me. But you must be careful that I don't take permanent offense."

"Right," said Theodenes. "Be careful."

She stared at him, waiting for him to say something more, but he bit his tongue. She lifted her chin, stood up, walked over to the balcony, and resumed her watch.

"The main event is about to start," she announced aloud. "Soon enough we'll see what Cazuvel and Vanderjack are up to. You might want to come over and watch too."

She let the guards position the gnome under cover; no sense torturing him any more. Besides, she was growing impatient. The sooner Cazuvel made his move, the better. "It's time to show yourself, wizard," she said under her breath. "Show yourself so we can get on with it."

CHAPTER TWENTY-TWO

Vanderjack was soaked in blood and rain.

The crowds were deafeningly loud, calling out, "Ergoth! Ergoth!" He swung his chariot, one of only two remaining on the track, to speed toward the other on a collision course. His lungs burned, and his head was drumming in time with the *thrum-thrum-thrum* of the chariot wheels on the mud. He could see out of only one eye, a cut above the other rendering it swollen shut. But he felt strangely alive.

He was drenched by the persistent rain. He wore an ornate helm to hide his features and was clothed in a scale mail hauberk and black leather trews, heavy boots on his feet. Still, he was recognizable as an Ergothian by the dark color of his skin and because Broyer had provided him with a large leaf-bladed Ergothian sword. It wasn't long after he entered the arena before he had his own cheering supporters.

Five bands of gladiators, besides his group, had entered. They faced a dozen armored chariots, bristling with spears, with wicked blades extending from the wheels and spikes upon the harnesses. Each band fought to gain chariots, which began the thunderous race in the hands of single charioteers instructed to defend against all footmen. The entertainment came when gladiators fought each other for the chariots, and when the charioteers lanced the gladiators with their spears or cut them in half as they charged by.

The bands had been whittled down one by one, either at the hands of other gladiators or by charioteers. Vanderjack assumed command of the survivors of his group, huddled near the center of the arena. He had been attacked by a Lemishite savage, a Khurish blade-dancer, and a Kothian minotaur. All fell. The blood and the rain were everywhere, pierced by swords and spears and screaming faces.

Then he saw an opportunity and leaped aboard a chariot whose rider had been wounded by a thrown spear. He could barely hear the rain hammering on his skull for all of the cheering. "Ergoth! Ergoth!" Those gladiators in his band who were still alive joined in, shouting the word even as they traded blows with their opponents or dodged the chariots.

He snapped the reins on the chariot, and the horse leaped to the gallop, sending him barreling along the outer track, where the deep ruts in the clay let the wheels find purchase. He felt the wind fill his lungs, the exhilaration of speed. It was like flying again, like riding Star. Vanderjack lifted his sword, alert for remaining foes; he watched the seventh gate, still unopened, for signs of the dragonne.

"Ergoth! Ergoth!" Who could do this for a living? he wondered. It was nothing like mercenary work. It was showmanship. They applauded him but didn't even know who he really was, and if he died there on the blood-wet clay, who would mourn his passing? A spear carrier ran at his chariot, and he cut downward with the sword. The spear fell away in two pieces, and the man carrying it tumbled over and over, struck by the side of the chariot. The competition continued.

Eventually there were only two left—Vanderjack and one other. The arena was strewn with broken chariots, the dead, and the dying. His final foe was a grizzled veteran with a plumed helm he'd probably stolen from one of the Plumed Jaguars of Wulfgar. They raced across the arena toward each other, Vanderjack's vision narrowed to a tunnel, rain spraying in his face, his opponent's feathered plume sodden and plastered to his helm, a barbed lance raised and pointed in Vanderjack's direction.

A roar split the wind and the rain and carried clear across the arena, echoing and vibrating through the stone of the arena walls and under the feet of the cheering spectators. That was when the portcullis in the seventh gate lurched upward and a maddened, winged, brass-scaled creature emerged. The dragonne was shackled to twin lengths of chain, each of which was anchored on the inside of the seventh gate. Although he could probably lift himself several feet off the ground, the dragonne's wings would not provide him with the means to escape by flight.

Meanwhile Vanderjack was committed to his final charge, crouching slightly, the Ergothian sword raised high in a ready stance. The wheels underneath his chariot struck bodies, chunks of wood, and low basins of bloody water as he urged the horse on. His opponent's chariot did the same.

"Ergoth! Ergoth!" screamed the crowd as one.

The two chariots swerved, skidded in the mud, and slammed into each other. Both chariots' horses broke free, galloping onward, tack and harnesses dragging behind them. Vanderjack had flung himself forward at the last moment, using the momentum of the chariot to send him at great force into the midsection of his opponent and taking him down with him. With a crash, both men landed several yards away in another ruined chariot, causing an explosion of earth and broken wood and metal.

Vanderjack thought his legs were broken. For a few heartbeats, he couldn't move them at all, struggling to pull himself free of the wreckage. Then his legs began to twitch and spasm, and he pulled himself into a half-standing position.

The gladiator with the plumed helm was dead, impaled upon the twisted metal and wood, his eyes open and staring. Vanderjack swallowed back his gorge and, with difficulty, pulled his own helm free. He tossed it aside, drew himself up to standing, and heard the deafening adulations.

"Ergoth! Ergoth!" the spectators shouted. Vanderjack wiped the blood out of his eye, forcing it open despite the swelling so he could survey the cheering masses. It was hopeless. He'd never find Cazuvel in the crowd, and Rivven Cairn would be sure to recognize the sellsword as the champion standing in the middle of her arena.

There came a roar from Star. The dragonne was straining against his chains, roaring and bellowing. The crowd was spooked by the ferocity of his roar and many ran. Some fell or collapsed and were trampled by their fellow spectators. Vanderjack noticed that Star's eyes seemed wild and unfocused; the beast was probably under the effects of a spell.

Vanderjack cast his mind into the void in which the memory-voices of the Sword Chorus were nestled, hoping for some insights. He couldn't recall anything they had said in the past that might help. "Don't dwell on the pain, the injuries. You can always die tomorrow," said the Cavalier's voice in his mind, a familiar reproach. "Die tomorrow."

"Rather not die at all," he muttered to himself and hobbled across the arena toward the dragonne. The crowd saw that, and, eager for more entertainment, the panic began to subside. Some began to shout, "Kill the beast!" and "Ergoth! Ergoth!" At least the rain had lightened enough that the sellsword could see more than a dozen yards ahead. He had lost his sword after he threw himself off the chariot. He hoped Star remembered him.

Vanderjack raised his hands as he approached. Star was flapping his wings and leaping around, claws tearing up mud and chains rattling fiercely. "Star!" the sellsword said, shouting over the noise of both the crowd and the creature. "It's me! It's, uh, good old Vanderjack!"

The dragonne responded by lashing out with one huge clawed paw and raking Vanderjack across the chest. It tore through his scale mail, knocking him backward, and he landed ignominiously in the muck. He looked up to see the dragonne rearing and clawing at the air before coming down with a terrible splash inches from Vanderjack's legs. The chains were holding the dragonne back—but only barely.

Vanderjack scuttled backward and got up again. A battered circular shield in the mud caught his eye, and he ran to pick it up, sliding it over his arm and bringing it up just in time to block another sweeping blow from the dragonne's claws. That, too, knocked the sellsword over. He shouted out again, "Ackal's Teeth, Star! Shake it off!"

The great dragon-cat leaped and ducked, snapping at the air with his jaws, narrowly missing Vanderjack's head. The beast's wings were whipping up rainwater and mud from the arena floor, making it almost impossible for the sellsword to maneuver around the dragonne. He wondered what the Conjurer or the Hunter would suggest and decided that the only way to snap Star out of his rage and frenzy was to risk delivering a blow to the creature's head.

The crowd loved the new battle. Many, frightened of Star's roar, had climbed up the stands to a higher vantage point. They saw a weary and bloodied man doing battle with a great beast that seemed like an amalgam of two of the most dangerous and predatory beasts they knew. From where they sat, they couldn't tell Vanderjack was trying to reason with Star or neutralize him, not kill him.

"Sorry about this, big guy," Vanderjack said and threw his shield with all of his might at Star's massive skull. The shield rebounded from the beast's head with a clang. Star barely blinked from the blow. He turned his head fully around to face Vanderjack, opened his jaws wide, and roared at the sellsword from a distance of only ten feet.

Vanderjack's head felt as if an ogre had kicked him, and his chest shook with the unleashed rage tied up within the roar. It sent him flying backward, stunned, muscles strained to the point of exhaustion. As he lay there, the crowd shouting for him to get up and fight, everything from his concussed skull to the shredded tendons in his arms and legs screaming at him to just give up and die, he heard the one sound he knew would just make things worse.

It was the sound of the chains snapping.

******

Theodenes had had enough of the spectacle.

He'd watched the whole contest at Rivven Cairn's side, under the cover of the canvas awning stretched over part of the balcony, but the rain still soaked his boots as it showered upon the balcony floor. The highmaster, meanwhile, kept dry by some minor cantrip.

Theodenes had watched it all, occasionally wincing but steadily becoming confident that the dark-skinned stranger in the scale mail shirt and helm who had fought his way to the chariots would win.

The highmaster must have recognized Vanderjack too, but she didn't move to do anything about it. In fact, as Vanderjack and his last gladiatorial foe raced their chariots toward each other, he had decided that Rivven wasn't going to lift a finger until Cazuvel was drawn out of hiding.

Then the arena's big seventh gate was lifted and Star emerged, crazed, not at all the warm, intelligent creature he'd grown fond of. Theodenes was certain that they had done something to the dragonne to reduce him to that angry, almost mindless brute. Was it Rivven's magic? Perhaps some herbal concoction prepared by the beast masters of the Horseman's Arena to whip animals into a state of rage? Either way, Vanderjack looked in serious trouble.

Rivven continued to do nothing as Vanderjack tried pathetically to counter the berserk dragonne. She turned her head just enough to meet Theo's gaze and smiled.

Theo had most definitely had enough.

It was a widely known fact that gnomes have a low resistance to stress. Never in his entire life, however, had Theodenes responded to stress by running into a room, the chains on his ankles clanking and bouncing, grabbing a polearm from a guard, running back out of the room, hooking the polearm onto the canvas awning above the balcony, then leaping from the balcony into open space in a vain attempt to use the awning and polearm together as a makeshift hang glider. And yet, that is exactly what he did.

The guards were astonished, no less Rivven Cairn, but the gnome was already up and over the rail of the balcony before they could do anything but stare and gape and point.

"What in the name of—!" was all Rivven could get out before she watched Theodenes vanish from the railing.

Theo hung on to the polearm, jaw set, wind catching in the awning and lifting him swiftly up and into the air, easily putting some distance between himself and the palace. He made a mental note to add a glider function to his ultimate melee weapon device, for it was extremely useful and more than a little exciting. One end of his stolen polearm was a standard axe blade backed by a spike, the spike firmly hooked into one corner of the awning. The other end of the polearm was fortunately caught up in a loop of cord lining the other end of the awning; otherwise Theo would be dropping like a stone.

The triumphant gnome managed a sort of strangled war cry as he angled himself toward the far end of the arena, where Star and Vanderjack were circling each other. Star was busy straining against his chains, and the links stretched, groaned, and finally gave way against the dragonne's monstrous strength. The crowd was busy flinging itself toward the edges of the stadium seating, looking down over the high walls into the arena below, shouting and gesturing at the frightening display of bestial power.

Somebody in the crowd noticed Theo's rapid descent and pointed upward. The cheers of "Ergoth! Ergoth!" were joined by "Kender! Kender!" As drenched and worn out as Theo was, with his luxurious white hair clinging to his scalp and his fine traveling clothes hanging awkwardly off his limbs, he looked to the idiot masses like a wet kender.

He landed in a sodden, muddy heap near Vanderjack. The awning fell forward, flapping in the wind, and, as luck would have it, flew right into Star's face. The dragonne, finally free of his bonds, sailed right over Theo and the prone sellsword, jaws and forelimbs caught up in the canvas. Theodenes lifted the polearm out of the mud where it had landed and stood, prepared to defend himself and Vanderjack—once and no longer his enemy—against all comers.

"Star!" he shouted, watching the dragonne leap and flap crazily around the arena until he managed to claw the canvas away from his face. "Star, you are under the effects of some kind of pharmaceutical or metaphysical stimulant! Remember who we are! Theodenes and Vanderjack!"

The dragonne spun around, spraying water so hard that it splashed all the way up the nearby wall and into the faces of the throng watching from high above. There was more cheering, but the crowd's mood had sobered somewhat. It was strange entertainment, a kender fighting a dragonne that flopped around as though it were confused.

Star tensed, his muscles bunching up, drawing himself back on his haunches. His wings spread wide and angled upward, as a bat's might before it propels itself forward to snare an insect from the air. Theo gulped. Star was big enough that he could swallow the gnome in one bite if he wanted to.

Theodenes felt rather than saw the stirring of the sellsword beside him in the mud. Vanderjack was trying to pull himself up into a sitting position, but he looked terrible.

"No good," said the sellsword. "May as well say whatever prayers you gnomes have to whatever gods you have, Theo. Star's—"

Theo finished the sentence. "Charging right at us," he said, gritting his teeth. He thrust the butt end of the polearm into the thick clay and braced himself for the impact. He thought of closing his eyes, afraid to look, but something made them stay open. Gnome curiosity, perhaps?

The dragonne beat his wings and launched himself up and into a swift and deadly arc, claws outstretched on the way down, wings pushing him halfway across the arena in the direction of the gnome and the Ergothian, jaws opening. Then, at the moment of impending collision, the wings beat once feverishly, and Star flew past overhead.

"He missed!" said Vanderjack, seized by a coughing fit.

"No, he didn't," said Theo, smiling. "Look!"

Star was flying around in a lazy arc over the stands of spectators. There were screams and cries of "The beast is loose!" and "Call for the guard!" and "It's all the kender's fault!" Then, without any signs of wrath or madness, he landed before the gnome and breathed a warm, wet greeting in his face.

"I apologize," said Star. "It took me this long to overcome the enchantments the bozaks placed on me."

"No apologies necessary, Star. We are simply glad that you have come to your senses."

Star looked at Vanderjack, who was kneeling and trying to stand up all the way. "Are you going to be all right?"

"Never felt better," said Vanderjack. "Feel like I could go a few more rounds with those gladiators."

Star suddenly whirled around, and the large feline eyes widened. "Be ready!" he bellowed. "Cazuvel comes!"

"Is that Etharion talking to you? Are the Sword Chorus here?" asked Vanderjack, using Theodenes as support. "Where's Cazuvel?"

Star looked down at the ground. With a thunderous rumble like the sound of a hundred chariots clattering over rock, a colossal mechanism beneath the arena began its work. The puddles and lakes of water on the surface trembled, ripples disturbing their surfaces. The crowd fell into a hush, and the rain had stopped for the time being. Star said simply, "Cazuvel rises."

The sucking sound of mud disgorging its contents followed as enormous doors in the arena floor lifted and slid open. Hundreds of gallons of water drained around the doors, but from inside the dark cavity, the rumbling noise grew even louder. A stone platform, clearly designed to lift large numbers of people or animals into the arena, rose from the new opening at the center of the arena. Underneath it, four columns of stone rose, forming a solid foundation for the structure as it climbed into the air above the arena with surprising speed and stability.

Upon the platform was what appeared to be an elaborate cage fashioned from iron. It was the same cage that Star had been locked up in at Castle Glayward. Even from that distance, Theodenes could see that on one inside wall of the cage a woman's body was chained up; her wrists and ankles had been secured to the bars.

"Gredchen!" said Vanderjack, pointing. "What in blazes has Cazuvel done to her?

On the opposite wall of the cage was a rectangular object that both Theo and Vanderjack recognized as the painting of the baron's beautiful daughter.

Cazuvel himself, still dressed in black robes, his hood thrown back and gaunt albino features boasting an exultant grin, stood on top of the cage. His arms were raised in the air. All of the crowd's eyes were on him, having left Vanderjack, Theodenes, and Star for the magnetic appeal of the new surprise.

"People of Wulfgar!" screamed the wizard, his voice unnaturally loud. "Your time to bear witness has come!"

Theo suddenly remembered the highmaster. His gaze shifted to the balcony. He saw her there, a figure in black and red with a billowing cape and that hideous armored mask she wore. Her gauntlets gripped the balcony railing. Her two thugs were by her side. Theo wondered where her red dragon was, but only moments later, he saw the enormous bulk of Cear ascending the roof of the palace, squatting there with wings folded by his sides, waiting.

"Now that you have reveled in your blood sports and cried out for death, it is time to reflect on the future of Krynn!"

Vanderjack said, "He's going to give a speech?"

"We need to get onto Star. You have to get up there!"

The sellsword nodded wearily. He looked pretty grimy and bloodied and bruised, from the gnome's analytic point of view.

But Vanderjack climbed quickly onto Star's back, joined by Theo. "I have a plan," said Vanderjack.

"I have a better one," said Theodenes.

"Would you shut up for once and listen to my idea? Trust me, for once."

The gnome sighed. "All right."

"Star," he said, bending over and whispering instructions to the dragonne. "That was going to be my plan," said Theo sulkily as Star sprang up from the floor of the arena and sped toward Cazuvel and the cage.

The crowd cheered. Theo cringed. The wizard looked down at the approaching dragonne and laughed maniacally.

"People of Wulfgar!" crowed Cazuvel, gleefully pointing at the dragonne and his riders. "See how even now, facing certain doom, the brave heroes ride upon their mighty winged steed to the rescue of the fair maiden!"

The wizard reached into his robes and withdrew something long and sharp. The heavy clouds above the arena, which had until then permitted only a watery gray sunlight to filter through the rain, split apart. The object in Cazuvel's hand shone brightly, almost dazzling.

"Lifecleaver!" said Vanderjack. "There's my sword! Star, where are the ghosts? What's he planning?"

Star rumbled, "I fear they are not present. There are dark forces I do not fathom at work up on that pedestal."

Cazuvel was still pontificating. "Behold, people of Wulfgar! You will be the first to see the power of the Abyss made manifest!" With a single swift motion, the wizard drove the sword into the top of the cage, midway between the chained figure of Gredchen and the painting. The sound of metal scraping against metal rang throughout the arena.

Cazuvel intoned, *"Cermindaya, cermindaya, saya memanggil anda dan mengikat anda!"* Almost immediately afterward, a burst of vivid blue and orange light flashed from inside the cage as ribbons of energy began to dance between Gredchen, the sword, and the painting.

They were almost there. Theo gripped his polearm for an attack, but just as they swung close, to his surprise, Vanderjack shouted, "Take Theo clear, Star!" The sellsword leaped off with nothing but a battered shield.

"No! Vanderjack! Wait for me! Wait!"

"Trust him," said Star, winging away from the platform. "Vanderjack knows what he is doing."

Theodenes, looking over his shoulder as the sellsword closed on the wizard, fumed . . . and feared for Vanderjack's fate.

CHAPTER TWENTY-THREE

Vanderjack leaped toward certain doom.

The fetch in Cazuvel's form stood amid a storm of energy, a storm that linked Gredchen and the painting, holding the sword Vanderjack had inherited from his mother, the queen of the pirates. *His* sword—one of the fabled nine-lives stealers and fashioned from unbreakable star metal ore—was undoubtedly the lynchpin of magic holding the storm together.

The wizard below lifted his hands and channeled the surging power filling the cage; it haloed him in alternating coronas of blue and orange. Seeing the sellsword plummeting toward him, he gestured with one hand and directed a bolt of the energy in Vanderjack's direction. The ribbon of power struck the sellsword full in the chest, holding him there for a moment, surrounding him in the same coruscating light. Cazuvel tugged his arm back sharply, and the stream of magic acted like a fisherman's line. Vanderjack was flung forcibly down and to the side of the cage, slamming into the stone platform.

The crowd screamed out its disappointment,

although there were some cries in the stands applauding the wizard.

Cazuvel's stunt with the magical snare had drained Vanderjack, rendered him almost unconscious. He struggled to breathe, but it was as if his lungs were filled with broken glass. The shield had buckled and folded around his left forearm, rendering both it and the arm useless. He couldn't tell whether or not his hip had shattered, but did it matter anymore? The wizard walked along the roof of the cage and stood on one corner, looking down at him with the light from the magical storm shining in his eyes.

"Get up, get up, get up," Vanderjack said to himself, speaking what he imagined the Sword Chorus would say if he could hear them. "Ignore the pain; die tomorrow."

He reached out, the fingers of his right hand wrapping around a bar on the cage, and felt the thrumming power within the cage channel through his arm, his shoulder, up his neck, and into the base of his skull.

"Get up, get up!" cried the Sword Chorus, outside of his mind, coming from somewhere else. They were really speaking to him. He opened his eyes, pulled himself up against the side of the cage, and realized that the cage was acting as a conductor between him and Lifecleaver.

"Glad to . . . hear your voices," he said, coughing blood. "Little late to the party, though."

"The wizard cannot hear us," said the Apothecary.

"He is distracted," said the Hunter.

"Vanderjack!" shouted the Cook, whose wavering image seemed to hang beyond the bars, within the cage itself. "Cazuvel is using the link between the painting and Gredchen to open a gateway into the Abyss. You have to stop him!"

"Right. I figured as much. I'll get . . . right on that," he said and flung himself to the left as Cazuvel tossed another bolt of lightning down at him. He almost tore his right arm out of its socket. The pain was intense, but it sharpened his senses, cleared away some of the fog.

"You are broken!" cried Cazuvel. "You are finished! Even now, I draw upon the powers of the Abyss! I wield the power unfathomable! Look at what great works I can accomplish while your life slips away from you!"

Another surge of power came from the cage and flooded the fetch's mortal body, making him crackle with even stronger mystical forces. He spread his arms, and intoned, *"Mati santet, mati sihir! Mati semuasaya daya!"*

In the arena below, motes of orange and blue light winked into existence above the dozens of dead bodies of the gladiators. Threads of light seemed to unwind from those points of light, traveling at great speed toward the center of the arena, toward the cage, toward Cazuvel.

Vanderjack stared, but at least for the moment he felt invigorated by the same power Cazuvel was drawing upon. As long as he remained in contact with the cage, he seemed able to ignore the constant pain setting his nervous system on fire.

"He's gathering the souls of the dead," hissed the Conjuror.

"An abominable act!" said the Aristocrat.

"For what purpose?" Vanderjack asked. He moved one step at a time around the cage in Gredchen's direction.

"To open dozens of smaller portals, using the souls as a bridge to the Abyss," said the Cook.

Vanderjack winced. Why isn't Rivven doing anything about this? he wondered. He took another step

289

and watched as all of the myriad threads from the arena floor made contact with the fetch. It was becoming harder to look at Cazuvel, with all of the violent light radiating out from him. He looked away, toward the palace of the khan. She wasn't standing there on her balcony anymore. Where had she gone?

The crowd was fleeing again. There was no more cheering, not for the man who had survived the games and the dragonne, nor for Cazuvel. All Vanderjack could hear from the stands was screaming, yelling, people climbing up the benches, scrambling to get to the exits.

"The fetch has expanded upon the basic theories that Cazuvel had once used to create the painting," said the Philosopher.

"Souls as templates . . . he's going to bring more fetches through those portals. Bring them through and into the bodies of the dead. You need to do something quickly!"

Vanderjack would have rolled his eyes if one eye hadn't swollen almost completely shut and the other wasn't streaming with tears from the unceasing light. The hand gripping the cage was starting to blister, and the energy flooding into him didn't feel right anymore. It felt unnatural. He was using the fetch's own ritual to keep himself going—the very power of the Abyss.

"Gredchen!" Vanderjack shouted above the roar of the magical storm in the cage. He could see her face. She didn't seem conscious. The ribbons of energy and light leaping from her to the sword and the painting at the other end of the cage formed a rippling afterimage of her, a half-real image that had begun to shift from her body toward the center of the storm.

Vanderjack reached up, felt Gredchen's wrists, and found that they were securely manacled. The only thing that was close at hand that might cut through those bonds and free Gredchen was his sword, and that meant he would have to climb up on top of the cage and pull it free.

Cazuvel had been so caught up in his necromancy, and so dismissive of Vanderjack, that he hadn't registered the sellsword moving around the cage toward Gredchen. However, since the web of souls was in place, the fetch turned to his hapless foe and laughed. "Are you still alive, Ergothian? I should take pity on you—put you out of your misery."

"About time too," muttered Vanderjack, seeing a series of iron rungs in the cage beside Gredchen. It appeared to be fashioned in such a way as to grant access to the roof of the cage, and that's where he needed to be. "What are you trying to do with the ugly woman, by the way?"

"I admire your ability to continue with these pointless jokes as you face death," Cazuvel said. "Gredchen here is the result of the true Cazuvel's early experimentation with soul magic. While flawed, she is nevertheless living proof that his theories were viable. In fact, had he not overreached his own abilities when plumbing the depths of this magic, he might have perfected the immortality of body and spirit."

That was interesting—and Vanderjack wouldn't mind prolonging the discussion with a fiend from the Abyss about one of Rivven Cairn's pet Black Robes. Keep the braggart talking. Yes, that was the plan, such as it was.

"I have the ghost of the Cook to thank for reminding me of that experiment." Cazuvel smiled, gathering power in his palm, holding it there, nurturing it, as if biding his time before delivering the sellsword's fiery end.

"As I unravel the magical bonds that secured the life force of the baron's daughter in this painting, bonds secured by energies wrought from the Abyss, I shall replace the baron's daughter with my own spirit. Then *I* shall be the template, the progenitor of a new race of fiends on Ansalon. No longer will I need Rivven Cairn and her crumbling army. I shall lead an army of my own."

As Vanderjack thrust his hand into one of the pockets sewn into his trews, his fingers closed around the thing he was frantically looking for. He coughed again and used the wracking motion to fall against the cage near Gredchen.

"Which reminds me. Where is my dear highmaster?"

"I really don't know," said Vanderjack. "But I think I'll send her a message." He pulled his hand from his pocket and, thrusting both arms into the cage on either side of Gredchen, produced the small parcel Rivven had given him. It was the talisman for sending the mage's body back to Rivven after Vanderjack had killed him. Well, that might not happen, but Vanderjack had a more immediate use for it. If only he could block out the pain burning his arms, searing his skin, setting the sleeves of his tunic on fire.

Cazuvel's eyes widened and he drew his hands back, focusing the power of the cage through them. Vanderjack was faster. He slipped the parcel on its thong around Gredchen's neck, even as the parcel itself glowed with the heat of the eldritch fires within the cage. He fell back and allowed himself a scream, his arms smoking.

Cazuvel roared in anger, unleashing the lightning bolt he'd stored up, and watched it streak into Vanderjack, an Abyssal lightning that blew the sellsword back to the very edge of the platform. But it was too late. A burning smell like roasting cinnamon wafted up from the cage.

Vanderjack lay on his stomach, feeling all but dead. He could barely to look up to see that Gredchen had vanished. The raging vortex of soul and planar energy within the cage had lost one of its vital elements.

Cazuvel shrieked and was lost in a towering column of nightmarish light, fire, and darkness. The vortex exploded upward, straight up into the sky, a tornadic firestorm that carried the too-mortal body of the fetch up as it went. Cazuvel spun about, end over end, screaming, before being torn apart by the winds of the Abyss.

"That's what I think of your army," Vanderjack whispered before passing out.

******

Rivven spoke the words in her mind.

Cear. I need you.

The wind increased briefly, heralding the great red wyrm's arrival. His wings buffeted Rivven as he descended, dropping to just below the balcony level. The highmaster made sure her sword was secure on her back, adjusted her knee-high boots, and leaped over the railing onto the dragon saddle.

She looked down at the arena and saw Vanderjack hugging the cage, silhouetted by the blinding blue-orange light churning around within it. She saw the wizard, threads of magical power extending from almost a hundred small blue and orange points of light in the arena. She shifted her vision magically with a spoken word, expanding her senses to penetrate into the eldritch realms.

"By the Dark Queen, he's done it," she whispered.

"Are we going anywhere in particular?" asked the dragon. "Or am I just hovering here to give you a better view?"

"Take me down there. I have a feeling Vanderjack's about to die, so I need to—"

"Rivven Cairn!" cried a familiar voice.

She turned in her saddle, looking up to the left. "Theodenes? Are you insane? Get your flying cat out of the way of my dragon, or I'll personally give the order for him to burn you out of the sky."

"How much do you know, Rivven?" the gnome said defiantly. He was astride Star, who had flown up and in front of Cear, as brazen as his scales. "About this. How much did you know before today?"

Rivven looked down at the battle then back at the gnome. "Are you asking me about the painting? I knew all about it, of course. Well, Cazuvel being an imposter, that was new to me, but I can adapt."

"You knew who Gredchen really was," the gnome said. "That she and the painting . . . "

"Yes, yes. The painting was crafted by Cazuvel to preserve the baron's only daughter, but she died anyway. So I had Cazuvel use the painting to bring the daughter back, and Gredchen was the result. I've kept the painting ever since."

"And you promised the baron that one day, if he kept funneling you information about the Solamnic Knights, you'd have your wizard fix everything. He'd get his real daughter back, not an ugly copy."

Rivven sat up a little straighter in the saddle. "That was the deal. Now if you're through with this line of investigation, I've got a precariously balanced portal to the Abyss to take off the hands of a demonic wizard."

"That's all I needed to know," said Theodenes. "Star? Did the ghosts get all of that?"

The dragonne rumbled. "Yes," he said. "They will pass this information to Etharion, who is watching over Vanderjack."

"Ghosts?" asked Rivven with a frown. "What ghosts?"

The gnome smiled. "Vanderjack's sword is haunted," he said. "Didn't you know that? Seven ghosts, always giving him advice. And an eighth ghost, a cook he accidentally killed and whose spirit joined the others."

Rivven cursed. "So that's the secret of that sword! Of course! A nine-lives stealer. Cazuvel must be using the sword's properties to—"

The highmaster was cut off by the sudden arrival of Gredchen, whose unconscious body simply materialized immediately in front of her. Cear craned his long neck around and said, "Hey, isn't that—?"

"Gredchen!" cried Theodenes. He spurred the dragonne forward. Before either the dragonne or the highmaster on her dragon could react, there was a titanic explosion.

A bright column of roaring magical fury shot into the late-afternoon sky from the cage. The force of the column's creation released shockwaves that struck Star and Cear and sent the wyrm crashing into the balcony. Marble tumbled to the palace below, smashing through skylights and breaking apart as it hit courtyards and gardens.

Rivven clung to her saddle and realized Gredchen was sliding off the dragon's neck. She reached out, hauled the girl back up, and looked at her. The teleportation amulet she'd given Vanderjack was around her neck, still smoldering.

"Oh, you clever bastard," she said. She stood in her stirrups, held Gredchen aloft, and looked up at Theodenes. Star had flown back up again, a little shaken by the fiery column's explosive arrival, and the gnome was intact.

"Theodenes!" Rivven shouted. "Here. Take her. Now that your friend's removed her from the arcane equation, the Abyss is about to empty its contents upon Ansalon."

"But Vanderjack . . . "

"Probably disintegrated. Just like Cazuvel. Forget about him. Go now. Save yourself. I'm going to go down there and see what I can salvage of that mess."

"You'll be killed!"

Rivven laughed. "Don't sound so pleased, gnome. No, I think I can take care of this little dust-up. I'm Rivven Cairn. I walk the Left Hand Path, just like Ariakas."

She gave a heave, and threw Gredchen out into the space above the arena. Star dived, intercepting the falling girl before she struck anything below them. Rivven didn't want to spend any more time arguing with a gnome.

Rivven rode Cear at great speed from the palace of the khan to the center of the arena. The red dragon made one circle around the pillar of Abyssal flame, allowing Rivven time to examine it with her eldritch sight. As she feared, Vanderjack had succeeded in disrupting Cazuvel's plans to channel magical power into his mortal body and conduct his demonic rituals, but removing Gredchen had upset the delicate balance. The painting was probably still intact, but what she needed was the enchanted sword. Where was it?

"Impossible," she said as Cear flew back in close to the platform. There, standing barely ten feet from the whirling inferno, was Vanderjack. He'd struggled to his feet, and in his hands was the sword. It had been thrown clear, and the seemingly tireless mercenary had recovered it.

Cear unleashed his dragonfear upon the arena. Rivven saw Vanderjack recoil, shudder, and simply shrug it off. He raised the sword before him; he was keeping himself going by sheer will alone. That and maybe his ghosts were helping.

"Bring us close," she said to Cear. The dragon obeyed, his wings beating at the air then dropping them to the edge of the platform. Perched like a monstrous red gargoyle, Cear exhaled his hot, blanching breath in Vanderjack's direction.

"Rivven," said Vanderjack, gritting his teeth. "I know everything."

"Almost everything," she said. "Hand me the sword, then get out of the way. I'm taking over for Cazuvel."

"You want an army of Abyssal monsters of your own?" the sellsword said, cocking his head to one side and adjusting his grip on the sword.

"That's something I'll have to think about in future. Right now, though, how about you do us all a favor and give me your weapon?"

"You said I could keep it. I killed the mage. Now I get my sword back."

Rivven looked away. "Oh, right. I did say that. Well . . . " She looked back at him. "I lied."

"Thought you'd say that," said Vanderjack.

Rivven tensed and sprang out of her saddle. Cear shoved away from the platform as she unsheathed her sword and brought it down in an impressive display of speed and skill.

Rivven bound all of her strength into the blow she was about to give Vanderjack. As she came down, her curving elven weapon, the weapon with which she'd cut down countless hundreds of foes in her lifetime, flashed in the light.

The blade sliced downward. Vanderjack brought Lifecleaver up in its path. With a high-pitched squeal of shredded metal, Rivven's magical scimitar struck Vanderjack's sword and was sliced in half. The end of the sword flew out to the side, and Rivven landed in front of Vanderjack with a gasp.

"My sword!" she cried.

"Star metal!" said Vanderjack. He brought the blade back and swung it forward. Rivven ducked, and the blade swept over her head. She couldn't believe how sharp and impossibly hard the sword was. Her own blade was magically reinforced, and it was half its original length after meeting his, the end jagged.

Furious, she reached out and grabbed Vanderjack by the shoulder. He buckled; there was a wound there, and she clenched her fingers hard. With her free hand, she grabbed at his sword and wrestled the blade free of his grasp. Wrapping her fingers tightly around Lifecleaver's hilt, she brought the hand up and delivered a solid right hook backed by the weight of the sword.

Vanderjack collapsed, coughing up blood and worse. She gave him a swift kick in the ribs and said, "That's for my sword." With Lifecleaver in her possession, she strode over to the edge of the screaming vortex and stared straight into the Abyss. The smell of power was even stronger, almost overwhelming. She needed to bottle the storm, but there was something about it . . .

She noticed, then, the ghosts surrounding her.

"Rivven Cairn," said the Aristocrat.

"You cannot do this," said the Philosopher.

"Enter the vortex, and you will die," said the Apothecary.

"I know what you are," said Rivven, her breathing heavy. "You aren't ghosts. I'm no stranger to divine forces. I walk the Left Hand Path, like Ariakas before me."

"But you are not Ariakas," said the Conjurer.

"No," she said. "I've been more careful than him."

"And yet you kept a black robe mage in your confidence," said the Balladeer.

"And never noticed when he was replaced by a fetch," said the Cavalier.

"If you know who they are, Rivven," said the Cook. "Then you know they have been watching over Vanderjack all this time."

"Did he realize it, though? Does he know who the seven of you truly are?" she asked. She was waiting, waiting to step into the vortex and take control of it.

"A man comes to faith in his own way," said the Philosopher.

Rivven took a deep breath. "So does a woman," she replied and stepped into the tumult.

She stood there on the edge of oblivion, looking down into a spiraling vortex of black. Above her, she saw the torrents of wind and fire, lightning flashes of orange and blue, everything laced with that howling darkness. Holding the sword tightly, she focused inward; she tried to do what she knew Cazuvel had been doing, using Lifecleaver as a lightning rod for collecting and controlling the power.

"We're sorry, Rivven," said the Aristocrat.

"You think you can harness this dark magic for yourself, but it is too strong for you," said the Conjurer.

"No, I can feel it ... even stronger. I see legions of ... soldiers, dragons, the minions of my Dark Queen.

I could bring them all through. No more highlord, no more requests to Neraka for more draconians."

"Rivven," said the Cook.

She closed her eyes and lifted her arms up, filled with the surging and seductive power of the Abyss. "Unlimited power! It's almost too much! Cear!"

She felt rather than saw the red wyrm land beside her. She felt something emanating from him—anxiety? Suspicion? Fear? "Cear! I have to share this with you!" She reached her hand out, felt it touch upon Cear's steaming snout, and heard the dragon howl in pain.

"Cear!" she screamed, turning around, looking away from the tremendous black vortex, seeing everything through a shimmering veil of energy. She couldn't move, couldn't step out of the wall of the fiery column, and watched helplessly as the red dragon tried to recoil.

Ropes of orange and cobalt blue energy snaked out and seized the dragon. Where she had touched him, his scales grew thick, calcified, and crumbled into dust as if he had aged a thousand years. The vortex howled, and her dragon was pulled sharply inward, into the middle of it. It drew him in, and he was gone, lost to the Abyss.

"Rivven, I'm sorry," said the Cook.

"Damn you!" she screamed at the ghost. "The sword . . . ?"

"It's the only thing keeping you alive," said the Cavalier.

"All this power!"

"Never really yours to take," said the Conjurer.

She opened her eyes again and looked out at the platform. Vanderjack was getting to his feet again. One leg hung limp; one arm was broken in several places. He looked at her and lifted a finger in her direction.

"I want my sword back," she heard him say.

She held the sword out before her and pointed it at him. "You can't have it. I need it!"

"That's what I used to think," the sellsword said, taking a step forward, "until a really ugly girl, who by rights should have been a really pretty girl, told me that I didn't need it nearly as bad as I thought I did."

"Don't come any closer," she said. "I'm warning you, Ergothian. I'll not surrender this power!"

"This is why history will forget about you, Rivven," said the Cook.

Rivven didn't have time to ask him what he meant by that. She looked at the ghosts arrayed about her, their spectral visages sorrowful, and when she looked back at Vanderjack, he was running at her.

The fool! she thought. He's running straight into—

Vanderjack leaped at Highmaster Rivven Cairn, the star metal blade in her hands piercing through his scale mail shirt, tunic, his ruined chest, and his heart. His mouth was near her ear, his ragged voice barely a whisper.

"Room in there for one more?" he said and she knew he wasn't talking to her.

With his last gasp, Vanderjack shoved himself away from the highmaster, taking the sword with him. She saw the ghosts descend upon him; they faded from her sight, and all that she heard was the howling siren of the Abyss behind her. The vortex fell in upon itself, an implosion of light and sound. Like a flame deprived of oxygen, the column of nightmares was extinguished. It yawned open one last time.

Rivven followed her dragon down into darkness.

CHAPTER TWENTY-FOUR

Vanderjack was dying.

He lay on the blasted stone surface of the raised platform, alone. Lifecleaver jutted upward from his chest. The pain was indescribable, but death had yet to claim him. He wondered if, by some bizarre stroke of luck, the sword had completely missed any vital organs and was just lodged in a rib or something like that. But every beat of his heart flooded his chest with a sickening warmth, blood pumping out of the wound formed by the sword.

It can't take this long to die. Death should be instantaneous. Wasn't that the way a soldier was supposed to die? He couldn't have asked for a better way to go, though. Run through with his own life-stealing sword, sending the highmaster off to her doom, somewhere in the Abyss. It was glorious. But it was taking far too long.

"Vanderjack," said a voice nearby.

He opened his eyes. He was surrounded by his ghosts. For some reason, they seemed brighter, larger, more real. He saw features on their faces that he'd never seen before. The Hunter's hawklike face, with phoenix feathers arrayed behind his ear. The Cavalier's mighty barrel chest, that helm with the curving bison horns he'd always kind of ignored. The Philosopher's thin, ascetic features, quizzical movements, like a praying mantis.

"Vanderjack," said the voice again. Etharion, the journeyman cook, was kneeling beside him too. "You won."

"I did?" Vanderjack groaned, wincing at the pain. "The portal to the Abyss is sealed?"

"Yes," said Etharion. "But I don't think anybody's going to remember. It was so chaotic."

"Typical," said Vanderjack. "Save the world and nobody's paying attention."

"They are," said Etharion, indicating the ghosts standing or floating around them. "I think they're waiting for you."

"The legend," Vanderjack said.

"Right. If the sword is used to kill somebody who should not die, they join the Sword Chorus. Nine lives."

Vanderjack groaned, hearing footsteps. He turned his head, trying to fight through the fog of pain and increasingly blurred vision. Somebody was approaching.

"Vanderjack? Vanderjack!"

It was Gredchen. He spoke her name, and she was there, kneeling beside the Cook. Of course, she couldn't see the ghosts, could she?

"You saved my life," she said.

"Figured it all out at the end," Vanderjack said. "You and the painting. I'm sorry it took so long."

He felt her hand on his head, cradling it. "I wish I could help you. I'm not a wizard. I'm just an ugly copy of a dead girl."

"Come on." Vanderjack coughed. The blood was

emptying faster. He didn't have that much longer. "You're not so ugly. You . . . you did kind of grow on me."

"Like a wart?" She smiled through her tears. The pain was setting Vanderjack's nerves on fire. He'd gone from intense pain to numbness to pain again.

"They're waiting for me," he added. "The ghosts. Etharion said it's my time. That's it. I'm gone, unless . . . "

Gredchen held his hand against her cheek. "Unless . . . what?"

"Unless I have something to keep living for."

No. Endure the pain. Die tomorrow.

Vanderjack gritted his teeth together and pushed himself up on his elbow first, then farther, feeling the sword slip deeper into his chest. He stifled a cry. The world swam around him. The only thing he could see clearly was Gredchen, up close.

Was she really that ugly? Did it matter? Vanderjack kissed the baron's aide right where her pretty smile had been only moments before.

He fell back, Gredchen sobbing loudly, and let his last breath escape his ruined lungs.

Lifecleaver shook; it rang like a tuning fork struck against a rock and claimed its ninth and final soul. A half second or a lifetime later, it *shattered*.

"Nine lives claimed and released," said the Apothecary.

"All is done," said the Philosopher.

"The sword's task is fulfilled," said the Cavalier.

"The baron's beautiful daughter is revealed," said the Balladeer.

"What was unfinished is now ended," said the Aristocrat.

"The hunt is over," said the Hunter.

"The magic comes full circle," said the Conjuror.

"I'm alive!" said the Cook.

"Ackal's Teeth," said the Sellsword. "So am I."

******

Theodenes was surrounded by Solamnic Knights.

Once again the Knights' Hall in North Keep, the capital of Nordmaar, flew the banners of Solamnia. Emblems of the Kingfisher, the Crown, the Rose, and the Sword were arrayed above the hall, unseen for more than ten years. The Knights themselves had returned, as control over Nordmaar had reverted to the young King Shredler Kerian, and old alliances were once again honored.

Theodenes had arrived there on the back of Star, who chose to remain outside in the courtyard while the gnome took care of his business inside. Theo passed rows of statues, of stained-glass windows and suits of armor. All of them were in various stages of cleaning, having been left to gather dust for a decade.

He was admitted into the waiting room, but he was the only one there. Minutes later, the doors to the Grand Council Chamber opened, and he walked in. Beyond the doors, a high table dominated the back of the room, and seated at the table were three lord knights, one each of Crown, Sword, and Rose. Their faces were hidden in darkness, and the only light shone right in Theodenes' face.

"Theodenes," said one of the Rose Knights. "We have looked over your report."

"I have to admit," said the Crown Knight. "It seems a very far-fetched tale."

"It is all true," said the gnome. "Why would I embellish it? Do I look like a kender?"

"Is that a rhetorical question?" asked the Sword Knight.

"Every word of it is the truth. I did as you requested and made sure to accompany the sellsword behind enemy lines, kept with him the whole time as much as possible. All that I witnessed, I wrote down."

The Crown Knight turned to the Rose Knight. "This does agree with the information we were provided by Lord Gilbert Glayward."

"And Vanderjack never suspected you were working for us the whole time?" asked the Sword Knight.

"I believe he was completely in the dark," said Theodenes.

"Not even with you showing up in Nordmaar just in time to travel with him?" asked the Crown Knight.

"We . . . resolved a lot of issues, but no."

"Magnificent," said the Rose Knight. "There's only one part of this that we don't fully understand."

"The part near the end," said the Sword Knight. "About the mercenary's final fate?"

"The legend that surrounded his sword," said Theodenes, "explicitly states that once the ninth soul is claimed by the sword, a soul whose time had not yet come and who still had much to live for, the sword will break."

"But surely Vanderjack didn't have anything left to live for," said the Rose Knight. "Unless you count the reward for rescuing the baron's daughter."

"Oh," smiled Theodenes. "Vanderjack had a lot to live for."

The knights muttered to each other. Finally, the Rose Knight spoke aloud. "Theodenes, we accept your account of the events leading up to the liberation of Nordmaar. However, as we agreed, these details must remain secret."

"Convenient that everybody in the arena stands

can't remember anything about it," said the Crown Knight.

"We must praise the gods for their blessings," said the Sword Knight, placing his palms together.

Theodenes nodded. "Indeed. Well, it's time I left."

"Where do you go now?" asked the Rose Knight.

"The Dragon Isles," said Theodenes. "Star's going to show me his homeland, and I've decided I would rather spend my last years in pleasant company."

"As you wish," said the Crown Knight.

Theo bowed, turned, and walked out of the hall.

"Blessings of the gods, indeed," muttered Theodenes to himself, as he set off to find the dragonne. "All seven of them."

EPILOGUE

Pentar, Winter, 351 AC

The Journeyman was surrounded by mercenaries.
The newly rebuilt Monkey's Ear tavern floated above the water, safe from dragon's fire, and boasting a larger common room. The tables were new, the ale was fresh, and the patrons were eager enough to test it.

The Journeyman set down his own tankard and tossed a coin into the middle of the table. "It's time I went."

"But it's early yet!" said one of the Brass Tigers.

"Yes, come on, Etharion," said another. "Vand and Gredchen will be returning soon from Willik. They say we have our first contract. You don't want to miss out on that, do you?"

"You know I'm not really a very good cook," the Journeyman said. "And besides, I've overstayed my welcome here in Nordmaar. Vand and Gredchen already know I'm leaving."

"But no good-byes?" said the first Brass Tiger. "After all, you're family, aren't you?"

The Journeyman smiled. Vanderjack and Gredchen had taken the last name Cordaric, in honor of him, but passed him off as a cousin. Nobody knew their true identities. Vanderjack and Gredchen didn't know his.

The others clasped hands with him and nodded; he felt a sudden pang of regret, a desire to stay there with his new family. But he had more places to go, things to chronicle.

It was a shame he couldn't tell Stella when he returned that he had known her grandfather and grandmother. Nor, he thought, could he tell her he knew everything there was to know about being a ghost.

Next time, he thought as he let the door of the Monkey's Ear close behind him, I would prefer to stay among the living. It was just easier that way.

On his way to the nearest out-of-the-way alley, he passed by the Temple of Branchala, with its familiar stone idol of a winged dragon-tiger, and looked down upon the street of temples and gods.

"That is, if it's all the same to you," he said.

There was no answer. But in his head, he was certain he knew what their response would be.

RICHARD A. KNAAK

THE OGRE TITANS

The Grand Lord Golgren has been savagely crushing
all opposition to his control of the harsh ogre lands of
Kern and Blöde, first sweeping away rival chieftains, then
rebuilding the capital in his image. For this he has had to
deal with the ogre titans, dark, sorcerous giants who have
contempt for his leadership.

VOLUME ONE
THE BLACK TALON

Among the ogres, where every ritual demands blood and every ally can
become a deadly foe, Golgren seeks whatever advantage he can obtain,
even if it means a possible alliance with the Knights of Solamnia, a
questionable pact with a mysterious wizard, and trusting an elven slave
who might wish him dead.

VOLUME TWO
THE FIRE ROSE

Attacked by enemies on all sides, Golgren must abandon his throne
to undertake the quest for the Fire Rose before Safrag, master
of the Ogre Titans can locate it and claim supremacy
over all ogres—and perhaps all of Krynn.

December 2008

VOLUME THREE
THE GARGOYLE KING

Forced from the throne he has so long coveted, Golgren makes a final
stand for control of the ogre lands against the Titans . . . against an
enemy as ancient and powerful as a god.

December 2009

JEAN RABE

THE STONETELLERS

"Jean Rabe is adept at weaving a web of deceit and lies, mixed with adventure, magic, and mystery."
—sffworld.com on *Betrayal*

Jean Rabe returns to the DRAGONLANCE® world with a tale of slavery, rebellion, and the struggle for freedom.

VOLUME ONE
THE REBELLION

After decades of service, nature has dealt the goblins a stroke of luck. Earthquakes strike the Dark Knights' camp and mines, crippling the Knights and giving the goblins their best chance to escape. But their freedom will not be easy to win.

VOLUME TWO
DEATH MARCH

The reluctant general, Direfang, leads the goblin nation on a death march to the forests of Qualinesti, there to create a homeland in defiance of the forces that seek to destroy them.

August 2008

VOLUME THREE
GOBLIN NATION

A goblin nation rises in the old forest, building fortresses and fighting to hold onto their new homeland, while the sorcerers among them search for powerful magic cradled far beneath the trees.

August 2009

Forgotten Realms®

A Reader's Guide to
R.A. Salvatore's
The Legend of Drizzt™

THE LEGEND
When TSR published *The Crystal Shard* in 1988, a drow ranger
first drew his enchanted scimitars, and a legend was born.

THE LEGACY
Twenty years and twenty books later, readers have
brought his story to the world.

DRIZZT
Celebrate twenty years of the greatest fantasy hero
of a generation.

This fully illustrated, full color, encyclopedic book celebrates the
whole world of The Legend of Drizzt, from the dark elf's steadfast
companions, to his most dangerous enemies, from the gods and
monsters of a world rich in magic, to the exotic lands he's visited.

Mixing classic renditions of characters, locales, and monsters
from the last twenty years with cutting edge new art by award-
winning illustrators including Todd Lockwood, this is a must-
have book every Drizzt fan.

LISA SMEDMAN

The New York Times best-selling author of *Extinction* follows up
on the War of the Spider Queen with a new trilogy that brings
the Chosen of Lolth out of the Demonweb Pits and on a bloody
rampage across Faerûn.

THE LADY PENITENT

BOOK I
SACRIFICE OF THE WIDOW

Halisstra Melarn has been a priestess of Lolth, a repentant follower of Eilistraee, and
a would-be killer of gods, but now she's been transformed into the monstrous Lady
Penitent, and those she once called friends will feel the sting of her venom.

BOOK II
STORM OF THE DEAD

As the followers of Eilistraee fall one by one to Halisstra's wrath, Lolth turns her
attention to the other gods.

BOOK III
ASCENDANCY OF THE LAST

The dark elves of Faerûn must finally choose between a goddess that offers
redemption and peace, or a goddess that demands sacrifice and blood. We know
what a human would choose, but what about a drow?

June 2008

THE KNIGHTS
OF MYTH DRANNOR

A brand new trilogy by master storyteller

ED GREENWOOD

Join the creator of the FORGOTTEN REALMS® world as he explores
the early adventures of his original and most celebrated
characters from the moment they earn the name "Swords of
Eveningstar" to the day they prove themselves worthy of it.

BOOK I
SWORDS OF EVENINGSTAR

Florin Falconhand has always dreamed of adventure. When he saves the life of
the king of Cormyr, his dream comes true and he earns an adventuring charter for
himself and his friends. Unfortunately for Florin, he has also earned the enmity of
several nobles and the attention of some of Cormyr's most dangerous denizens.

Now available in paperback!

BOOK II
SWORDS OF DRAGONFIRE

Victory never comes without sacrifice. Florin Falconhand and the Swords of
Eveningstar have lost friends in their adventures, but in true heroic fashion, they
press on. Unfortunately, there are those who would see the Swords of Eveningstar
pay for lives lost and damage wrecked, regardless of where the true blame lies.

Available in paperback in April 2008!

BOOK III
THE SWORD NEVER SLEEPS

Fame has found the Swords of Eveningstar, but with fame comes danger. Nefarious
forces have dark designs on these adventurers who seem to overturn the most clever
of plots. And if the Swords will not be made into their tools, they will be destroyed.

August 2008